THEODORA VAN RUNKLE

KERRY MITCHELL

A Birdy Black Book

Birdy Black Books
Melbourne

Publisher's Note: This is a work of faction – a combination of fact and fiction. Names have been changed, events have been embellished and dialogue invented or altered for literary effect. The reader should not consider this book anything other than a work of literature.

Book Layout © 2017 BookDesignTemplates.com
Printed by Ingram Spark USA

Theodora van Runkle/ Kerry Mitchell. -- 1st ed.
ISBN 978-0-6482301-3-7

{For the ones who lived}

ONE

Theodora van Runkle had the outward appearance of a completely normal person. But anyone who spent more than a minute in her company quickly realised their mistake.

She was disarmingly charming and could easily talk the leg off a table and, although she spoke a little too loudly and a little too quickly, it wasn't for either of these two reasons that people would take an uncertain step back from her. It's not so much how she spoke that unnerved them but rather precisely what she said.

To put it bluntly, everything she said was slightly outrageous. So, when she told us one wintry afternoon (as we were tucked up in a cosy nook of The Abandoned Book Shop) that the man in the shed was dead, we were appropriately speechless. And a little terrified.

Naturally we all assumed that she had killed him.

I suppose he had a name once, although at the time of his death none of us knew what it was. And Theodora, of course, only ever referred to him as the man in the shed. He lived in a garden shed at the edge of the Bellwether estate backing onto Wildwood. It once belonged to the Falconer. Falconry (as everyone surely knows) is the hunting of wild quarry in its natural state and habitat by means of a trained bird of prey. It was a lonely space but I think that's how he preferred it. Legend has it the broken lighthouse that stands on the edge of the clifftop beside the Bellwether house was a falconry observation tower in medieval times.

Clearly this is not true but it sounds good. I like the thought of the broken lighthouse having been useful once upon a time. We'd all like to believe we've been of some use to someone at some time. Even dopey slugs on the underside of wilted lettuces must feel that way. I know I do.

There were no falcons now, though, only crows but they belonged to me. I live in the crooked little cottage next door, hidden away by trees and undergrowth. I never disturbed the man in the shed and he never disturbed me, or my crows.

Theodora lived alone in the grand Bellwether manse. Well, not quite alone. There were always a lot of dead relatives clogging up the passages and cluttering the landings (with their rather morose-looking portraits lining the walls) and the ghost of Great Aunt Prunella (who occupied the attic) even continued to clean the house on a nightly basis. Some might say 'haunt' but she always left a spotless room in her wake.

Elizabeth and Emily Bellwether were still alive but far too busy with their own problems to worry about Theodora's. Elizabeth loved to travel and frequently sent back assorted trinkets collected along the way (which Aunt Prunella dutifully dusted and stored away in the attic). She once met a rather eccentric French woman fleeing Paris and that is how Mademoiselle Gabrielle came to take a room under the eaves.

More often than not, though, Mademoiselle could be found in The Abandoned Book Shop. That's Book and Shop, not Bookshop, because the books are abandoned, not the shop. The room was filled floor to ceiling with dusty and dog-eared second-hand books, with comfortable reading chairs full of soft, squidgy cushions, and reading lamps casting a warm glow in every corner.

Our little reading group would meet there every Tuesday to read books or buy books or swap books or talk books together but sometimes we would talk about other things, too. That's how we came to learn about the man who lived in the falconer's shed at the back of the Bellwether house.

'I don't like to muddy the waters,' Theodora had once said, 'but we do have a rather murky past together, the man in the shed and me.'

Theodora had the air about her of having lived a full and robust life filled to the brim with murkiness. I imagine there were a lot of skeletons in her closet (and a dead body or two under the floorboards), so when she told us the man in the shed was dead, I must admit we were not immediately surprised.

'How did he die?' asked Honey. She was never all that interested in the whys or what-fors but the hows always fascinated her. For example, how do people know when they're in love and how do they know when they aren't?

Theodora said that when a man moved into the shed, you could be fairly sure that romance had followed him out the door.

'He slit his throat,' said Theodora, 'and he was rather slap-dash about it.'

'Can a person slit their own throat?' asked Sunny, rather insensitively.

'Well, he did make a mess of it,' Theodora conceded, 'but in the end he got the job done. Mind you, the police seem to share your scepticism.'

'They do?'

'Yes. They've got it in their silly heads that foul play was involved.'

'Oh no!' wailed Lucille, falling back against a cushion. 'You don't mean that somebody killed him?'

'I don't mean that at all,' said Theodora. 'It's only what the police think.'

Clearly it didn't matter to Theodora at all what the police thought. Personally, I can't see how they could have thought otherwise. I agreed completely with Sunny. Whoever heard of a person cutting their own throat?

But Theodora was still convinced that this was exactly what happened.

'I think he was trimming his beard,' she said, 'with the garden shears and he nipped an artery in the process. He always was rather careless about the details.'

'Why was he using garden shears?' asked Honey. 'Wouldn't that be dangerous?'

'Apparently so,' said Theodora. 'I never said he was sensible. In fact, I think he was rather stupid. But now he's rather dead so I guess we shouldn't speak ill of him.'

'Are you a suspect?' asked Lucille, voicing what we were all thinking.

'How should I know?' said Theodora. 'I've left them to it. They've been combing the garden all afternoon, looking for clues or incriminating evidence. Though, of course, they won't find any.'

'Because you were careful not to leave any?' suggested Honey.

'Because there aren't any,' Theodora frowned. 'There is nothing to hide. I didn't kill him and I very much doubt anyone else would have bothered to kill him, either.'

'How sad,' said Sunny. But she didn't look sad. She looked frightened.

In fact we all did.

There was something unsettling about the way Theodora insisted that he'd died by his own hand, as if trying to convince us of such a ludicrous notion in the hopes of drawing attention away from her obvious guilt.

Hadn't she only just last week complained of what a nuisance he was?

I don't know about the others, but I wondered if I would have the nerve to tell the police what she had said. Who, I ask you, would ever dare to go against Theodora? Well, the man in the shed probably had, and look where that got him.

TWO

It was commonly believed that the man in the shed was one step away from being a tramp. He seemed hardly to notice that all around him his life was slowly disintegrating into dust.

'He thinks he's managing to keep his head above water,' Theodora once said, 'but he hasn't noticed that he's drowning in the drink.'

I'm rather surprised, actually, that she didn't tell us he drowned in the bathtub.

A little too obvious, perhaps.

When we met again in the reading room the following week to discuss Tolstoy and the state of Russian men, Theodora casually said that the man in the shed was once Russian (presumably when he was still alive) and that reminded us all of his rather unfortunate demise. And Lucille fell against the cushions again and needed a strong cup of tea to revive her. (I added three lumps of sugar when no one was looking.)

'Must our talk always turn to unpleasant things?' she moaned, when her spirit had been sufficiently revived.

'I don't see why not,' Theodora retorted. 'The world is a very unpleasant place full of very unpleasant things.' See what I mean about everything she said being a little alarming?

'I don't think that's true at all,' I said, 'and certainly this shop is a little oasis of calm and tranquillity. So perhaps whilst we are in it we could keep the conversation genial and light.'

'As you wish,' said Theodora, 'although if that's the case, I think you'll be hearing a lot less from me.'

No one said what they were thinking but I think we were all thinking the same thing, that a little less talk from Theodora would probably be very welcome.

None of us had slept all that well after what was said last week.

But, as Theodora allowed the silence to fill the bookshelves and bleed into every word on every page, I began to realise how much we depended upon her outrageous stories to liven up our rather dull lives.

There was something a little addictive about Theodora. She was exhausting and always seemed to dominate and yet when she wasn't around, the afternoon always felt a little flat. And, whilst none of us wanted to be reminded of how the man in the shed had died, we still couldn't help wondering in what direction the investigation was headed. Was it an accidental death or were the police still sticking to their murder theory?

'Did you know that Jack the Ripper's last victim was murdered on my birthday?'

'Surely not, Theodora!' exclaimed Sunny.

'Well, not the year I was born, obviously, but the same date and the same month.'

'Why are you bringing this up now?' asked Honey.

'Do you think someone like Jack the Ripper killed the man in the shed?' I asked. Well, it's who we were all thinking about, so why not say it? The man in the shed had been on our minds all week. I'd even hoped that the police had found their smoking gun (or blood-soaked garden shears, as the case may be) and had arrested Theodora before our little group could meet again.

Clearly that had not happened but perhaps she was ready to confess (and put us all out of our misery).

'I'm just mentioning an interesting fact,' she said.

'Genial and light,' I reminded her.

'This is as light as I can get. The man in the shed's aunt has been haranguing me all week and I'm ready to scream. If she tells me one more time how much she's going to miss him, I think I'll slit my own throat. Do you know she hasn't spoken to him in years?'

'Hadn't,' I corrected her. 'She *hadn't* spoken to him in years.'

'Oh yes, that's right, he's dead. I keep forgetting.'

Theodora had the most peculiar expression on her face.

It almost looked as though she were sad.

And that unsettled me far more than anything else about her ever had.

Surely, I thought to myself, she doesn't care one way or the other whether the man in the shed lives or dies? And yet, it was so very obvious that she did care.

And, from the looks on the others' faces, I'd say they'd realised the same thing I had. Theodora van Runkle had a heart. And right now it was clearly broken in two.

THREE

I admit I was curious to see where he'd died but I convinced myself that I was only going next door to Theodora's house to comfort her; a little tea and sympathy to help ease her pain.

The minute she opened the door I could see that my instincts were right. Clearly she was in need of a distraction to lift the black cloud hovering over her head. I could practically see it dropping wet tears upon her cheek.

So, 'show me where he died' was probably not the first thing I should have said. 'If you're up to it,' I feebly added and was properly chastised by the withering look she gave me.

'Of course I'm not up to it,' she said. 'I'm thoroughly fed up with the whole business but the police are obviously not going to let it go so I guess I can't assume that anyone else will. Mind your step.'

Elizabeth's curios were cluttering up the corridor and I stumbled over a pile of books at the foot of the grand staircase.

'Oh, they belonged to him,' she said, not needing to explain who 'him' was. 'I've been trying to sort his stamp collection albums from his aunt's diaries. Can you believe he kept them for her? Every day the nursing home sends more of her rubbish our way. This house is rapidly becoming her own private storage unit.'

'That explains all the chintz,' I said.

'Yes, I suppose it does. But why he would keep her diaries is a mystery to me. On every page, under every date, she simply recorded the miserable weather. She had an unspeakably boring life so I wouldn't expect her diaries to be full of anything remotely interesting but what sort of idiot religiously records the weather in a diary, year in, year out, and what sort of idiot stores them away for safe-keeping?'

'The sort that collects stamps?' I volunteered.

'You're right,' she snorted. 'He was just as boring as she was.'

But I knew she didn't really think that, and immediately upon saying it, a look of melancholy crossed her face so I hastily changed the subject.

'It looks like rain.'

'Good,' she said, 'maybe it'll wash all that blood off the path.' And she opened the back door and led me down the garden path towards the shed.

She was right. There was a lot of blood lingering on the blackberry bush. It reminded me of the knights in *Alice in Wonderland* painting the white roses with splashes and sploshes of red.

The patch of grass at the shed door had an arc of blood-splatter like a sunburst. There was almost a perfect outline of where his body had lain.

'He bled to death right here,' said Theodora.

'Were you the one who found him?' The instant I said it, I realised how stupid it sounded. She would have been the only one to notice him missing.

But she surprised me with her answer.

'No,' she said. 'Aunt Prunella did.'

Although the ghost of Aunt Prunella preferred to stick to the inside perimeter of the Bellwether estate, she had been known to visit her grave in the garden from time to time. The crows had a penchant for picking at carcasses so Aunt P inspected her gravesite periodically to ensure all her bones continued to rest unmolested.

'At first she thought he was lying on his back, admiring the stars and dreaming of endless possibilities,' Theodora snorted rather contemptuously, 'but then Aunt Prunella realised he was lying face down in a pool of blood. She sat with him for a while but it wasn't easy.'

'Because he was dead?'

'Why would that bother her?' Theodora looked at me like I was mad. 'It was difficult because she very badly wanted to mop up the blood.'

The Bellwethers once had a reputation for being the best undertakers around. They knew how to respect the dead and when to let them lie. But there hasn't been an undertaker in the family for quite some time and I couldn't see Theodora letting the dead (or anything else, for that matter) rest in peace for very long.

'Hadn't you noticed he was out there?' I asked.

'Good Lord, no,' said Theodora. 'I usually tried to forget that he was lurking about in the shadows.'

'What about when you went out to hang your washing on the line?'

'It was too cold for that. I used the airing cupboard.'

'Didn't you see him through the window?'

'I never looked out of the window,' explained Theodora, 'too creepy. He might have been standing outside waiting for me to notice him.'

'Yes,' I agreed.

A strange thought popped into my head. Perhaps the man in the shed slit his throat in order to get her attention. Maybe he only intended to nick himself and things got out of hand. What if he'd been lying on that path, gurgling for help, and she'd been steadfastly ignoring him for days?

I wanted to ask how long it took him to slowly bleed to death but I didn't want to see that stricken look on her face again. Clearly the thought had already occurred to her.

FOUR

'You know, I think she still loves him,' I whispered into the cosy corner of The Abandoned Book Shop.

Honey, Sunny, and Lucille, huddled in the corner with me, allowed their eyes to open wide in surprise.

'No,' breathed Lucille.

'Did she tell you that?' asked the ever-practical Sunny.

'Of course not. I read between the lines. Isn't that what we all do so well?' I swept my arms wide to encompass all the books on the shelves.

'You know, none of this feels real to me,' said Honey. 'It's like something you'd read in a trashy Gothic novel. You don't think she made the whole thing up, do you, just for a little entertainment?'

'I saw the bloodstains,' I began to say but then I remembered how the blood on the blackberries reminded me of paint splashes and another thought popped into my head. 'Has anyone ever seen the man in the shed?'

Many times I'd seen a man lurking around the falconer's shed but I realised now that I'd just assumed it was him. But what if it wasn't?

'Do you think she made the whole thing up?'

'What a brilliant storyteller she is,' said Sunny with admiration.

'Who's a brilliant storyteller,' asked Theodora, suddenly appearing in our corner and scaring the living daylights out of us.

'Jane Austen,' said Sunny, managing to recover brilliantly.

'Ugh!' said Theodora. 'Her books send me to sleep. She's all talk and no action. All those convoluted conversations cluttering up the drawing rooms.'

'I suppose so,' said Sunny, 'but then, no book could compete with your life.'

'Too true,' laughed Theodora.

'Any more news about the man in the shed?' asked Honey.

'Well, he's been very quiet since his death,' said Theodora, 'but I guess that's to be expected.'

'What about the police?' I asked. I'm not sure if I was hoping they'd rule it an accidental death or if I wanted something a little spicier, but I have to say even I was surprised by her answer.

'I'm their number one suspect,' she said.

Now I know that I said that we sometimes find Theodora a little too much to take and we try to rein in the more outrageous aspects of her personality, but right at that moment I could have hugged her. I've had quite a lot of experience with the dead so believe me when I tell you they don't do much at all once they're dead. This one, however, was getting more interesting by the minute and suddenly all of our dull, predictable lives skyrocketed into the stratosphere. I've no doubt we'll be dining off this death for many years to come.

'What are you going to do?' asked Lucille.

'Nothing,' she said. 'I didn't do anything so there's nothing I can do.'

'Maybe you could tone down your opinion of him,' I suggested.

'Yes, that's probably why the police suspect you,' agreed Sunny.

'But he was such a nit-wit,' said Theodora. 'I can't not say how I really feel.'

When you get right down to it, that's the truth of Theodora. She always says exactly what she feels. No mincing words or softening the blow. Most of the time Theodora will be your greatest champion, no one is more loyal, but if she thinks you are being unspeakably dull, she'll say so.

What Theodora needed now was our unwavering support against the court of public opinion.

Everybody would think she did it. Secretly even her closest friends believed it. But if she put her mind to it, I bet she could have even convinced Aunt Ursula that he'd got exactly what he deserved.

'You know,' said Theodora, 'there are a lot of stupid people who have accidently killed themselves in extremely reckless ways.'

I took a moment to check how I felt about that before realising with growing unease that I agreed with her one hundred percent.

The papers got a hold of the story and by Friday it was front page news. I rushed over to her house with a packet of TimTams, ready to dispense (what I considered to be) much needed tea and sympathy. But Theodora remained as brilliantly untroubled as ever.

She stood on the doorstep as dark clouds gathered overhead and boomed out my name and the crush of reporters parted like the red sea to allow me through. I felt as important as the Queen, especially when one of the reporters asked me how to spell my name and I must admit I felt secretly thrilled to see that several of them jotted it down. I had to stop myself from asking which paper they belonged to (in order to properly see my name in print). Quite a few of them attempted to shove recording devices under Theodora's nose (although, I note, none of them were brave enough to get too close) but she simply closed the door firmly in their faces.

'Goodness,' I gasped, falling into the nearest armchair. 'How on earth are you coping with all that?'

'All what?' asked Theodora, and, I must admit, she did appear completely unruffled. Her eyes lit up at the sight of my TimTam packet, though, so I can rule out a doctor's hand somehow sedating her or helping to dull her senses in any way.

She was as exuberant as ever.

'Aren't you flattened by all this unwanted attention?' I asked.

'I don't follow the news so I haven't the faintest idea what they're saying about me.'

'And you're not the slightest bit curious?'

'No, I'm not.'

If I were dealing with a normal person, I would say it was impossible. Most of us care very much what others think. But Theodora was a completely different kettle of fish.

Other people's opinion rarely came into it.

I also think that in spite of all her blustering and bluff, Theodora kept her true feelings very close to her chest.

All outward appearances steadfastly pointed to Theodora intensely disliking the man in the shed but I had seen that grief-stricken look on her face. And another thing was also bothering me.

'Why did you let him live in your shed?' I asked.

She stopped sucking her tea through the end of a TimTam and looked me square in the eye. 'Why do you think I did it?'

I decided to go out on a limb. 'I think you secretly loved him and wanted to keep him near.'

'If that's what you think, then it can't have been much of a secret,' she said.

'Well, I don't think anyone else has figured it out yet.'

'But you think you have. So presumably nobody else knows me quite like you do.'

'Well, I'm not sure what others think. What about your family?'

'Oh, they all think I'm perfectly capable of killing him,' she grinned. 'Even Sunny, who's known me since we were ten, thinks I did it.'

I imagine it would be difficult to be Theodora's friend for that amount of time. It would be like endlessly swimming with sharks. You'd have to always be ready for anything and not show fear at the first sign of blood.

'And there was a lot of blood, wasn't there?'

A picture of the blackberry bush flashed into my mind's eye.

'Yes, there was a lot of blood,' she said. 'I thought he was made of sterner stuff than that.'

'I don't suppose he meant to slash his own throat.'

'No?'

'What? You think it was suicide?'

Theodora seemed to consider this for a moment but I'm not sure if it was the first time suicide had occurred to her or if perhaps she was weighing up whether she should tell me what she really thought. Was I the sort that could be trusted with a secret?

I tried to adopt a conciliatory expression.

'Why are you looking at me cross-eyed?'

Oops, trying too hard.

'What did you tell the police?'

Which path, I wondered, was she sending them down?

'I didn't tell them anything.'

'But surely they've asked how you thought he died?'

'They asked me lots of things.'

'And what did you say?'

'Nothing.'

Theodora explained that the police called her in for questioning and cautioned that anything she said could be taken down in evidence and used against her in a court of law and so she'd sat in the interrogation room and uttered not one single syllable.

Clearly the police thought she would eventually crack but they underestimated her. She sat in that room for over an hour and said nothing. Not even when they told her that her silence was clear evidence of guilt.

'You're damned if you do speak and damned if you don't,' she said, dunking another TimTam into her tea.

'Did they arrest you?'

It seemed the logical conclusion.

'Not yet,' she said. 'They're looking for more evidence.'

She jerked her head towards the window and I suddenly realised the police were out there, prowling through her garden and traipsing in and out of the falconer's shed with hefty brown paper bags.

'What's in the bags?'

'His stuff.'

I glanced down the hallway and realised the books and boxes were gone. 'Oh no, don't tell me they're reading his aunt's diaries?'

'They're being bored to death as we speak.'

'She's putting up a good front,' I told the girls, 'but I think she might be feeling a little isolated.'

At this, Theodora strode into the bookshop followed by about thirty reporters with cameras held as close to her face as they could (safely) get. They shouted questions at her without waiting for an answer.

'She doesn't seem all that isolated to me,' said Honey.

Theodora plonked herself down in our corner and pulled out her copy of *To Kill A Mockingbird*.

'This is the book we're discussing today,' she said, addressing the throng of reporters. 'If you haven't read the book, you can't stay here and if you have read the book then you'll understand the concept of walking around in someone else's skin and you won't want to stay.'

The reporters looked suitably dumbfounded for a full second before carrying on exactly as before. Many of them started shouting at the rest of us. Lucille burrowed herself into the cushions again, Sunny looked thoroughly pissed off, and Honey looked frightened. I locked eyes with Theodora and tried to pretend we were the only two people in the room.

Theodora could pull it off a lot better than I.

Eventually each of us opened our books and quietly read to ourselves.

Theodora opened hers at the very beginning and settled herself in for a comfortable read. I knew she had every intention of waiting patiently for the reporters to give up and go away. They tried every tactic they knew of to break her concentration but she was stronger. I even felt a little sorry for them, thinking they stood a chance against her.

A lot of customers in the shop had been curious enough to follow the reporters in to see what all the fuss was about but they quickly grew bored with us. After all, what's so bloody fascinating about a bunch of middle-aged women reading quietly in a corner when that is what they were trying to do?

After a while the customers grew impatient and many complained that their peace and quiet was being unfairly intruded upon and the reporters were finally forced to leave although a few of them tried to argue that the shop was open to the public and so they had every right to be there. But the proprietor has the right to refuse entry to whomever they wish and when the reporters became too much of a nuisance, they were politely asked to leave. A few reporters staked out the back door to the alleyway but that just shows how much they underestimated their target.

Theodora van Runkle ran away from no one.

Eventually (and it took a lot longer than I expected) only one reporter remained. With a look of affected concern, she asked Theodora, 'What are you trying to tell us by reading this book?'

'Clearly she's not trying to tell you anything,' said Lucille. (I knew she'd be the first to crack.) 'She's trying to read.'

The reporter furiously wrote all this down.

'I do not give permission for you to quote me,' said Lucille.

Theodora kept reading. The reporter slunk off.

I exhaled sharply. 'I don't know how you do it.'

'Do what?' said Theodora, looking as innocent as a lamb.

'Well, if you did kill the man in the shed, rest assured, you will most definitely get away with it.'

'But you didn't, did you?' asked Honey, going red in the face.

Theodora gave her a look that (silently) spoke volumes.

SEVEN

The following week Theodora was late and so naturally I assumed the worst.

Mademoiselle Gabrielle sat on a battered old chair in the doorway of the bookshop with her tarot cards spread out on her lap. (She had once been a fortune-teller in a circus.) Mrs Dimple, who ran the teashop across the road, was a whizz at reading the tea leaves. I could have asked either of them to predict Theodora's future but I didn't.

'I think she's been arrested,' said Sunny. 'Anybody who's spent more than five minutes in her company knows that she's totally capable of murder.'

'And the police are terribly good at jumping to conclusions,' said Honey.

I kept glancing at the door, expecting her to make a grand and triumphant entrance.

'Perhaps she's fed up with those reporters following her around,' said Lucille. 'I would find it most upsetting.' She took a quick look behind her to make sure there was a cushion or two at her back.

'Maybe we should pay her a visit,' I suggested, 'to show that we've got her back, so to speak.' I stared pointedly at Lucille.

But in the end, there was no need. Theodora, a mere ten minutes late, walked purposefully over to our corner with a huge grin on her face.

'My bike had a flat,' she said.

'How did you get here?'

It was bucketing down outside but Theodora seemed to only be a little damp around the edges.

'Oh, those reporters come in handy now and again. One of them gave me a lift on his handlebars. I had an open umbrella in one hand and my copy of *Anna Karenina* tucked under my arm. I'm sure he thinks there's some hidden meaning to it.'

'Maybe he thinks you're going to throw yourself on the railway tracks,' suggested Honey.

Not to give away any key plot-points but Anna Karenina does come to a rather bleak end.

And we all laughed because there was nothing despondent about Theodora.

'Oh I couldn't wait for her to die,' she said (a little too loudly). 'If I was on that train station I would have gladly pushed the bitch over the edge. She was positively vile.'

None of what Theodora said was different to anything else she had ever said to our group but that was before a dead body was found in her garden. Somehow those words escaping rather ferociously from the mouth of a possible murderess made it sound much, much worse.

I began to wonder what we'd gotten ourselves into. What if the police hauled us in for questioning? Would loyalties be questioned? And what side of the fence did I sit on?

Naturally if Theodora ever felt the need to unburden herself and confess to the actual murder, I would consider it my duty to inform the police immediately (after I'd eaten the TimTams, of course) but I seriously doubted Theodora would ever do anything that foolish.

I couldn't help thinking, though, that if anyone ever confessed a murder to her she would take their secret to the grave.

Sometimes I think she deserved better friends than us.

'Totally selfish and completely self-absorbed,' Theodora declared.

I wasted several precious seconds wondering if she was talking about herself or the man in the shed, or maybe even me, before realising she meant Anna Karenina.

From the flushed faces of the others, I'd say I was not the only one to make this mistake.

'We don't have to talk about the book if you don't want to,' said Sunny.

'What makes you think I don't want to?'

'It's just that you seem a little upset.'

'I'm not upset.' Theodora looked around at the group to see if anyone else shared Sunny's opinion.

'We wouldn't blame you if you were,' said Honey.

'After all, you do have a lot on your plate,' added Lucille.

'You mean with the man in the shed being dead?'

'Yes,' said Lucille. 'If you want to talk, we're always here for you.'

'Ready to lend a willing ear,' said Honey.

'It's funny but the man in the shed is a lot more interesting to people now that he's dead. No one ever showed the slightest bit of interest in him when he was alive,' said Theodora.

'What was he like?' asked Honey, stuffing *Anna Karenina* into her bag.

'He was a bit of a loner and didn't like to be bothered much,' said Theodora. 'Truth be told, he annoyed the hell out of me. Never pulled his weight, and not much of a conversationalist. Glad to be rid of him, if I'm being brutally honest,' which, of course, she always was.

I diligently filed that information in my memory under MOTIVE.

'Had you known him long?'

'Ages. We were married once, a ghastly mistake that we both rectified immediately.'

Boy, that MOTIVE file was getting full.

'Married?' Sunny looked positively gobsmacked. 'But why did you never tell us?'

'It's not something I'm especially proud of,' said Theodora.

'Yes, but you can't keep secrets from us,' said Lucille. 'We've been friends since we were young.'

'We know where the bodies are buried,' added Sunny.

'Well, perhaps not,' said Honey.

'I'm sure I told you at the time,' said Theodora, a little vaguely.

'No,' said Sunny, 'you did not.'

'We would have remembered,' said Honey, 'if you had.'

'So did he move into the Bellwether house after you married?' asked Lucille.

'No. He moved into the shed long after our divorce.'

'But why didn't he move into the house? It's so big with all those empty rooms.'

'They're not that big... or empty,' she said, letting the implication hover in the air (for everyone knew the Bellwether house was haunted). 'Besides, we were close, but not that close.'

That pretty much sums up Theodora. All that loud and outrageous behaviour is just her way of keeping others at a distance. And it works, doesn't it? We always take a step back. How clever of her. If she took a step back from us, we would notice and probably take offense, or at the very least see it as a weakness.

But what about the man in the shed? Had he known the truth? How many times had he taken a step down that path towards her only to be beaten back by her forceful personality?

Had he tried to get closer and she needed to take more aggressive action to hold him back? Was that slit throat a close shave, not just for the man in the shed but for Theodora as well?

How long had it taken him to realise that the shed was not just his sanctuary but banishment from the castle? And Theodora was the princess, alone in the tower, untouched and unaffected by it all. No wonder it was so easy for her to ignore all that questioning by the police and the press. She knew exactly how to keep them out of her inner sanctum.

She'd had a lifetime to perfect it.

EIGHT

Talk, as usual, veered away from the book at hand and on to our messy, complicated lives. Of course Theodora's life was hands down more interesting than our own but, nonetheless, we all managed to throw a few interesting titbits into the pot. Honey's husband's prostate came up again and we all agreed that the hardest part of men's health was getting them to the doctor.

We talked about breasts and bras and all the usual topics that men expected women to talk about until eventually we got back around to mentioning the book which led us, once again, to Russian men and back at last to the man in the shed.

Still dead, I'm afraid.

'Any new discoveries?' asked Lucille.

'They found a few spots of blood on his mirror,' said Theodora.

'What does that mean?'

'It means he could have been trying to trim his beard, which is what I've been saying all along.'

'So what was he doing on the path?'

'Probably coming to find me,' said Theodora.

'Looking for a Band-Aid?' asked Sunny.

Typical male, we all agreed, underestimating his injury.

'I bet his last thought was, it's only a flesh wound,' said Theodora.

We laughed but it quickly ended in silence as we pictured the man in the shed realising, too late, that his troubles were far more serious that he thought.

NINE

W e were so used to Theodora arriving late and making a grand entrance that it threw us completely when the following week she didn't show up at all. We sat in The Abandoned Book Shop pretending to read but I knew the others were just as worried as I was.

Finally Sunny slammed her book shut and announced, 'I'm off!'

'Are you going home?' asked Lucille.

'Don't be daft. I'm going to Theodora's house. Who's coming with me?'

We all jumped to our feet, jamming books into our bags or tossing them haphazardly back on the shelves, before Sunny had a chance to finish her question.

Ten minutes later (and with the threat of a thunder storm looming) we cycled through the Bellwether gates. As we reached the front door (trying our best to rein in our enthusiasm), I swear I saw the curtains twitch.

It was a little discombobulating. One doesn't normally ascribe a curtain twitch to a person like Theodora van Runkle. She was the type to fling open a window and shout at the top of her lungs, "Get lost!" It didn't seem right to witness such furtive behaviour.

I was almost too frightened to knock but Sunny had no such qualms. She hammered on the door until Theodora opened up.

'What are you doing here?' she asked, blinking into the light.

'You missed our reading session.' Sunny had a way of saying it so that it almost sounded like an accusation.

'I did?' Theodora opened the door wider and we trooped in as if it were our right.

'Why are you hiding away in your house?' demanded Lucille.

'I'm not hiding,' said Theodora, 'I just forgot.'

'When do you ever forget anything?' said Honey.

'My mind's been on other things, I suppose.'

No points for guessing what that could be. Clearly the man in the shed was causing just as much trouble dead as when alive.

The media storm had died down and town gossip had moved on and even the police-tape had been removed from the path.

'Are they letting you into the shed yet?' I asked. I know from experience that clearing out a dead person's clutter can sometimes help you to move forward and accept life without them.

Had you told me that Theodora might be the type to succumb to paralysing grief if the man in the shed ever left her, I would have laughed in your face. Ha! Right in your face. And called you mad. Bonkers, I would have said.

And yet here she was, looking bewildered and, dare I say it, fragile.

Yes, fragile! *Poor Theodora*, I thought, and, believe me, I never thought I would ever think that. I would have been far less surprised if Theodora had thrown a party and wished the man in the shed good riddance.

You know, I don't think I ever heard her say a kind word about him. She said he was her cross to bear; someone who was never going to go away no matter how hard she wished it.

Perhaps she grew to rely on that and was now shocked to find that the thing she presumed to be impossible had actually happened. Was this what disbelief looked like on a person as fearsome as Theodora van Runkle?

I will admit I was inwardly patting myself on the back for having pegged the situation sooner than the others and although I stopped short of actually crowing, I was already mentally picturing myself comforting the sobbing Theodora as she wept buckets of tears upon my stoic shoulder. And I even went so far as to unzip my bag so that I might proffer a hankie when needed.

I should have known better.

Some things just aren't meant to be messed with. You don't fix the smile on the Mona Lisa or straighten the Leaning Tower of Pisa and you don't put Theodora van Runkle in the timid or meek or fragile box.

'They still won't let me in the shed,' she said, 'but that's of no concern. There's no need for me to go in there because he's not there anymore.'

The first time I noticed recent activity in the Falconry shed, I put it down to the police searching for more evidence.

Once, I saw a man standing with his back to me, staring silently at the Bellwether house and I marvelled at how similar he looked to the man in the shed.

It wasn't until I came face to face with him and he spoke to me that I realised he was back.

Now, before you get all excited and start thinking that I've lost my marbles, let me explain. I see dead people. I'm a hedgewitch. It's kind of what we do. We help the dead come to terms with the fact that they are dead.

You would be surprised at how many people seem to have difficulty adjusting to their death. They still live in the same house and look exactly the same and most have no concept of the passing of time because time doesn't really exist. It's just something the living have developed to make our lives run smoother. And help us keep track of things, like birthdays and anniversaries and meeting on a Tuesday to chat about books.

Things that are no longer relevant when you're dead.

The dead hardly seem to notice when those around them continue to age and yet they themselves don't. It's a bit like when you look at your child fully grown but can still see the small child holding your hand to cross the street. I think mothers still instinctively reach for their hands.

Usually a dead person will notice that everyone around them, everyone they love, is unbearably sad and no one is speaking to them or looking at them, not even when they are standing beside them with their arm over their shoulder and whispering, 'It's alright, I'm okay,' into their ear. Most of the time the living just cannot hear.

But the man in the shed didn't have a lot of loved ones and those (like his aunt) had not shed a single tear. And Theodora ignored him most of the time so I'm sure he thought this was just one of those times when he should give her some space and wait for her to get over her black mood.

But I'm afraid I couldn't let sleeping dogs lie (or die, for that matter).

'I'm sorry,' I said, 'but to Theodora, you're dead.'

He nodded sadly. 'I thought so.'

It's the job of a hedgewitch to help the dead transition. The dead don't go to heaven or follow a tunnel into a bright light. They sort of just fade and stay exactly where they are, doing exactly what they were doing before. Think of all those radio waves swimming all around us completely unseen. Think about air. Without it we die but we cannot see it or touch it or slip it into our pocket.

The dead are just like that.

I've heard the bereaved say that their dearly departed loved one is now tucked away safely in their heart but that's different. They're talking about memories and that overwhelming feeling of love that you keep with you even after someone is gone.

And the dead are very much aware of that, so keep doing it. And by all means talk to them as though they are still in the room. Because they are. And don't worry about picking your nose in front of them. They don't care about stuff like that. They've got more important things to worry about, like being dead.

Bitterly Bay was like most towns. The dead mostly ignored the living and the living mostly ignored the dead.

And witches were stuck in the middle, straddling both realms like a broomstick. A foot in each camp, so to speak.

It's not an easy thing to do and I have to be careful not to say things like, 'I was talking to your (long-dead) relative yesterday'. People don't like it when you do that. It upsets the delicate balance that the living have with the dead.

That's why I didn't stop the other day and talk about Theodora's possible state of mind with Mademoiselle Gabrielle (as she sat out the front of the bookshop) or Mrs Dimple (as she poured tea in her teashop). Both of them are dead; mere ghosts living in the otherworld, invisible to most living eyes. People would have thought me mad had I appeared to be talking to myself. And seriously so, had it appeared that my invisible companion had given me a reply.

Most people, you will find, prefer not to think about dying one day.

That's why I think some people run around and achieve enormous success and tell the people who sit on the couch all day eating potato chips that they are wasting their lives away. They want to be doing something that matters but in reality none of it does. Do whatever you like. There'll be no reckoning (or fanfare) when you're dead. Saint Peter will not be standing at the Pearly Gates, clipboard in hand, ticking off your achievements and only letting the worthy in. I know a lot of dead people who are still happily sitting on the couch eating potato chips.

But not the man in the shed. He was a brooder. He liked to stand at cliff's edge, staring down at the angry sea, and ponder the wisdom of it all. Now he spent a lot of time staring into the back window at Theodora. Waiting for her to notice him.

For the record, Theodora's favourite book is Emily Brontë's *Wuthering Heights*. Clearly the brooding, complicated man in the shed was her Heathcliff. Her second favourite book is Mary Shelley's *Frankenstein*. Make of that what you will.

Theodora had a love-hate relationship with the dead. She quite enjoyed the company of ghosts in that draughty house of hers but she didn't like them interfering in her business.

Normally I would hesitate in telling her that the man in the shed still clung to her like wet clothes on a drowning man (sorry for that ill-chosen metaphor) but when Theodora said he was not in the shed anymore, I knew that was because she could see him standing right beside her.

The others, though, had no such insight.

'That's right,' said Honey, watching her intently for signs of a crack (and looking a little too eager in the process). 'He's gone, Theodora. The man in the shed is sadly no longer in the shed.'

'I know,' said Theodora. 'He's in here.'

'That's right,' said Honey, tapping her chest, 'He now occupies a special place in your heart.'

'No,' said Theodora, patiently, 'the bloody bugger's haunting my house and I haven't had a moment's rest.'

'Good Lord,' said Lucille, casting her eyes around for a cushion.

Sunny gave a little sigh. 'Why do the best things always happen to you?' she said.

TEN

'Perhaps we should do an exorcism,' suggested Sunny.

'If Theodora's head starts spinning around, I'm out of here,' declared Lucille.

'Don't we need holy water?' asked Honey, watching Theodora fill the kettle.

'What, to make a cup of tea?' asked Theodora.

'No, to do an exorcism.'

'Oh, he's not going anywhere,' said Theodora with just a trace of bitterness.

'Well of course he isn't,' I said. 'He's finally managed to gain access to the house. That's something he could never do before.'

Theodora laughed. 'Oh, yes,' she said, 'he's thrilled to bits to have finally slipped past my locked doors.'

'Wouldn't he have scarpered as soon as he saw us advancing upon your door?' said Sunny.

'I think he's a lot more tolerant now that death is on the table.'

As Theodora poured the tea, the others moved from room to room trying to ascertain where the man in the shed might be.

Lucille looked for indentations in the cushions (she didn't like the idea of sitting on him), Honey looked for cold spots (before realising the heating was on) and poked her nose into the loo (because that's where blokes like to hide, she said), and Sunny stood frowning in the kitchen.

'He's very irritating, isn't he?' said Theodora, misinterpreting her scowl.

'I thought you were far too sensible to believe in ghosts,' she said. 'Should we start calling him the moan in the shed?'

'He's not a ghost,' said Theodora. 'And he doesn't moan or groan or rattle chains or walk through walls. He's just here, all around me, leaning over my shoulder and poking his nose into everything.'

'When Harry died I could still hear his voice in my head,' said Honey.

'Well, I don't hear anything,' said Theodora. 'I just feel him, lurking about, sticking to my skin. It's very bothersome.'

She carried the tea tray into the front room and we all joined her.

'You have to let him go,' said Honey. 'Tell him that it's time for him to move on.'

Theodora waved her hands in the air as if shooing a fly. 'I tell him to rack off all the time but he refuses to listen.'

'Let's talk about Jane Austin,' said Sunny. 'That'll make him leave.'

'That'll make me leave, too,' said Theodora.

I was glad a little of the old Theodora had returned but I couldn't shake the image of her opening the door to us in such a bewildered and agitated state. Nor could I stop imagining her sitting alone in her house with the curtains drawn, arguing with a ghost.

Or, worse still, learning to get along with him.

ELEVEN

Over the next few weeks the police called Theodora in for questioning several times. They recommended she retain the services of a lawyer but Theodora refused to spend any money on anything to do with the man in the shed.

They even threatened to toss her into a jail cell but she didn't care.

'It makes no difference to me,' she said 'whether I sit at home or in jail. I don't have any place to be or anything else to do and I know they can't keep me there forever because I didn't do anything.'

'But if you don't speak up,' I said, 'they could pin the whole thing on you.'

'Don't you see? They're desperate for me to start talking so they can find some way to twist my words. I've seen it happen dozens of times. Think of all those

Shakespearean plays where words were misinterpreted with tragic repercussions.'

'That's not real,' said Honey. 'They're just very entertaining stories.'

'Well, I can't be bothered with any of it,' said Theodora.

And she continued to sit mutely in front of investigators. And they continued to let her leave after several frustrating hours of watching paint dry.

I'm surprised she didn't tell them that the man in the shed was now haunting her night and day. Sure, they'd have thought she was crackers, but it would have been much easier for a jury to believe a plea of insanity.

Meanwhile, we continued to meet in The Abandoned Book Shop and talk about books and we probably would have been quite happy to continue on in this way were it not for the man in the shed's Aunt Ursula deciding to rear her ugly head.

The police finally allowed his aunt to clear the shed but she was disappointed to find there were no valuables in amongst all the junk. She was convinced Theodora had gotten to his stuff first and taken anything of worth and so she knocked on Theodora's door, demanding access to the Bellwether house.

Well, that's a first; somebody wanting to get in.

Theodora, who had never liked the aunt, refused to let her in. 'I've given all of his things to the police,' she said, 'so there's no need for you to poke your nose where it doesn't belong.'

The aunt thought otherwise.

She accused Theodora of still being married to her nephew and therefore he legally owned half the Bellwether house. Why else would he have been living there?

'He was living in the Falconer's shed,' said Theodora.

'As if he would live in that hovel,' said the aunt. And she threatened to sue Theodora for her nephew's share of the house. 'I'm his next of kin,' she stubbornly argued.

'If you think we're still married,' said Theodora, 'then I'm his next of kin and you can get your greasy mitts off my house. It will never belong to anyone but a Bellwether.' (Forgetting momentarily that it now housed a van Runkle.)

There was a time when I thought that perhaps the man in the shed might be a Bellwether and Theodora had married into the manse but had that been the case, he never would have put up with living in a shed, not when he had a choice of so many grander rooms. It seemed more likely that van Runkle was her married name, which might make it the man in the shed's surname only I'm fairly certain Theodora's been married more than once. Perhaps another ex-husband was a Bellwether but I doubt it. If he were still living, he'd have kicked Theodora out of his family home and if he were dead then he'd be haunting the halls along with all the other family ghosts so I guess that makes Theodora a born Bellwether with Bellwether blood flowing through her veins.

And so she ignored the steady parade of real-estate agents knocking at the door. The man in the shed was never given a key to the house, so Aunt Ursula was locked out. But she came up with a devious plan. If she couldn't get in, then she'd get Theodora out.

'Can you believe it?' fumed Theodora. 'She told the police that I'd made threats to kill the man in the shed. They were so excited to finally get a lead that they didn't even bother to check if it were true!'

And that is how we all ended up in a jail cell.

TWELVE

Rest assured, only Theodora had been arrested. The rest of us decided there was no point in meeting at The Abandoned Book Shop if Theodora couldn't be with us and so we met in the jail instead.

Rodney, the young pup left in charge, thought it was unwise to allow so many visitors in her cell but we ignored him and forced our way in.

Theodora was sitting in her small cell, uttering not one word, and I suspect Rodney's superiors (whom he telephoned to ask for direction) hoped that by allowing us in, they might be able to glean some vital information from her. After checking each of our books (for hidden contraband), Rodney positioned himself on a stool outside the cell with pencil poised and ears alert.

'I hope this doesn't scar him for life or cause him to leave the force,' I grinned. But secretly I hoped Theodora would be in top form today.

She did not disappoint.

'Oh, I could kill that bitch,' she said, and poor Rodney nearly broke his pencil trying to quickly write it all down.

I'd only met the aunt once, many years ago, and she had been mean and miserable then, too.

'Ixnay on the itchbay,' said Honey.

'What? What does that mean?' asked Theodora crossly.

'It's Pig Latin slang,' explained Honey, 'so that prying ears don't know what we're saying.'

'Forget about Rodney, I don't know what the hell you're saying.'

In fact none of us did.

'It's easy. You take the first letter of a word like nix, the Latin term for stop, and you place it at the end of the word and then add 'ay' on the end of it, so nix becomes ixnay.'

'That's way too complicated,' said Sunny, 'and now that Rodney's heard you explain it, there's no point in going on with it.'

Honey reluctantly agreed to speak sense from now on.

'You don't really mean you want to kill her?' she said.

'Yes, I do,' said Theodora. 'I want to wring her scrawny little ecknay.'

Rodney scribbled like mad and his ears turned pink.

'Surely the police must know she has an ulterior motive for pointing the finger at you,' I said, staring pointedly at Rodney.

'They don't care,' said Theodora. 'They've got the media breathing down their necks so I'm not surprised they cracked under the pressure.' She waited patiently for Rodney to catch up before adding, 'It takes a lot of strength of character to stand up to a bully.' And she gave a little smile.

I think she was thoroughly enjoying the moment. She finally had a chance to speak her mind and tell the police exactly what she thought of them.

I would have cautioned her to hold back a little but I was having too much fun. We'd each brought in a copy of Stephen King's *The Shawshank Redemption* and a poster of Rita Hayworth, and Theodora gleefully tacked it to the wall.

'It's hard to believe that a man who is famous for his horror stories is also responsible for something as poignant and wonderful as this,' said Lucille, hugging her book to her chest.

'You never know what people are truly capable of,' said Theodora, calmly.

Poor Rodney didn't know what to make of that. He turned bright red and muttered, 'We'll know soon enough.'

'What's that supposed to mean?' demanded Theodora.

Rodney didn't want to say but Theodora wasn't about to let him off the hook that easily. He knew something and she was determined to find out what it was.

The rest of us sat back quietly and patiently waited for Rodney to crack.

It didn't take long.

'We found your diary,' he blurted out, and, oh, the look on Theodora's face.

I don't think I've ever seen a look quite like it.

I knew then that this diary, wherever it was, was clearly something that Theodora had not intended for anyone else to read.

She grabbed hold of my arm and hissed in my ear, 'You have to get that diary.'

'He doesn't have your diary,' said Sunny. 'He's bluffing.'

'Don't you need a warrant to search her premises?' said Honey.

'We got that,' said Rodney. 'At least, I think we did.' He looked nervously about, saw the thundercloud gathering over Theodora's head and very wisely grabbed his stool and fled.

'That's our cue,' said Sunny, gathering up her bag and book.

'Thank goodness,' said Lucille. She had almost begun to panic upon discovering there were no cushions nearby.

'Chin up,' said Honey. 'This'll all be over before you know it. Storm in a teacup,' I heard her say as she made her way out of the jail.

The others followed but Theodora held me back until we were the only ones left in her cell.

'They can't have found my diary,' she said. 'I've hidden it well. But you'll need to check, just to be sure.'

I didn't like the idea of rummaging through Theodora's belongings but I was honoured to be chosen. Theodora did not find it easy to put her trust in others but I guess she had no choice. She was stuck in jail and the vultures were circling.

'It's hidden in the attic, in a secret compartment in the wall panel. Watch out for Aunt Prunella. She doesn't like people disturbing her dust.'

What dust? The attic was as spotless as the rest of the house and, luckily, ghosts didn't bother me, although in hindsight I probably should have heeded Prunella's advice.

'Don't you-oo poke your nose into-oo other people's business,' she moaned.

'I've got Theodora's permission,' I said.

But the ghost of Great Aunt Prunella waggled her ghostly finger at me and groaned, 'No goo-ood shall come of this.'

And I'm afraid Aunt Prunella was right.

THIRTEEN

I told myself that just because I had the diary in my hot little hand, that didn't mean I was going to violate Theodora's privacy by reading it but sometimes even with the best intention, you find yourself behaving rather badly.

This was Theodora's private thoughts and intimate moments. Clearly the police hadn't found it so Rodney was either bluffing, as Sunny had said, or they'd found another diary that wasn't this one. All I had to do was retrieve it and keep it safe. But I couldn't help thinking that I might be the only one to find out who the man in the shed really was and what he really meant to her.

Maybe I would even find out why he lived in the shed.

Perhaps it would help her case and get her released from jail. Yes, I think a pathetic, deluded part of me actually thought that I would be doing Theodora an enormous favour by reading her secret thoughts.

And so I settled into a comfortable chair with a pot of tea and a packet of biscuits and turned to the very first page...

I have six brown cardigans, ranging from a light beige to a chunky chocolate brown that pills a lot so I only wear that one when it's freezing, on account of the chunkiness (Theodora began).

I have packed them all into my suitcase. Except for the one I'm wearing. I am also wearing my mustard polo shirt with the Johnny collar (a smaller opening that does not require fastening) as it is the most striking item of clothing I own and today requires a little more effort than usual. It is July 14, 1986 and, at the tender age of twenty, I am on my way to London.

Thanks to my koumpounophobia (an affliction that I have taken great pains to hide), I have always thought that my (rather crippling) irrational fear of a certain everyday object ought to narrow my horizons (and to a certain degree they have affected all of the clothing I wear, everything being either snipped or zipped or belted or buckled or even left open to flap in the breeze) but here I am, nonetheless, broadening them. I suppose I have Sunny to thank for that.

I'm not exactly sure how she talked me into this. Ever since we met in primary school, when Sunny put her hand on my shoulder and told me that I was her new best friend, I have been swept along in her tidal wave and talked into doing a great many things. On the whole, though, it has afforded me many opportunities that I would have otherwise missed… although I can't think of one example at the moment.

Perhaps this trip to London will be the making of me. At least that's what Sunny thinks. My mother thinks I'm crazy. Almost three months ago Chernobyl (somewhere in Russia, I think) had a nuclear disaster and she's convinced the wind is going to carry the side effects across to England and choke us all in our sleep. Sunny says she doesn't plan to sleep much anyway so I guess we'll be okay.

'Oh, what have you got packed in here,' she says, heaving my suitcase onto the airport scales.

'Six brown cardigans,' I mutter.

'And…' she prompts.

'*Jane Eyre, Nicholas Nickleby* and *Oliver Twist*,' I sigh, unzipping the case and removing the weighty tomes.

'You know you can buy books in London.'

'These are for the flight.'

Just getting to the airport has been an adventure in itself. We have had to catch a ferry from Bitterly Bay to the mainland, then a train from Pixy Point into the City and a bus out to the airport. It has been an arduous, miserable trek.

Somehow, leaving Melbourne in the pouring rain seems quite fitting. We arrive in London in the middle of their summer. It is twenty-four degrees Celsius, quite pleasant actually. I remove my brown cardigan and get a look from the Customs Officer. Mustard has that effect on some people.

'Business or pleasure?' he gruffs.

'Pleasure.'

He looks me up and down. 'Really?'

Sunny is the very last passenger through Customs. Uncle Reg, who has been waiting for us at the gate, seems rather annoyed by this. Perhaps that's why he drives like an absolute maniac all the way to East Sussex. We careen down a narrow country lane and a green blur shoots by. We bump into an embankment, slide down a ditch, and pass a tractor on a bend before arriving in Crowborough where Aunt Flavia and Uncle Reg live.

'How fortunate that you have included our niece in your travels,' says Aunt Flavia to Sunny, 'since she has family willing to put you up for a spell.'

Personally, I do not think this is the reason why Sunny insisted I tag along. We are on an adventure together. Sunny says it's what young people do nowadays. Sow some wild oats.

I have been working for Mr Nichols' accountancy firm for two years and eleven days and Sunny says that is two years and eleven days too long.

So now I am a temp secretary in London. There is no job security and the pay is considerably less but Sunny says it's what young people do nowadays and who am I to disagree?

I think I shall wear my walking shoes tomorrow. Sunny and I intend to hit the ground running. Or so she says.

FOURTEEN

S unny's clothes are strewn all over the bedroom floor. I packed hangers with my six brown cardigans, etcetera, so I hang my blouses, skirts and trousers over the back of the spare bedroom door. The rest of my clothes can stay in the suitcase. They will not crease.

Sunny says we must do the sights of London and we haven't a moment to lose. Unfortunately it takes us sixteen minutes to walk into Crowborough village and nine minutes wait for a bus that takes twenty-one minutes to get to Tunbridge Wells train station where we wait another eighteen minutes for a train to take us to Charing Cross Station, the centre of London. This takes one hour and nineteen minutes.

So all in all it takes us two hours and thirty-eight minutes to reach London. Sunny's right, we haven't a moment to lose. At this rate, it will be midnight before we get home. It costs us five pounds, twenty pence (thirteen Australian dollars), which I consider to be rather expensive, especially if we are to be doing this on a daily basis. Sunny agrees and suggests we immediately find a place to live in London.

I am afraid her idea makes perfect sense. I purchase a London A-Z guide (it contains all the maps of London) for three pounds, twenty-five pence and we both agree that somewhere near Hyde Park would be acceptable. I prefer a little nature in amongst the smog and Sunny wishes to be right in the thick of things. It takes almost the entire day to reach Hyde Park as Sunny insists we take in a few sights along the way. I am not averse to Trafalgar Square with the pigeons or The National Gallery but I begin to suspect that Sunny's agenda may be different to mine when she agrees to The Tower of London in order to see the crown jewels and Westminster Abbey to see where Fergie married her prince. At Harrods department store I buy a one pound, fifty pence sachet.

'Last of the big spenders,' says Sunny.

Finally our double-decker bus speeds past Big Ben and the Houses of Parliament and deposits us in Bayswater Road outside the gates of Hyde Park. It is thirty degrees Celsius and apparently this is considered a heatwave, which has the unfortunate effect of causing the British to remove most of their clothing in order to turn their grey skin pink. They call this a 'tan'. I have no idea why. I am wearing my pink polo shirt, beige cotton skirt, short-sleeved fawn cardigan, stockings and sensible walking shoes. I feel a tad overdressed and a little self-conscious.

'Nonsense,' says Sunny. 'Sensible walking shoes are all the rage.'

'I was referring to my cardigan.'

Sunny removes her denim jacket and ties it around her waist. She suggests I do the same.

'Don't be absurd.' (If I were to tie it anywhere, it would be around my shoulders not swinging from my hips.)

Her t-shirt says '*Too fast to live… too young to die*'. 'You know we've probably already wasted a quarter of our lives,' she says. 'We haven't a moment to lose.'

'According to you, we have another sixty years to live.'

'All the same, we need to find somewhere to live.'

'Fine, there's a place just down the road that might be able to help us.'

Sunny allows me to guide her to The Walkabout Club. Perhaps she is suffering from heatstroke. Don't forget it is a whopping thirty degrees Celsius.

According to my guide book, the Walkabout Club is a meeting place for Australians. They have a little shop that handles accommodation and travel and across the road is a basement club where young travellers go to drink and mingle. I am fairly certain we shan't need that facility. We are given a list of addresses and set out to find a flat.

In the first one there is an enormous hole in the middle of the stairs.

'Don't worry,' grins the landlord. 'Everyone just shimmies up the banister.'

I do not, so we scratch that one off our list. The next one has a pile of cardboard boxes in the corner of the kitchen.

'Think of all the rats and cockroaches,' I gasp and we leave.

The third one is a share flat and Sunny and I would need to also share a bedroom. The rest of the flat consists of more squalid bedrooms, a filthy living area, a festering kitchen and a bathroom with no sink and a continually flushing toilet. For this, we would each pay twenty-three pounds per week. Oh, and we'd be sharing with three men. Sunny is keen to take it. I cannot get out of there fast enough.

'We don't need to panic just yet. We still have Aunt Flavia.'

If the truth be told, I would be happy to stay with them indefinitely. The village is nice and quiet, Aunt Flavia and Uncle Reg are very civilised and it isn't that different to my life back home but Sunny is having none of it. We came to England to find adventure and live an exciting life and Crowborough just doesn't cut it.

We return to The Walkabout Club and they have one more flat to show us. Sunny wants to give it a miss. 'My feet hurt,' she whines.

'You should have worn sensible walking shoes. I hear they are all the rage.'

'The flat is just a little further up this street,' says the man at The Walkabout, 'and I think you will find it worth your while.'

That's the thing about me. People tend to form an opinion at first glance. I am neat, precise and to the point (and I would never say no to a nice cup of tea) so when the man says he thinks I will find the next flat worth my while, I am confident that he is right.

With a determined air, I bustle Sunny down Gloucester Terrace to a basement flat at number one-three-three.

'Isn't this a handsome street?' We pass row upon row of tall, elegant white-painted Victorian houses. 'To think that we could afford a place like this.'

'They're probably all subdivided into poky little flats,' says Sunny.

'Good. Then we'll definitely be able to afford it.'

I fall in love with the basement flat even before I have made it down the big concrete steps leading to its door. There are red geraniums in pots on the bay windowsill. The flat is clean, nicely furnished and comes complete with a landlady named Mrs Quist who vacuums, dusts and changes the sheets once a week. There are three beds and Mrs Quist will find the third flatmate.

'No men,' I specify.

'Certainly not!'

'Sunny, we are home,' I sigh.

She is a little disappointed that we're not exactly roughing it but she can't argue with the location. The Lancaster Gate Underground tube station is down one end, right next to Hyde Park, and Paddington Station is up the other.

'Rent is thirty-five pounds each, paid weekly at my door. I live on the very top floor,' says Mrs Quist.

'Lucky you've got those sensible walking shoes,' says Sunny.

Our first evening in our new flat is an absolute disaster and I blame Sunny entirely. For reasons inexplicable to me, she has decided we must 'assimilate' with the locals. I can think of nothing more distasteful but reluctantly accompany Sunny on her assimilation attempt. It involves a noisy pub and a couple of pints of ale. Why am I not surprised?

We meet two sleazy lads, one named Douglas, the other named Kev and within an hour they are back at our flat and I find myself in the kitchen, politely making tea, when suddenly 'You rat,' Sunny is shouting from the living room. 'Where's my money?'

'I don't know what you're talking about,' says Doug, the dropkick.

'Give me back my money!'

'I don't have it.'

'Give it back!'

This goes on for about ten minutes until I ascertain the cause. It would appear that Douglas swiped Sunny's purse and hid in the toilet. He stuffed the banknotes down his trousers (that would explain the bulging pockets) and tried to flush the coins down the toilet. I suppose idiots can't be expected to get away with the perfect crime. Sunny discovered the coins, which led to the purse, which led to the shouting in the living room. This, of course, led to the lads legging it out the door.

Now Mrs Quist says we are to get a new flatmate. She will be moving in next week. I rather hope she has a sensible head on her shoulders or I fear that we are sunk.

FIFTEEN

Her name is Bebe and she enters our flat like a hurricane, wearing a furry cardboard bowler hat. She is wearing the bowler hat, not the hurricane.

'Oh, it's a tacky tourist souvenir,' she laughs, 'but don't you just adore it?'

I do not.

'Where do I sleep?' she enthuses, 'or do we just line up in the corridor and slumber on our toes?'

It is a very small basement flat and, granted, her sleeping quarters are the size of a cupboard but at least she has some privacy, except of course when one of us needs to step into the corridor to use the telephone. There is a mustard-coloured velvet curtain separating her room from the kitchen. I have to be careful not to stand in front of this whilst wearing my mustard polo, lest I blend into the background – a skill for which I am frequently known. Dull clothing and sensible shoes do not an impact make. I am, however, used to being overlooked and not entirely against it. It makes for less unpleasant conversation and more time for productive thinking. Besides, Sunny garners enough attention for the both of us.

When Bebe first makes introductions, she says, 'I think everyone should have an interesting moniker, don't you agree? It sets the tone, right from the very beginning.'

Sunny says, 'I'm Sunny Skies,' and Bebe says, 'I love it!' Of course she does. Everyone does. Sunny has hippy parents (and a brother named Blue). Unfortunately there is nothing she likes about my name, it's too long, too pompous, and Bebe declares it much too old-fashioned for her liking and so, in the time it takes to boil the kettle and drink a cup of tea, my name is changed to Teddy.

'I don't like it,' I say.

'Nonsense,' says Bebe. 'It fits you to a tee, more tea?'

I don't like to say that I stomp on Bebe's furry cardboard bowler hat on purpose, but I definitely think the punishment, in this case, fits the crime.

With barely a minute to catch our breath, Bebe bustles us up and out, down the road and through the mews, around the corner and up the stairs into The Royal Eagle Hotel. She works on Reception and has been eyeing the bar in the far left corner of the foyer for almost a week.

'Hello lads, these are my flatmates, Sunny and Teddy.'

My nickname has stuck but if I think, even for one minute, that my racy new nickname will garner me some attention, I am wrong. The men in the bar circle Sunny like flies to a rubbish dump.

Within nought-point-three seconds she has caught the eye of the Assistant Manager. He has a girlfriend, sitting not two feet away, but this is irrelevant now. William Abernethy has lost his head. I can almost understand his position. He has a very responsible job, not exciting in the least, and yet every day he must deal with guests who are going somewhere and doing something different with their lives. Whilst he stays put, in the same dull job, doing the same dull things with the same (by the looks of it) dull girlfriend. He looks like a man who lives vicariously through the lives of others. And yet, I think he quite enjoys being the one who stays put. It gives him an air of authority. In a way, I feel an affinity towards this dull, dependable soul. I, too, prefer to watch the excitement from the sidelines. Even now, having been swept up into the action, I still prefer to sit on the sidelines and watch.

I watch William Abernethy coolly and calmly lose his head, with his girlfriend sitting not two feet away. I must admit I am more than a little impressed that

Sunny has managed to snag a pasty-white Brit right out of the gate but then she always was a fast mover.

I, on the other hand, put turtles to shame with my apathy. At this point, I would rather not hitch my wagon to another man's belt, or however the adage goes, but it has become abundantly clear to me that this is the only way I can move forward. Sunny is going on dates with William to restaurants and theatres and Andrew Lloyd Webber productions whilst I am sitting at home, alone, twiddling my thumbs. Bebe is working most evenings at the hotel and there doesn't seem to be any other option. I must 'bag a bloke' if I am ever to leave this flat.

So, back to The Eagle I go.

Bebe waves me into the bar. I order a packet of crisps and a glass of lemonade and sit in a corner and wait. No flies come buzzing around my table. I am wearing my pretty pink blouse with the Peter Pan collar, a light brown cardigan with a flower appliqué along the hem, a light cotton skirt and brown lace-up shoes. My hair is scraped back from my face with an Alice band. I sit with my hands folded neatly in my lap, taking the occasional nibble of a salt and vinegar crisp, trying not to make a face when the vinegar hits my taste buds.

Jack walks in and asks if I've eaten dinner.

Let me explain before you get all excited and think I've scored a date.

Jack is the hotel cook. He has dark hair down to his collar and a warm and charming smile. He's the type that causes you to lose your balance and tip you off your feet. He is an Australian, no pasty skin here. He has a bronzed complexion and a trim physique. I can almost see his tight abs through his chef's jacket. It almost tips me off my feet. Have I said that already?

Bebe has sent Jack into the bar to see if I've eaten dinner. I decide to stick around until her shift is over, which, coincidentally, is also when Jack finishes his shift. I am not sure I am being entirely alluring but Jack strikes me as the type of man that needs little encouragement and so he walks me home.

He takes one look at the flat and suggests we go to his place instead. My bed is in the living room, right beside Sunny's bed. Between our beds is the door to the bathroom. At the foot of our beds is the living space: a couch, two chairs, a coffee table, a bookshelf and a dresser. Compared to Bebe's cupboard, it's a palace but there is little room for privacy. I am expecting Sunny and Bebe to arrive at any moment so clearly there is little chance to conduct a private discussion where one may get to know another a little better. I, therefore, have no objection to accompanying Jack to his own apartment, situated around the corner in Cleveland Square, where I imagine a nice pot of tea and gentle conversation will be the order of the day.

Except, of course, it is night. Eleven p.m. to be precise.

His flat is poky, dirty and messy and I am utterly enthralled. It is my first time in a dump and it feels so worldly to me, if you know what I mean. His motorbike sits in the entrance hall (he's a courier by day). In the living room there's a broken skylight with a giant saucepan in the middle of the floor, presumably for when it rains. In the toilet is the kitty litter box. I'm guessing it is never emptied. There is something quite enchanting and, at the same time, disgusting about sitting on a toilet with poo at your feet.

Jack leads me into his grubby bedroom and closes the door. He begins removing my pretty pink blouse with the Peter Pan collar and I am too stunned to speak. Is this how things operate in London? I was expecting fast-paced action, but the speed with which Jack is removing my clothes has left me gasping for air, which I think is sending out the wrong impression. Jack takes my quick, short gasps for something else entirely.

'Shall we?' he asks in a throaty, husky voice.

'Shall we what?'

'You know.'

I wish I did. It seems clear to me now that this is the sort of situation where one needs to be infinitely aware of what the other is thinking but all I am thinking as he lowers me onto his bed is that his bedding is pretty disgusting. I think he changes his sheets as often as he changes the kitty litter.

'Let's go over to the windowsill,' I suggest. 'You can see the moonlight so much better.'

'Wow, Teddy, you really are a little kinky, aren't you? I never thought of doing it on the windowsill.'

Actually, neither did I.

SIXTEEN

I have a boyfriend back home. His name is Dan and he is very sweet. We met five weeks before my trip. Sunny says that is not long enough to fall in love and I suppose I have to take her word for it since I have never fallen in love before and according to Sunny she has done it dozens of times.

I rather suspect she is doing it now, with William, who, of course, doesn't know what hit him.

Dan and I met at one of those noisy nightclubs that my rather bossy friend Helene dragged me to. I remember I was wearing a pearl necklace and, as far as I could tell, I was the only girl in the club wearing one. Dan said he liked the 'cut of my jib' from halfway across the room. I have no idea what a jib is but I knew at once that he appreciated my style, and that included my pearl necklace, so at that point I stopped worrying that I was the only girl in a pearl necklace and agreed to a spot of dancing on the pulsating floor. I tried not to look at the neon lights flashing at my feet. I lifted my chin and looked squarely into Dan's eyes, something I have never done with a boy before, and Dan looked squarely into mine (something a boy has never done with me before) and smiled.

He was rather upset when I told him that I was running off to London with Sunny.

'I can't believe you're leaving me,' he said, 'and I don't know when you'll be back.'

'I'm going for a year, Dan. I told you that already.'

'A year? It may as well be a lifetime. I don't think I can wait that long.'

'I'm not asking you to wait. I don't think you should.'

'Not wait? Are you mad? Of course I'm going to wait. Aren't you?'

To be honest, I quite liked the idea of a boy pining for me... perhaps out on the moors – Cathy! Cathy! Heathcliff! My Heathcliff! – That sort of thing.

I'd even hidden a copy of *Wuthering Heights* in my suitcase, to sort of get me in the mood. But Sunny said that Dan had no right to wrap me in cellophane for a whole year when no doubt untold adventures and fascinating men-folk awaited me and I must admit that the thought of fascinating men-folk awaiting me in some far-flung country did rather appeal to me. Was that really something that could happen to a girl like me? It sounded more than a little impossible, but Dan seemed quite willing to entertain the notion.

'I can't believe that I've finally found a terrific girl like you and now you're leaving me,' he said.

I tried to explain. 'I'm not leaving you per se, I'm leaving Bitterly Bay,' but he whispered in my ear that we'd only just found each other and 'a love like ours is hard to find. How can you let it slip away?'

He pressed his chest against my bosom and my pearls were nearly crushed beneath his hot and heavy ardour. I felt my resolve begin to weaken and my voice wobbled a little as I squeaked, 'Sometimes a girl has to follow her dreams.'

'What dreams?' he hotly contested and my brain scrambled to remember what dreams Sunny had told me I possessed.

'There's a great big world out there,' I weakly protested, 'and I've got to see where it takes me.' He flung himself away in sheer frustration and I quickly smoothed down my tweed skirt and patted my hair back into place. 'Besides,' I gulped. 'I've already booked the flight and paid for my ticket. It's non-refundable, you know.'

He sighed. 'I shan't wait. After all, we made no promises.'

I tried to hide my disappointment. 'I would like to see you when I get back.'

He grabbed my hand and squeezed tight. 'You promise?'

'Sure. Maybe we'll even write.' (If I can ever get my hand to work again.)

'I'm not good at putting my feelings down on paper,' he countered.

'Perhaps a postcard or two?' I suggested.

And that's when he told me that he'd think of me every day and that I mustn't tell him about all the men sniffing around me because it would break his heart.

'Just remember me when you're gone.'

'Sure.' I said. 'I'll think of you often.'

My emotions were a tangle of confusion. Were we Cathy and Heathcliff calling out to one another across the moors or was this just a silly little fancy sent to test my resolve?

I have to admit I do like him, quite a lot, but surely it's far too soon for love? He is cute, though, and he's just opened his own business, a video store in the mall. Working hard at establishing himself, my father says. Not to mention he's very attractive in a tall, blonde, broad-chested way. In fact, he is the perfect specimen of a bronzed Aussie but haven't we seen enough of those to last a lifetime? Sunny thinks as much. She says we're looking for pasty-white Brits who huddle in darkened corners talking existential angst.

'Is that too much to ask?' she says. And, at this point, I am ashamed to say that I very much think it is.

How else can you explain my stumbling at the first hurdle? I mean, here I am in London with nary a pasty-white Brit to be seen. Of all the men in London Town, how have I managed to end up in the grubby little bedroom of an Australian? I watch him toss my pretty pink blouse with the Peter Pan collar onto the floor of his filthy bedroom and hope the collar won't look too crushed in the morning. It makes me think of Dan pressing his chest against my bosom (was it heaving? I can't be sure) and crushing all my pearls.

SEVENTEEN

My first temp assignment is with The Family Planning Association. Someone up there has a sense of humour, wouldn't you say? It is in Oxford Circus, only three stops up on the tube. It's one of those buildings full of rabbit warrens with periodicals piled up to the ceiling and I have come to realise that the British office worker cannot be rushed at anything. They also seem to thoroughly enjoy morning tea and afternoon tea. It involves a lot of tea. I sit at a tiny desk, overflowing with yellowed paper and look out at the grey buildings pushed up against one another and try to remember wide open spaces and clear blue skies and Dan's clear blue eyes.

A pamphlet extolling the virtues of safe sex and contraceptive options gets caught under my heel as I leave the building at the end of the day and, unbeknownst to me, I carry it onto the tube and out of the station before it joins a pile of rubbish in the gutter not far from The Royal Eagle.

I wait in the bar for Jack to make an appearance but after several hours the horrible truth dawns on me. He is avoiding me. Now I look ridiculous. What am I doing drinking lemonade in a bar and waiting for a man that will never show up? Bebe finishes her shift and introduces me to Dave, a hotel guest that she's been sleeping with between shifts. He explains that his house is being renovated and he's been forced to make this hotel his temporary home. He says he hates the domestic staff encroaching upon his space. I grab a napkin off the bar and scribble down some words…

I'm sleeping in my big warm bed
I'm hearing a buzzing in my head
I open my eyes, the room is moovering
Damn those cleaning ladies hoovering

They move my things to a different corner
The telephone rings with another 'Good morner'
Don't they know that I've been boozering?
Damn those cleaning ladies hoovering

The later to bed, the earlier they ring
It's so annoying to have a cleaning lady sing
Perhaps they think the sound is soothering
Damn those cleaning ladies hoovering!

'Are you a writer?' asks Max.

Max is a friend of Jack's. On our first night at The Royal Eagle, when William had fallen head over heels for Sunny, I had been squashed into a corner with Max. He is an American writer, terribly serious about his craft, and on that first night he leant into my drink several times to reiterate just how important his opinion was, although what that opinion might have been was a little hard to gauge. He used awfully big words and they sounded quite political to me. I just nodded and grunted and hoped he wouldn't ask me any questions (which he didn't). The topic was all about him, anyway, so I guess he was more than happy to hog the conversation.

He is an ugly man, hairy to the point of bestial. He reminds me of that *American Werewolf in London*. A werewolf who wears a brown corduroy jacket with brown corduroy pants. He has messy black hair and a scruffy black beard and he's short and rotund.

He grabs the napkin from my hand and reads my poem out loud.

'You're good,' he says, but I don't care what he thinks. I just want to sink through the alcohol-infused carpet and disappear. I am wearing a cream blouse under one of my brown cardigans over a brown knit skirt with my hair scraped severely back off my face.

'You look like someone with no imagination,' he says, pulling his stool closer to me, 'but I bet beneath that bland exterior there beats a wild and passionate heart.'

'No.'

Jack walks in on the tail end of our conversation and with a wink says, 'Don't let 'er fool ya, mate.'

Max drains his glass and says, 'Right, back to my place. Let's go.'

Everybody gets up out of their seat and follows Max out the door and I don't know why but I do, too. It's like a tidal wave carrying me down the footpath but when I think about, there were really no more than four of us. Bebe and her new beau stay behind in the bar. William and Sunny are at a performance of *Starlight Express* and that leaves just Max and Jack and a girl whose name I haven't caught yet. She has shaggy orange hair and looks like a cross between Boy George and Bananarama. She is South African and, along with her South African boyfriend, shares the filthy flat in Cleveland Square with Jack. Her boyfriend is off travelling to parts unknown.

I know how he feels. I have absolutely no idea where we are going but we walk, catch a train, walk again, catch a bus, and then do yet more walking (thank goodness I'm wearing my sensible shoes) until we end up a long way from home. The night is getting chilly so I pull my cardigan tighter around me. The other three wrap ratty thin scarves around their necks. I make a mental note to buy a scarf in order to fit in. Do you think an Hermès would do?

Max lives in a tiny flat on the top floor of a building with no elevator. He puts on a Blondie record and croons tunelessly about rolling in designer sheets.

I wonder if Max has clean sheets.

Then he stares right at me and commands that I call him and I go cold from my head to my toes and glance across at Jack. Has he told the others what transpired between us? Does a gentleman tell? For that matter, is he a gentleman?

The girl sniggers into her Boy George layers. 'What is your name?' she says.

I think about this for a minute. Should I tell her the truth, try to connect with her in a real and honest way, and stretch out my hand in friendship?

'Teddy,' I answer and an imaginary line is drawn. I don't know how I ended up with friends like these but they are not going to get the real me. I am going to wrap her up in soft, pink tissue paper and pack her away with the mothballs at the bottom of my suitcase under the six brown cardigans, etcetera. I sit there, pulling an imaginary thread from my woollen cardigan and steal glances at their clothing and I come to the conclusion that they probably trawl flea markets for second-hand finds. But I don't think I can do that. The thought of wearing someone else's dirty clothes gives me the heebeegeebees. Tomorrow I am going to buy an oversized man's sweater from Selfridges and poke a couple of holes in it.

After about twenty minutes I finally say, 'What's your name?' It's just occurred to me that I ought to have asked her sooner.

She gives me a smirk and says, 'Not Teddy.'

She makes it sound like a piece of dirty lingerie. I know she thinks we have nothing in common but we have more in common than she thinks; it's not my name, either.

I am an idiot. Obviously this little get-together at Max's place was planned in advance and my tagging along at the last moment is something of a faux pas and now I am stuck. We are spending the night on his cold, hard floor and this time Jack has no intention of helping me to undress. I am well out of my comfort zone. I have no pyjamas, no clean underwear and, horrors of horrors, no toothbrush. I suppose it's just as well Jack is keeping his distance. I would hate to think that my morning breath alone was enough to knock him off his feet.

In the morning, I tag along with Jack and the orange shagball whose name I have discovered is Shelley. It's clear, however, that I'm a third wheel. I fear that with all the eye-rolling Shelley is doing, her eyes will roll right out of her head but at least she's looking my way now and then. Jack just looks right through me. They do a little dance at our tube stop. Shelley decides to stay on the train and go shopping. Jack says he'll tag along, it sounds like fun. I have no idea what the protocol is in such a situation and, not wanting to appear rude, I politely agree to go shopping, too. Perhaps I shall buy a warm winter coat. They say the winters in England are brutal.

Suddenly, Jack leaps out of his seat and sprints for the door. 'I've changed my mind,' he calls out over his shoulder and steps out onto the platform. I quickly follow. I am all at sea. I don't wish to offend Shelley but if Jack is going to bow out of our little social excursion, then surely it won't appear rude if I follow suit?

Shelley rolls her eyes again. Clearly, I have made another unforgivable blunder. It's not until I'm alighting from the Underground at Jack's side that I realise (aided by his body language) that he has been trying to (unsuccessfully) extricate himself from my (unwanted) company. Unfortunately, we live in the same direction so I am forced to trot on down the pavement at his side. I can feel the indignation rising like bile in the back of my throat.

'I realise you consider yourself irresistible to women but, contrary to your belief, I am not, in fact, pursuing you,' I finally blurt out. 'It may have escaped your attention but it was you who propositioned me, you who insisted I enter your bedroom and you who undressed me and threw me down onto those grey and grubby sheets. I am merely trying to find my footing in a strange new town. I wish to make some friends, that is all, and I would have thought that your little trio would be flattered that someone found your company appealing. Who knows, you might have even found my company appealing, too. But I guess we'll never know because you have decided to not even give me a chance. I think it's grand that you can use a person for your own pleasure and then toss her aside so callously but you'll forgive me if I don't fall at your feet and grovel in gratitude. And I suppose you're right, a kind, intelligent, interesting person who has made the terrible mistake of being interested in you is surely not the sort of person with whom you would wish to waste another minute of your precious time. So sorry to have ruined your day, Jack. Goodbye!'

Luckily we have reached the departure point between our two streets and I am able to execute a dignified retreat.

I hear him say, 'Bye Teddy' in a rather mystified tone but I refuse to turn around. I scuttle down the concrete steps to my basement flat, feeling my spirits rise a little at the sight of those pretty red geraniums and then rush inside, find Bebe's cardboard bowler hat and stomp on it again.

Then I make a cup of tea. You know, I think the British are onto something here. I certainly feel better for it.

I don't know where that outburst came from but clearly it was in me all along. It was very easy to let it out and although I'm fairly mortified at the scene I have caused, there's definitely something inside me that has stirred itself awake. It is now sitting up and paying attention.

When Sunny said London would be the making of me, I don't think she meant for it to make me into a monster but now that the Teddy is out of the bottle, I wonder if I'll ever be able to lock her back up again.

EIGHTEEN

I decide a quiet night in is the order of the day. I pull on my all-weather anorak and set off down the well-lit streets to the pizza shop. Now I know what you're thinking, is it safe to walk the streets at night? But Sunny has assured me that it is and if anyone knows, it would be she. She has been out almost every night.

There are a million and one cars travelling along the thoroughfare at all hours of the day and night and all I really need to worry about are the rich Arabs who cruise up and down in their big, expensive cars, asking every girl on the street, 'How much?' I figure with a pizza box in my hand and wearing the hood of my anorak tied tightly around my head I should be safe but I am wrong. Within minutes, an Arab approaches me.

'How much?'

'Are you kidding? How many hookers do you know in all-weather anoraks with a pizza in their hand?'

I guess this being London he figures anything goes. Sunny was once offered five hundred pounds but I don't get offered anywhere near that amount. Perhaps if I shared the pizza?

Once safely home, though, I'm feeling a little flat, having rejected the Arab's paltry offer and eaten all the pizza, so I decide to throw caution to the wind and sort out my coin collection. I need ten pence coins for the public telephones, twenty pence coins for the Laundromat, and fifty pence coins for the electric meter in the flat and for the ticket machine at the tube station. That sorted, I settle down to catch up on correspondence back home.

Dan has written to tell me that he wants me to have a good time but not *too* much of a good time, you understand, and he wants to know if I plan to return home anytime soon.

Mother wants me to dress warmly and buy more thermal underwear.

My bossy friend Helene seems rather miffed that I am enjoying life in London and is dropping rather broad hints that she ought to join me. Whether it's to join in the fun or wrench me out of it, I'm not sure.

And then there's Great Aunt Ida in Birmingham. She wants me to visit her as soon as possible, now that the pomp and pageantry of the Royal Wedding (Fergie to Prince Andrew) is over, the gooseberries and blackcurrants have been picked and preserved, and they've had a first feed of new peas and potatoes from their allotment. She writes about making Uncle Bill a cup of tea (he's watching the Test Match on telly) and it sounds exactly like my cup of tea so I write back immediately with plans to visit her in the near future.

I have a job, so it will depend on what assignments I've got. I work for temp secretarial agency Kelly Girl. I'm sent to companies all over London, sometimes at a moment's notice. I earn good money, over four pounds an hour (about nine Australian dollars) and my duties cover answering phones, typing up documents, and other secretarial duties. I don't have to fetch too many coffees as most of the larger companies have a tea-lady who wheels her trolley down the aisles. The British love their tea.

I also write a thank-you note to Aunt Flavia and Uncle Reg. I visited them on the weekend and they took me down to Brighton Beach. I hobbled across the stony shore, past flabby white bodies, and along the pier to the Penny Arcade. I even saw the scaffolding and tarpaulin on the hotel where the IRA tried to blow up Prime Minister Maggie Thatcher. Far from being disappointed, I was elated at having experienced a typical British summer, nothing at all like the ones back home. I even wore a sweater!

I've seen very little of Sunny. She has spent every evening with William. I rather suspect we are having two entirely different experiences in London.

I wash my hair, hang my wet stockings over a chair and am just about to put on my pyjamas and go to bed when there is a knock at the door. It is eleven p.m. and, surprise, surprise, Jack is standing on the threshold. I pop the kettle on.

It seems my little speech on the pavement has made an impact on him. He wants us to be friends.

'Come down to The Eagle tomorrow night,' he says. 'I'll cook you dinner.'

I'm tickled pink, or at the very least beige. I've made a friend and scored a decent meal and it would appear I'm no longer a desperate interloper at The Royal Eagle Hotel.

Well done, Teddy!

NINETEEN

Max is trying to get into my pants. I had my suspicions the night he put that Blondie record on but lately he's been positively persistent. I'm afraid he doesn't make me go weak at the knees so there is little opportunity to get me in the horizontal position, although I can't fault Max for trying. Sometimes he is very trying indeed.

For example: William and Sunny invite me to join them on an evening out. I'm rather excited in the beginning, imagining a fine live performance of feline thespians or perhaps a nice curry at the local Indian restaurant but, alas, it's movie night.

We go to see *9½ Weeks*. It's all sado-masochistic nonsense wrapped up in whipped cream and striptease and certainly not the type of film one wishes to watch with a couple still in their honeymoon phase.

Back at The Eagle, I sit in the bar with Max as he goes in search of a pseudo-intellectual dissection of the piece. 'Women like to be dominated and controlled,' he says.

'No,' I correct him. 'Men like to dominate and control women. Kim Basinger would like a hit film and a movie career. Other women would like to look like Kim Basinger and some women, like me, don't give a damn about any of it.'

Max leans in closer, a habit for which he seems especially fond of, and says, 'Some women like to do the dominating and be the one in control and some men find that very appealing.'

Ugh!

I wonder if Jack has told him about my rather forceful outburst.

Max thinks I have a rather dim view of America's artistic endeavours and the only rectification that he can see is to take me to an avant-garde American play. Finally I get to sample the theatre in London, even if it is miles away from the West End and populated by Yankee-doodle-dandies.

I can see at once, though, that I have made a terrible mistake. The play is awful – the acting dreadful, the plot dreary – and Max still has that annoying habit of leaning. He whispers into my ear that Jack 'has herpes' and at first I think it's another baffling plot point in this tedious play before realising he is talking about my Jack.

And an infectious sexual disease.

'Why are you telling me this?' I whisper back. None of the other patrons around us ask us to shush because most of them are asleep. The gentleman beside me is reading a book in his lap by torchlight.

'I don't want you to get hurt,' says Max.

'Or you're trying to eliminate the competition,' I counter.

'That too.'

So what is the truth here? Does my delectable Jack have herpes or is this just an attempt by Max to weasel his way into my affections? Jack is quite the ladies' man so I suppose it could be possible.

It is not until we are standing on the train station at midnight and Max is refusing to accompany me home that I come to the conclusion that all men are bastards. Max reasons that he has to work in the morning and cannot afford the extra hour it will take to see me to my door. Best I return to his flat and spend the night with him. I don't have any work in the morning (no one does – it's a bank holiday although apparently Max's workplace is the one exception) so he thinks it makes sense for me to stay the night with him.

Hmm.

I acquiesce, simply because I have no choice but, 'No funny business,' I warn as I strip down to my underwear and climb into bed beside him. It's a small single bed so the chance of an unmolested slumber seems slim. Max stuffs his fist into his mouth and whimpers.

'Perhaps I should sleep on the floor?' I suggest.

'No, no, no. You don't have to lower yourself to that level.'

'I would gladly lower myself to the floor than consent to lowering myself even further by subjecting myself to a grope or two.'

'Nonsense. I won't lay a hand on you. We're just two friends bunking together for the night.'

Hmm. I've heard that before.

Max, however, is a man of his word. I wake in the morning to find him curled up in the foetal position on the bedroom floor.

'I couldn't take the pressure,' he says.

I return home and William takes Sunny and me down the M4 in a borrowed MG to Windsor Castle. It's pouring with rain so we go to the pub instead. I natter on about Jack and Max and Shelley (who's actually beginning to like me) and Dave's aversion to cleaning ladies and Sunny gives me a blank look and says, 'Who?'

It appears that even though she is spending most nights at The Eagle, she has made no effort whatsoever to get to know any of the natives. Sometimes she'll sit in the bar with us but she's not all that interested in what the rest of us are doing. Not even when we're all glued to the big screen television, watching the Australian mini-series *Return to Eden* (the Brits are totally addicted to it). Sunny has the ability to be an island even in a room full of people. She just detaches herself a little so that not all of her is all there.

Perhaps that's another reason why I was so desperate to make friends. It gives me someone to talk to. I once thought I was the shy, wallflower type but that was before Teddy burst onto the scene. Teddy likes to get into intellectual stoushes with Max over poetry and plagiarism and poorly-acted plays. Teddy likes to eat Jack's meals and debate whether rice and potatoes belong on the same plate together. Teddy loves whooping and hollering at the screen when Stephanie, who is horribly disfigured by a croc attack courtesy of her evil hubby, returns to Eden to wreak revenge.

And when Bebe's shift finishes, Teddy likes to walk home with her, laughing and singing and shouting out to those rich men in their fancy cars, 'You can't afford us!' And I don't even mind that everyone calls me Teddy.

But these busy days and busy nights are beginning to wear me out. I develop a sore throat and then a kidney infection and spend the week in bed. William and Max and Jack send fruit, cranberry juice and well wishes. Sunny finds me a fluffy red hot water bottle to ease the pain and I lie in bed and accept copious cups of tea.

Bebe drapes herself across my mustard-coloured eiderdown (why is everything in this flat mustard?) and the truth is finally revealed. Sunny and I are both aged twenty, doing what young people do, as Sunny says, and although Bebe could never pass for a woman that young, I take her twenty-eight years at face value. Granted, that face is a little more weathered than expected but I am shocked when she finally admits that she is thirty-eight.

'You're not,' I gasp.

'Oh, all right, I'm actually forty-two,' she confesses. (Old enough to be our mother!)

At first I think she's far too mature for us but then she tells me what has brought her to London and I realise her emotional level is pretty much on a par with ours.

'A broken heart,' she sobs, 'a tragic, twisted love story involving a groom – not mine – and star-crossed lovers. I met him on his honeymoon.' She sits upright and bugs her eyes out at me. 'That's right, his honeymoon. Just two days too late, I was. You know, he's often said that if only he'd met me first then he would never have married her. Of course he could hardly leave her so soon after their wedding, bad form and all that. And, really, you have to admire his scruples, don't you?'

At first I think she says you have to admire his balls so I answer, 'You sure do,' before realising my mistake. 'How long have you been together?'

'Seven years,' she sighs. And even I know that's an awful long time to wait to ensure his wife doesn't lose face. 'Of course in the end I just had to make an ultimatum. Damn ugly business.' And she blows her nose on a tissue. 'I told him either that grasping wife of his goes or I do. For some ridiculous reason he refused to leave her so here I am. I'm making him miss me, you see.'

'Is it working?'

'Of course. He is simply begging me to return. Naturally, I am making him suffer.'

I look at Bebe and her quivering smile and decide that she is probably the only one suffering in this scenario.

Is this to be my own fate, I wonder?

TWENTY

Max has taken to begging me to bounce my bottom on his balls. How on earth did I end up with such colourful cohorts? I never would have imagined that such people could exist but in London it seems to be the norm. I am certainly expanding my horizons and embracing opportunities but my nights and days are like, well, night and day.

I have taken to office temping like a duck to water. The varied assignments handed to me have been most enjoyable and it's such a nice change from the dull monotony of the accountancy firm back home. Sunny is also a Kelly Girl but my skills and neat appearance (brown is a very secretarial colour) seem to have afforded me much better opportunities than Sunny. She grumbles that her assignments are dull and dreary but I have been thoroughly enjoying mine – The

Family Planning Association, Trust House Forte, and Media Audits. The British accent over the telephone, however, is a little hard to comprehend.

Once I've recovered from my bout of illness, I decide that even though I love working, I ought to take a little time to relax and be a tourist. I join William and Sunny on a cruise down the Thames to the Tate Gallery. Those Turner paintings are so awe-inspiring. The next day it's Madam Tussauds Wax Museum. I take a photograph of myself with a waxy Bob Geldof and send it to my mother who has a heart attack (thinking it's my new boyfriend). And that night a group of us go to the Laserium for a laser light show set to the music of Genesis. On the Wednesday, I join Bebe and Sunny on a canal trip to Little Venice where Sunny calmly informs me that she's moving out of the flat and into William's tiny room at the hotel. It makes sense, I suppose. Why pay rent when you're never there? Still, it leaves me in a bit of a pickle. I will have to share a bedroom with a complete stranger. I want to object but Sunny says this is what young people do. And who am I to disagree?

Apparently what they also do is go to parties. I take a long time trying to find a suitable outfit. Bebe says if I'm to catch a young man's eye I need to make a good impression.

'Why do I need to catch a young man's eye?'
'To have fun.'

'Can't I have fun without a man?'

'No.'

'What about my mustard polo shirt?' Don't forget, it's the most striking item of clothing I own.

'I've had enough of mustard,' moans Bebe.

I hold up the oversized man's sweater that I've studiously avoided washing. There's a loose thread unravelling at the hem like nobody's business and a hole in one of the elbows.

'Perfect,' says Bebe. 'What are you going to wear on the bottom?'

I hold up a knit skirt in one hand and a knit trouser in the other.

'Don't you own a pair of jeans?'

'Of course not. Don't be ridiculous.'

Bebe disappears behind her mustard curtain and reappears moments later with a pair of freshly laundered jeans. 'These are too small for me,' she says.

'They're too small for me, too,' I protest.

'It's called making an impression.'

'It's called cutting off my circulation and losing the use of my limbs.'

'Beauty is pain.'

I squeeze into the jeans and throw on the sweater. Bebe pulls the Alice band out of my hair and messes it up a bit, then grabs her kohl pencil and rims my eyes in black. I look in the mirror and a stranger looks back.

'Go get 'em,' says Bebe.

And I go. And get 'em.

The party is down a flight of stairs in a basement flat a block and a half from home. William says they're 'chasing the dragon' down there. I have no idea what he means but I know as soon as I reach the door that this is not the place for me. Drunken girls in Aussie accents are singing (loudly and off-key) about being Londoners (which clearly they are not), as they drape themselves across the doorway and kiss everybody's cheeks. Jack seizes me as soon as I step inside and says, 'Thank God you're here.'

'I was just leaving,' I say.

'Great idea.'

And he bustles me out the door, up the stairs and back onto the footpath.

'You don't know how glad I am to be out of there,' he says. 'Let's go back to my place for a cup of tea.'

Don't look at me that way. His proposal makes perfect sense. His flat is on the way home, I'd have to pass it in order to get back to Gloucester Terrace, and after such a harrowing experience I could do with a restorative brew.

We sit on a lumpy couch as water from the ceiling drips into the saucepan on the floor and I try to align my cup with the stains on the coffee table.

'I'm so glad we're friends, Teddy.'

Uh oh. I know where this is going.

'No really, I mean it. Most girls just want me for my body.'

Is he kidding?

'But you're different. You see beyond the exterior.'

I do?

'When I'm with you I feel like I can truly be myself.'

I suppose that's true. I seem to be the only one who's taken the time to get to know my fellow travellers, although it's not that hard to do. Most people love to talk about themselves. The trick is to get them when they're sober. Then at least you can make sense of all their rambling. For instance, the story of how Jack came to London is quite unusual. He used to work on a building site until a pallet of bricks conked him on the head. He suffered a little bit of brain damage and got a sizeable compensation payout (and a sizeable lump on the head, no doubt), which he spent on a one-way ticket to London. We stay up chatting half the night and then we go to bed.

Asking someone if they have herpes is far too awkward but, thanks to that safe sex pamphlet stuck to the heel of my shoe, I know how to take precautions. I figure if I can handle dirty sheets then I can handle anything but I'm afraid nothing prepares me for the shock that awaits me in the cold, hard light of day.

A complete stranger bursts into the bedroom and plonks himself on the floor where he proceeds to roll the biggest joint that I have ever seen. I nearly vomit. I am that repulsed by him. He is thin and wiry and wears more scarves than Keith Richards from the Rolling Stones. He's probably more stoned than him, too. His dirty blonde hair stands up in all directions except for one long piece that keeps flopping over his eye. He looks like a scarecrow that has spent too many seasons out in the rain. I would run screaming from the bedroom were it not for the fact that I am naked under the bedsheets.

And that is how I meet Sean, Shelley's boyfriend, well, sort of boyfriend, just back from a visit home to South Africa. Apparently they're on and off on a regular basis, much like the man himself.

'Boy, am I glad to be home,' says Sean.

'I thought South Africa was your home?'

'Not any more. They kicked me out.'

'Drugs?' I raise an eyebrow at the enormous joint dangling between his dirty fingers.

'No, political propaganda.'

He lights up and offers me a puff but I shake my head. 'I don't do that stuff.'

'I've never met anyone like you,' he says.

Clearly he has met many a naked girl, with panda eyes and hair mussed up, curled up in Jack's sheets – he barely raised an eyebrow when he burst into the room – but this, a girl who doesn't smoke weed, this shocks the pants off him.

'I've never met anyone like you.' I try to sound scornful and scathingly judgemental but a little fascination creeps in.

'I'm a musician, too.'

Is he puffing out his chest?

'I play the sax.'

A little string in my heart tightens but my brain intervenes before anything can get out of hand. He's just a dirty junkie, nothing to get excited about.

But then he adds, 'I write poetry, too.'

I am seriously thinking about throwing this holey jumper in the bin. It is giving people the wrong impression. They think I am... what's the word... cool?... hot?... when how I really feel is luke-warm (like a cup of tea) and strung out (like a used teabag). Not sure why I'm thinking of tea right now but it's kind of soothing so I decide to go back to my (clean) flat and make myself a (fresh) cup.

I walk home with my hair dishevelled, make-up smeared, and clothes crumpled, and far from looking out of place, I actually fit right in. I meet a man coming out of my flat and he seems neither surprised nor scandalised to see me coming in.

I wish I could say the same.

What on earth is a man doing at 133 Gloucester Terrace, and at this time of the morning? It takes me a moment to place him. We met last night. He is the new young and attractive Aussie barman at The Eagle. His name is Mick. Apparently his girlfriend, also an Aussie, was missing in action last night and Bebe has seized the day (or night, as the case may be). To say I am scandalised and disappointed is an understatement.

'Nothing happened,' she says, but I'm not buying it.

I know people in (grotty) glass houses shouldn't throw stones, but my little dalliance was with a man who was free to dally back. Mick belongs to another girl. It's the married man on his honeymoon all over again, only this time the bloke is young enough to be her son. I have to remind myself that the people in London are far more cosmopolitan than the folk back home but it still feels wrong to me.

I'm still struggling to work out where I stand with Dan. He made it clear to me when I left that we have no obligation to each other whilst I'm overseas but then he writes me letters telling me how much he misses me and cannot wait for my return so I'm a little confused. Am I a free agent? And just because we're missing one another terribly does that mean we have to remain celibate for a whole year?

We're in the prime of our lives, Sunny says, on an adventure of a lifetime, doing what young people do, sowing wild oats, throwing caution to the wind (and every other cliché you can think of). When we planned this trip, I was a single gal, looking forward to 'endless possibilities' and 'fascinating men-folk'.

If I had a choice, of course I'd pick Dan (who wouldn't? He's gorgeous!) but he's not here, is he? The last thing I want is to be a wallflower, sitting in the corner of the room and missing out on all the fun. This is my time to shine. I might have sensible walking shoes and six brown cardigans but I intend to make every effort to step out of my comfort zone and embrace new ideas, tight jeans, and holey sweaters. And I shall loosen up my moral standards, if that's what it takes.

I am not prim and proper Theodora anymore.

I am a Teddy-Bear with panda eyes.

And over here, love (and fidelity) is a dirty word.

So is cooking, for that matter. I remove my make-up, Bebe puts hers on, and we go down to The Walkabout Club for a Sunday roast. And all thoughts of who's cheating on whom with whom are quickly forgotten.

As you may remember, Sunny and I joined The Walkabout Club on our first day in London. We made use of the accommodation assistance and they were very helpful indeed, having found us the place in Gloucester Terrace, and since then I have used their travel agency to book a coach tour through Europe, which I intend to take in October. At the time of us taking the lease at 133, Sunny agreed to a three-month stay and I adjusted my plans accordingly. Of course, she ended up moving out way ahead of schedule but I am still sticking to the plan.

At the time of joining The Walkabout Club, I was of the very firm opinion that we would never make use of the social part of their membership but, as you are well aware, London has proven to be quite the eye-opener for me and any expectations previously held have been forcefully abandoned.

The Club is in a basement (what is it with the Brits and their basements?), beneath The Elysee Hotel. It is a long, low room with a buffet-style restaurant at the front, a stage at the rear and a giant-screen television with seating area to the side. It would appear that on Sundays every Aussie within a one hundred-mile radius turns up for the traditional Sunday roast. Apparently, it reminds them of home. They sit there with a tear in their eye and a tinny in their hand and try to eat themselves out of a hangover.

William, whom you may remember lives vicariously through others, joins us at our table, bringing yet another stranger into the mix. I am almost reluctant to look this man in the eye for fear of what I should encounter but Elliott turns out to be an absolute delight. He is softly spoken and polite with a friendly smile and a twinkle in the eye. He comes from Liverpool but cannot really call any place home anymore. He is somewhat of a rambler, travelling all over the world, but he returns to London when funds are low and does work at The Eagle until he can afford to take off again. He reminds me a little of Sting, with his closely-cropped hair and his angelic face and I am very happy to see that he is not 'putting the moves' on me in the slightest. Finally, a man who doesn't need to bed every woman he meets.

Alas, I fear I may have spoken too soon. Less than a week later, Elliott is off again, grape-picking in the south of France but this time he is not alone. Sunny has run off to the south of France with him.

I can hardly say that I am surprised. The poor girl was fairly itching to find adventure in a far-flung land. Not two weeks earlier she had planned to join Rose, the barmaid, on a trip into Turkey but, not surprisingly, those plans fell through. Sunny quickly spotted the flaw in her plan and made changes accordingly. With Rose, she'd have to pull her own weight and pay her own way but with men... well, they have that thing between their legs that stops them using that thing between their ears.

William is trying to convince himself that it's purely platonic, but who is he kidding? He claims to be devastated but I notice that his long-suffering girlfriend is suddenly back on the scene.

I have little time to miss Sunny, though. Apart from being forced to make my own friends and find my own fun, I have also been busy at work. Fitch & Co. were a delightful little design company, tucked into an overcrowded warehouse; Liberty were the complete opposite – an enormous department store filled with the most exquisite fabrics and accessories, and even though I worked upstairs in the Publicity department, I spent many a lunch hour with nose pressed to glass cabinets. After that, there was Chappell Music, a recording studio where everyone wore denim; and then Goodge Street... I can't remember what they did at Goodge Street. I have a vague idea it might have been advertising.

And we have a new flatmate. Her name's Liz and she's ex-army so her disciplined point of view is right up my alley, although now, of course, that we are in London, we are walking on the wild side. One night we walk to the cinema in the rain to see *Pretty in Pink*. And we don't take umbrellas. In hindsight it's probably not such a daring idea as we sit soggy and steaming in the cinema but it feels oddly liberating to be a little reckless now and then.

It appears, though, that I may be wrong about not missing Sunny. Let's not forget, she is the reason I am here in London and I had hoped that we would be sharing a lot more adventures together. I don't like to say that Sunny has abandoned me, but it certainly feels that way. Max encourages me to express myself more in my poetry but I am fairly appalled at the result.

It's not the rain
Against my window
Or the voices
In groups walking by
It's not my empty room
Or empty wine bottle
Or even empty bed
It's just
That I'm lonely

I don't even drink so what's that about? And here's another:

- Windows of Pain –
Criss-crosses pattern my brain
Reflected in windows of pane
They cross over again and again
These patterns made from the rain

At the end of September, before I stick my head in the oven, I board a bus for Birmingham.

TWENTY-TWO

I feel like I am drowning in doilies. They appear to be on every surface in Uncle Bill and Aunt Ida's warm and welcoming home. I am pampered from the get-go with a cup of tea in bed each morning and sightseeing trips in the afternoon. The pork pies, however, I could do without. They take me to the house in Finstall where my father was born and the house where he lived until it feels like I am stalking him and I have more tea (and cake) and hear stories about every person in Britain that is even remotely related to me. It's weird to see so many people who look uncannily like my father but thinking of family and knowing that I am not that far from home has lessened the anguish of losing Sunny.

I return to London wrapped up in the warm hug of kith and kin, thanks to the lovely knitted cardie Aunt Ida has given me. It is blue. Not a colour I would normally wear but she says it lifts my face and gives me pep and where once such a thing would have filled me with horror, I find myself now embracing the idea.

And how lovely it is to return to my basement flat with the pretty red geraniums in the bay windowsill. I have a lovely cup of tea with flatmate Liz then take a walk down to The Royal Eagle Hotel to catch up with my friends. Bebe is on Reception and shouts in delight at my return. Jack makes me a delicious dinner and I sit in the bar with Shelley, who is turning into a good friend, and Sean, who is (worryingly) growing on me. I'm not sure if their relationship is on or off, it's hard to tell the difference. Mick, the young and attractive Aussie barman (who dallianced with Bebe) pours me a lemonade, as Dave dishes the dirt on his latest disastrous dealings with the domestic staff. He says my witty poem pulls him out of his domestic funk each and every time. Max, no doubt furious that his own talent is being ignored, challenges me to a poetry slam.

Now that I'm no longer channeling Sylvia Plath, I feel confident that I can rise to the challenge.

William, who believes he's the unofficial leader of our group, thinks we should put our creative talents to better use. So far he's mentioned a book deal, a song-writing business and something akin to New York's Algonquin Hotel's Round Table where a host of talented wits famously met on a regular basis. I am only too happy to compare myself to Dorothy Parker, if that's what William wishes, because I am a huge fan, but it would take a lot more than a few fancy poems to reach her heights. I do, however, rather enjoy the little thrill that tickles in my tummy when everyone praises my own efforts, inferior to hers as they invariably must be.

And thanks to my new friends (and family) I find myself missing home (and Sunny) a little less.

I am spending the working week at The Royal Institute of British Architects and am not in the least surprised when they offer me full-time employment. I am exactly the sort of worker they seek. But I surprise even myself when I politely decline their offer.

'I am not looking for long-term employment,' I hear myself explain. 'I have plans to travel in the future and am looking forward to new endeavours.'

I even find myself wearing my tight blue jeans and my new blue cardigan to a Jackson Browne concert with Jack and Max. My mother told me to stay out of crowded places because the IRA keep bombing them but they recently bombed a McDonalds and there's no way I'm staying away from fast food outlets so I figure everywhere in London is a possible target and I may as well just get on with it, as Sunny would say.

My tight blue jeans have the desired effect on Jack but Max is outraged that a mere wink from Jack has me weak at the knees and flat on my back. He decides affirmative action is required and the next evening whisks me off to the cinema to see *About Last Night*, starring Demi Moore and Rob Lowe. He is hoping that all that sex will get me in the mood but, alas, it is not to be.

'Why won't you sleep with me,' he whines.

'Because I don't love you, Max.'

'What's that got to do with anything?' he sulks.

What indeed.

This is London, where anything goes and nothing holds you back. People tumble into bed before introductions have been properly made. I've been banging on about loosening morals and grabbing every opportunity that comes my way so I'm not surprised Max is petulant and perturbed.

How can I tell him that he's just too damn ugly to see naked? Perhaps if he blindfolded me first and tied my hands together (so that they don't accidentally get tangled up in all that body hair) but, no, you're right, that sort of talk would just encourage him. Men (especially the ones in London) go bonkers for a bit of bondage.

William has spent the week sobbing on my shoulder. Sunny has telephoned (him, not me) and he is beginning to fear that she is not missing him in the slightest.

Well of course she's not. She's stomping grapes and drinking red wine by the barrelful and passing out on cobblestones with chunks of puke in her hair. Who has time to miss anyone with all that going on?

William invites me to a party in the country with some old school pals. They are all terribly posh and I get the impression he wants to dazzle them with his continental connections. There appears to be some confusion over which bed I am to sleep in but I make it perfectly clear that all will be above board where my virtue is concerned. After all, a girl has to draw the line somewhere.

Yes, I know I drew it with Max, but I draw it again with William.

I have no doubt that once Sunny returns home she will be picking up where she left off. Why else the telephone call? I don't like the idea of muddying the water with my best friend, even if she has run off to the south of France with William's best friend.

We are staying at the stately family home of Charles Llewelyn-Smyth (you know how these wealthy old families like their hyphenated double-barrelled names). Sunny had met him briefly and told me that she had 'fancied him like crazy' and I can see what the attraction would be for her. He is fabulously wealthy, insanely good-looking and clearly out for a good time. He also has one of the nicest girlfriends I've ever met. Her name is Lucy and she, too, is fabulously wealthy and insanely good-looking. She is also one of Britain's leading female racing-car drivers but that doesn't stop Charlie from expecting her to skim his swimming pool.

We take a tour around the stables and a leisurely stroll down to the quaint village pub for lunch before Charlie drives us to the train station in his gleaming red Porsche. You know, I had no idea cars could go that fast. It is not until I step out onto Paddington Station amidst the hustle and bustle that I realise I am changing. I am actually beginning to enjoy the fast pace of City living. I mean, sure there's grit and grime and a whole lot of unnecessary pushing and shoving, but there is also a delicious sense that something rather exciting is about to happen. I can feel it hanging in the air as William and I advance towards The Royal Eagle Hotel and we have placed barely one foot in the foyer before we are rushed off to The Walkabout Club.

Rose, the barmaid, is back from her travels abroad but we have barely time to hear the gory details before it's off to Le Beat Route, a nightclub in Soho. We are joined by a few guests from the hotel and Sean but not Shelley (so I guess their relationship is off again). Mick is working in the bar but his Aussie girlfriend decides to come along, too.

Her name is Lucille and she is a little bundle of fabulous. I have a thumping disco beat blaring in one ear, and Lucille rabbiting away in the other and instantly I adore her. I can tell that she is not the type of girl to be messed with and I admire that immensely. She is honest and forthright and says what she means and, as Dan would say, I like the cut of her jib. I feel a kinship with her immediately and it would seem the feeling is mutual.

I am wearing my pretty pink blouse with the Peter Pan collar in a cotton/silk blend, and Lucille says, 'I love your top. You look so elegant.'

Of course the music is distorting everything so she might have said, 'What's with the top? You look like an elephant.' But I think not.

On Monday I start a new assignment at Carlton Magazine in the Publicity Department of 'Options', a very successful women's magazine. I must say it's turning out to be quite a lot of fun. I spend an inordinate amount of time poring over their back issues and they seem quite impressed by my 'avid research' into their product. I am even pressed into service one evening when the magazine holds a male fashion parade in a department store. My job is to hand out free copies of their magazine. I know. It's insane. I actually get paid for this. I know what you're going to ask next and, yes, they did model underwear and, yes, it was every bit as good as you imagine.

All in all, a pretty fabulous day and to top it off a postcard arrives from Sunny:

Dear Teddy and Bebe,

Having a great time, heaps of sun, good wine, food and grapes. Tomorrow we are off to Nice or somewhere - who knows!!! Get your arses out of London – travelling is where it's at!!! Miss you guys heaps. Don't know when I'll be back but will keep in touch.

Love, Sunny.

To be honest, we barely have time to read it. Bebe has quit work at The Eagle and wants to become a Kelly Girl like me. Better hours, better pay and better perks (hello, male underwear models!) so we head down to The Walkabout Club for some celebratory drinks. I'm not much of a drinker, in fact I've been drunk exactly once – at a friend's brother's twenty-first. I had two glasses of vodka and orange, went to the toilet and puked in my underwear. I then pulled them back up and passed out on a bed. You can imagine what greeted me in the morning when I went to empty my bladder. As I said, I haven't really been much of a drinker since. But Bebe is drinking enough for the both of us. Even our flatmate, Liz, gets into the swing of things. She has extremely long hair, the colour of straw, which she combs over her face and tops with a pair of sunglasses. She looks exactly like Cousin Itt from The Addams Family. I think it's safe to say she's had a bit too much to drink, too. I tire pretty quickly of them and head off to The Eagle for a quieter night in the bar.

And that's how I meet Emily Oliver... back in town after picking grapes in the south of France where, yes, she encountered our Sunny. And what a tale she has to tell. It seems that Emily Oliver was the one-time girlfriend of Elliott, presumably before he turned up with Sunny on his arm. But what seemed to rankle her the most was that Sunny had taken a hairdryer to the ramshackle pig-pen that the grape-pickers called home.

'A hairdryer,' she says. 'Can you believe it?'

I am not surprised in the least. Good hair is Sunny's trademark.

What does surprise me, however, is that Emily Oliver gave up without a fight. She doesn't look the type. For starters, she's an Aussie and from my experience we are a lot feistier than our British counterparts. And secondly, she's scrappy. You can see it in her eyes; sharp, black pebbles that fire up at the mere mention of a hairdryer. And I imagine men would find her quite attractive in an earthy, unpretentious way. She's a true hippie; very buxom and shamelessly braless with long, flowing locks (a little greasy if you ask me) and hairy armpits but I can see how appealing she would be to a no-nonsense nomad like Elliott. She must have thought Sunny with her blonde cockatoo hairstyle, blow-dried and lacquered to within an inch of its life, didn't stand a chance. But then, men have a habit of losing all sense when Sunny is around.

I am keen to hear about their grape-picking in the south of France but all that toiling in the hot sun with no modern conveniences does not sound like my cup of tea at all. Travelling is where it's at? I don't think so.

Emily Oliver is sleeping on Jack's couch so we walk home together and it's still early yet (three a.m. to be precise) so I stick around for a while and let Sean serenade me with his sax. Alarmingly, he is beginning to grow on me, like fungus under a rock.

When I eventually make it home I find a crudely made note stuck to the front door. It says: *Massage Parlour*. Really? I find Liz passed out on her bed and Bebe in the bathroom, weeping uncontrollably. I put her to bed and set the alarm for ten a.m. We're having brunch at a posh hotel and I don't think the dress code extends to bags under the eyes and stonking hangovers.

TWENTY-THREE

Bebe is contemplating Africa. We arrive at the posh hotel where my tweed skirt, cream blouse and brown cardigan meet with the doorman's approval. I drag Bebe, hunched over in dark glasses, into the hotel lobby to meet with a friend of a friend who has connections to Africa. Her parents live in South Africa and she suggests to Bebe this should be her jumping off point. It sounds lovely to me until they start talking about man-eating lions and no running water.

Bebe says her head feels like someone poured concrete in her nostrils and do I know anything about this? There's nothing for it but to head off to The Walkabout Club for a nourishing Sunday roast. I hear hangovers always hurt less when you've eaten. We collect Liz and join William, Jack, Sean and Shelley for lunch before migrating to a couple of lumpy sofas in front of the big-screen television. There's a hockey match on between Australia and the U.K. Bebe slept with the Aussie coach when he stayed at the Hotel, and somehow it makes us feel more connected to the team so we shout like lunatics all throughout the match.

William is still moaning about how much he misses Sunny and I know I'm his designated crying shoulder but I'm a little distracted at the moment. I feel funny every time Sean looks my way and lately he's been most attentive...

Shelley says they're 'off' again so that makes him fair game, right? Even though I keep getting tangled up in Jack's crusty sheets, he keeps insisting we're just friends so I'm fair game, too, I suppose. But just because I can, does that mean I should?

So, the hockey match is heating up, they're closing the doors to the Club because it's after three p.m. and they can't serve alcohol to the public, William is blubbering into my armpit, Sean is whispering inflammatory poetry into my ear, Bebe is revealing salacious details about the team and everyone else is shouting profanity at the screen when...

Sunny and Elliott casually stroll into the bar.

After the initial shock wears off and Australia wins the hockey match, I discover that Sunny's next exotic and exciting travel destination is... the basement flat at 133 Gloucester Terrace. I put the kettle on.

'Did you miss me?'

'Yes.' (No.)

'Was it boring here without me?'

'Yes.' (No.)

'Don't you wish you'd gone to France?'

'Yes.' (No.)

'Aren't you glad I'm back?'

'Of course.' (Not.)

It's not that I'm sorry Sunny has returned, it's just that I know she won't stick around for long. She seems a little disappointed that I've gotten on with my life but she says it doesn't surprise her that I've made a safe little haven for myself in amongst all this maelstrom. I like to think that I'm a welcome port in everybody's storm but the main thing is I'm a welcome port in my storm. I need to feel that I'm still safe, dependable Theodora, even if I'm now called Teddy, and I won't apologise for that.

Sunny follows Elliott back to The Eagle, Bebe and Liz trot upstairs to visit the Kiwi girls in Flat 2 and I take a bath. Then Bebe takes a nap and I make tomato soup. At seven-thirty we grab a pizza and head over to (where else) The Eagle. I have made a point of wrapping my scarf (10% staff discount at Liberty) around my neck to show Sunny that I do, indeed, fit in but it would seem that my place in the world is not the issue here. Elliott is spending the night on William's floor so where does that leave Sunny? There seems to be some grey area about who she's hooked up to but it's good old Theodora to the rescue and she ends up sleeping on my sofa.

Two days later she's off again. Elliott is going back to his hometown in Liverpool and, a little bewilderingly, Sunny is going too.

I've little time to worry about Sunny's ménage à trios as I seem to have my own triangle developing with Sean and Emily Oliver. On the one hand, it's good that Sunny and Elliott are no longer here since Emily's not as forgiving as William. On the other hand, I wish she wasn't staying at Jack and Sean's place. She seems to be hanging around Sean like a bad smell and that's not just a figure of speech. She stinks! I don't think she bathes. She certainly doesn't look like she does. But that sort of thing doesn't seem to bother anyone around here and she does have those draping long dresses and droopy breasts to act as a distraction.

Obviously she is still furious with Sunny for stealing her man over in France but she seems oblivious that she is about to do the same thing to me right under my (permanently wrinkled from her offensive stench) nose. And when it comes down to it, where on earth is Shelley? Why isn't she getting annoyed that Emily Oliver is sniffing around her on-again, off-again man?

In the meantime Bebe has a new boyfriend, named Joseph. He's South African and tests products on defenceless animals (mostly monkeys). He tells me they shoot the monkey in the head when the experiments are over. This, he assures me, is the humane way to dispose of them. It turns out he knows Sean from back home so I trot over to Cleveland Square to collect him. Emily Oliver comes too. Why is she always with him now? Are they joined at the hip or something? Sean seems to be playing it cool – he's not acting like they're together and he's still flirting with me – so I'm a little confused. And why won't that girl bathe? Is she allergic to water?

Sean confesses to me in private that he always thought Joseph was an arsehole. I can't say that surprises me. I would like to consider myself a good enough friend to be emotionally invested in my friends' romantic entanglements but I am certain Bebe (and Sunny, for that matter) can fend for herself. Besides, who has time to worry about their dalliances when I have my own rather dubious dalliance to contend with.

It all comes to a head when I decide (rather foolishly) to get into the spirit of things, literally – as in alcoholic beverages. Perhaps I feel unstable thanks to Sunny leaving town again. Perhaps it's Joseph shooting monkeys in the head that tips me over the edge. Or, more likely, the odour of Emily Oliver has driven me to drink. All I know is that I have found my way to The Eagle's bar and Mick is making me cocktails.

I don't know what possesses me. I am putting the last dregs of my drink into my mouth when Sean says, 'Oh wait, I wanted to taste that'. God knows what I am drinking but I haven't swallowed yet so I simply lean into him and put my lips to his. When he opens his lips I transfer the liquid into his mouth. I know that sounds totally gross but really it's just a kiss with alcohol so in a way it's win-win.

Sean looks me square in the eye and says, 'Mm, delicious.'

So I bring him back to my flat and we make mad, passionate love on the linoleum floor in the kitchen. Very hot and heavy. We even break a teapot.

Naturally, I pen a poem.

It's so quiet
Here in my kitchen
Alone
2 a.m.
But still I hear
Your breathing
Feel you fingers touch
Upon my neck
Feel your sharp intake
Of breath
Your lips pressed lightly
Against mine
Then fiercely possessing
My mouth

It is so quiet
Here in my kitchen
So very alone
But still
I feel you

Yes, I am very, very drunk. Thank you for noticing.

TWENTY-FOUR

It does cross my mind that perhaps this means Emily Oliver is finally out of the picture but all hopes are dashed when I turn up at The Eagle the following night and am thoroughly snubbed by one ratfink. He acts like we've never even met. No, worse than that, he acts like I am an annoying little pest that he simply cannot shake. Ah yes, I remember that behaviour. Practically a carbon copy of how Jack behaved the day after our first dalliance. Perhaps men think all women want is to trap them into monogamy? Funny, I don't recall suggesting such a thing and to be perfectly honest the only man who's come close to making my heart go all aflutter is sitting on the other side of the world, pining away to his heart's content. Dan is not afraid to tell me how he feels and, quite frankly, he is the only one I have any feelings for and I'm certainly not going to let some scruffy pot-head ruin a perfectly good night of passion. I had an itch, he scratched it, and it's as simple as that. Why do men have to ruin things by behaving so beastly afterwards?

William is back to mooning over Sunny, which seems a little insensitive considering his old girlfriend is sitting right beside him. She is convinced that another girl is hiding in the wings and is putting the stink-eye on all the girls in the room, except for me. I'm not sure if it's the brown cardigan that convinces her I'm not a threat or if it's our easy manner together (comfy like an old cardie) but clearly William and I are not on the brink of a grand love affair. In fact, we have more of a brotherly-sisterly thing going on. We do seem to have quite a bit in common, not least our fondness for Sunny.

William can clearly see that the rat has upset my little apple cart and gallantly suggests a trip to the cinema to lift my spirits and his old girlfriend even offers to drive us there, although I suspect that's to ensure no other girl surreptitiously tags along. Like I said, I am not a threat, not in the slightest. I feel safe in the hands of William. He can be depended upon not to muddy the waters and so we enjoy *Top Gun* and spend the rest of the evening saying silly things, such as, 'I feel the need... the need for a cup of tea.' And, 'I feel the need... the need for sleep.'

I also feel the need to write tortured poetry about you-know-who.

Softly breathing
Cool, serene –
The wind
Presenting me
With a gift –
The man
Stormy passion
Strong, brave –
The man
Opening eyes
My dream becomes –
The wind

The candle
Basks your shadow
In a mellow, yellow glow
The dripping wax
The bluesy sax
It took a while to grow
The candle
Shining on your face
In a pale, frail light
Illuminating
And understating
Deceiving me of sight
The candle
Melted to a stub
There was nothing I could do

No more wax
No more sax
And sadly no more you

Max is furious with me. He has read my poems, you see, and what I thought was subtle references turn out to be blinking, blazing billboards to such a perceptive writer as he.

'You slept with Sean as well? Good lord, woman, am I the only one who hasn't tasted your sweet nectar?'

With words like that, is it any wonder?

'What's gotten into you, Teddy? You're behaving like a slut.'

'Am I? I sleep with two men and suddenly I'm a slut?'

'It's just not like you. You used to be so shy and quiet. A little mouse in the corner.'

'I'm still a mouse and, in case you hadn't noticed, I still wear brown cardigans and sensible walking shoes but I came to London for adventure. It's what young people do nowadays, or so Sunny says, and who am I to disagree? To be perfectly honest with you, I'm finding the whole experience a little overwhelming.'

'Then why don't you scuttle home?'

'Don't think the thought hadn't crossed my mind, especially when Sunny deserted me.'

'You've probably got another guy stashed away back there.'

'I do, as a matter of fact. His name is Dan and he's worth a hundred of all you lot. But I didn't come to London just to get laid. I'm here for the whole kit and caboodle.'

'Which one am I? The kit or the caboodle?'

'You're the thorn in my side, Max. That's what you are. Why do you have to spoil everything all the time? Why can't you just accept my hand in friendship without trying to wring it off my wrist?'

'God, Teddy, you're so infuriating!'

Really? I've never been infuriating before. Most people find me inconspicuous or inconsequential or even invisible but never have I been anything as explosive as infuriating. It must be the nickname. It's having the most remarkable effect on me.

Of course, at work Teddy is covered up in modest attire and a no-nonsense manner. And everyone calls me Theodora.

And a good thing, too. Obtaining new assignments depends entirely on my reputation and the feedback I've been getting is most encouraging. Apparently I'm a beautiful typist, buoyant, hardworking, quick to adapt to a new environment, a great help, happy to do what's asked of me, and very competent all round.

Who could ask for anything more?

My latest assignment is a happy one. I'm at St Georges Hotel, very posh and right in the centre of London in Regent Street. Did you know that the reason you rarely see staff wondering up and down the corridors is because they have their own hidden stairwells and secret passageways, separated from the guests? Next time you stay at a posh hotel, keep a look out for all those Staff Only doors. You'll find there are quite a lot of them. The restaurant at the St Georges Hotel is on the fifteenth floor, offering spectacular views and delicious meals and I get it all at a staff discount, lucky, lucky me.

Before I know it, it's October. The days are getting colder and I go shopping for a coat. I find an electric blue wool coat with a black velvet trim (and enormous shoulder pads) at Selfridges that I would never have considered purchasing but Teddy marches up to the counter, waving her two hundred pounds, before I can stop her... I mean me. Honestly, this split personality can be a little confusing at times. To tell you the truth, I'm not even sure Teddy is an alien entity anymore. I rather suspect this part of me was lurking somewhere deep inside, just waiting for the opportunity to spring forth. Who knew she'd choose to do it in an electric blue coat!

On the way out, I stop at the New Arrivals rack and Teddy seizes the opportunity to purchase a grey marl suit – a pencil skirt with zip jacket – and a form-fitting black knit dress with a zip all the way to the chin. Clearly Teddy has a zip fetish and I can't say I'm all that surprised.

My plan was to give up my lease and take a coach tour around Europe but my bossy friend Helene has put a spanner in the works. She wants to join me in London in November and the idea is that I wait for her before commencing my travels. After the callous way Sunny tossed me aside, it feels nice to be wanted again so I ask Mrs Quist if I can extend my lease and she's only too happy to oblige. Apparently I am a model tenant. Bebe is staying put, too, but our lovely flatmate Liz moves on to greener pastures (she returns home to Australia) and we are joined by another ex-pat Aussie named Joan. This one is closer to Bebe's age than my own and what a dour sourpuss she is. She actually has the gall to look down her nose at my wanton, wicked ways. Me, wanton and wicked? Teddy kicks up her heels in sheer delight whilst I plant my sensible ones firmly on the hearth.

In the local bookshop, I find myself drawn to *Dr Jekyll and Mr Hyde* and, really, can you blame me?

Surprisingly, the one constant in my love-life is Dan but that just makes me feel even more conflicted. The boys in London are just playful diversions, adding to the rich tapestry of my experience over here. Stories to tell my grandchildren. Well, maybe not them. But when I look back on my youth with fondness, will I even be able to remember them at all?

But, Dan, well, that's another matter entirely.

He is still writing me letters, telling me how much he misses me and wishing I would return and I find myself thinking about him far more often that I would have thought possible. Even when I'm with another man, he is lodged firmly in my heart. Is it true what they say? Does absence make the heart grow fonder?

I'll tell you what it's doing to me, though. It's making me feel worse about pursuing romance in London. I feel like I am cheating on him. Which is absurd and ridiculous and utter nonsense, I know, but there you go. I feel bad.

I have gone halfway around the world only to discover that the man of my dreams was living right next door to me.

What is a girl to do?

Jump on a bus and head back to Birmingham, that's what. It's less than two weeks until my twenty-first birthday. Theodora would rather not have a fuss made about it but Teddy wants a party and she has vowed not to return to London until somebody throws her one.

I do the touristy thing for a bit, visiting Shakespeare's Tudor home at Stratford Upon Avon and going for long drives with Uncle Bill and Aunt Ida down charming country roads and eating at charming country pubs until William finally calls me home, just two days before my birthday, with the promise of a special surprise.

'Is he your boyfriend, dear?' asks Aunt Ida.

'Oh no, he's just a friend,' I say. 'All my boyfriends in London have been rather horrid to me. This one's much too nice.'

'Then don't you think he'd make a much nicer boyfriend?'

Huh. You know the thought had never occurred to me. My first instinct, when a boy treats me with care and respect, is to look upon him as a brother. Isn't that funny? I guess I've always expected men to be disinterested in me. Even now, I think it's only the appearance of my daring alter-ego, Teddy, that has garnered me this much attention.

That being said, I board a bus back to London and rush over to The Eagle to let William know that I have returned. He is sitting in the bar, naturally, looking thoroughly offended that the barman has presented him with his bar tab, which, as usual, is inordinately long because he is always shouting everyone a drink, and there on the couch beside him, snuggled into his warm embrace, is Sunny.

Oh.

'What are you doing here?' I blurt out.

'You didn't think I'd miss your birthday, did you?'

'Well, yes, as a matter of fact, I did.'

'Don't be silly.' She snuggles into William's chest and he grins like a Cheshire cat.

'She missed us, Teddy-Bear. How about that?'

'Yeah. How about that.'

Sunny seems a little surprised that a party has been arranged in my honour. William has strung up balloons in the dining room and Jack has cooked lasagne. Shelley arrives with Sean (he's the official photographer) so I guess they're on again, which makes us well and truly off. I'm just glad Emily Oliver isn't following him around like a bad smell (literally!). Perhaps she's off travelling again or, miracle of miracles, perhaps she's taking a bath.

The gorgeous Lucille turns up with Mick and I discover her birthday is two days before mine, so no wonder we get on so well. Bebe brings Joseph and our new flatmate, Joan, and a few of the staff from The Eagle join in. There's Alan, he's a daggy Australian with even more plain clothes in his wardrobe than me and he works on Reception at night. And there's Eve, the stern, matronly type who guards Reception by day. She brings her boyfriend, Lester. He's a beefy Birmingham lad with a neck wider than my waist and tattoos all over his arms. He has spiky hair with blonde tips, which I find a little disconcerting. He's a blokey construction worker but he goes to a salon to get his hair tipped. How odd is that?

Dave is still staying at the Hotel so he's invited, too. Shelley has brought a friend and Lucille has brought her brother and by the time the night porter wanders in, followed by the Kiwis from Flat 2, the party is in full swing. Later on William bustles us into black cabs to take us to Le Beat Route nightclub in Soho where a private VIP booth is waiting with a massive birthday cake for Lucille and me.

I am wearing my new form-fitting black dress (the one with the zip to the chin) with black leather gloves and Bebe has rimmed my eyes in black again and slicked back my hair so I'm not surprised when Jack slides into the booth beside me.

'Are we still friends?' he asks.

'Of course we are,' I smile. 'Isn't that what we've always been?'

But what exactly does that mean?

Shelley goes home and Sean's interest in me suddenly kicks into high gear. One could get whiplash with this guy. He walks me home at the end of the night and gives me a long, lingering kiss in the kitchen....

TWENTY-FIVE

I know what you're thinking but you'd be wrong. Now that I am officially twenty-one, I am older and wiser or maybe Sean just isn't attractive enough to stomp all over my heart and have me coming back for more. (Jack, of course, is another matter entirely.) I'm not averse to the occasional snog, mind you, but that's where I draw the line, particularly at seven a.m.

I crawl into bed (alone) and slumber peacefully until noon.

Don't ask me how but Sunny has lugged an enormous Staffordshire jug and bowl set all the way from Liverpool. How on earth am I going to get that home on the plane?

It's not until Max turns up on my doorstep, pouting and sulking, that I realise he wasn't at my party last night.

'I am at the end of my rope, Teddy,' he says. 'I can't go on like this. Something has to give. This is the moment of reckoning. I refuse to step inside until the matter is resolved.'

'What on earth are you talking about?' I sigh.

Have you ever had that feeling when the whole world around you shudders to a stop and you almost step out of your body? You are suspended in time and every minute detail around you is suddenly brought into sharp focus. I can smell Bebe's coffee, cooling on the kitchen table. From the corner of my eye, I can see the crack in the teapot (courtesy of that hot and heavy night with Sean). Behind Max a petal drops from the geranium pot. Above his head the clouds scud across the sky. A car honks its horn. A dog trots by on the footpath, lifting its leg at the railing. My left ear pops – it's been blocked since I woke up. Joan flushes the toilet. And Max does what Max does so well, he leans in...

And what do I do? I lean out.

I cannot bring myself to be kissed by him.

Max looks like I have just shot him in the heart. His face crumples to the consistency of his corduroy jacket. He says he can see the revulsion in my eyes. He says that it's a shame I cannot see the forest for the trees. He says that he will never bother me again. And he hopes I have a nice life.

And then he says goodbye and walks away.

What a way to ruin a birthday, hey?

I would like to say that I realise immediately the enormity of this event. That I know the instant it occurs that I have lost a very dear friend who means a great deal more to me than I ever thought. But I don't have a clue.

I shrug my shoulders, make myself a coffee, take the tube into Charing Cross Station with Sunny and hang out at Trafalgar Square for a while. We watch the tourists with their faces all lit up feed the pigeons and take photographs, just like we did on our first day in London. Was it only a mere four months ago that I was excitedly pouring over the London A-Z and hoping that a pigeon wouldn't poop on my head?

'I can't believe how quickly London has become my home,' I marvel. 'It feels like I've been here forever.'

'You have,' says Sunny. 'I've been to France and Liverpool already and who knows where I'll be heading next. You really ought to get out and see a bit more of the world.'

'And leave all this?'

Sunny looks at the grey, drizzly sky, the million-and-one tourists, the honking horns and abusive drivers, the chaos and noise and pooping pigeons and says, 'Yes!'

I think that's the moment when I realise Sunny is not a Londoner.

On Tuesday Elliott arrives and within twenty-four hours they are flying to America. William is in shock. I think he actually thought Sunny had come back to him. I never for a moment thought she'd come back for me so I am left relatively unscathed.

> The cactus flower has no fears
> And from its leaves it sheds no tears
> No need for warmth or light or rain
> The cactus simply feels no pain
> Yet it can hurt if you should touch
> It doesn't care for company much
> To crack their shield is hard to do
> The cactus is a lot like you

And now the cactus flower is in the United States, driving cars with Elliott through the American landscape.

Here's how it works: Someone moves from one end of America to another but they don't want to drive there so they catch a plane and arrange for a service to deliver their car at a later date. Elliott and Sunny work for that service and deliver the car to its owner. In the meantime, they get to see America and the transportation is free.

Bebe is thinking of moving on, too. She has bronchial asthma and the doctors think the air in London is toxic. Before she came to London she was living in Florida Keys but she couldn't get a Green

Card. She's thinking about Africa next but I think what she really wants is to go home to Australia. But she's waiting, isn't she? For her married lover to call. In the meantime, she has Joseph with connections to South Africa. He works in Oxford and he assures Bebe that the air is much clearer over there but I don't want her to go.

It's the nature of the beast, I guess. Everyone is always moving on.

I wish Max were still around. I am only now starting to realise what I have lost. One of my poems is published in a feminist magazine called Aurora and I want him to dissect it as only he can. Instead, I rush over to The Eagle and show it to Jack – he was after all my inspiration.

- Mouth to Mouth -
Whilst catching all the flies
You fell into my mouth
I ate you
I think
You burned my tongue
And gave me an ulcer
But you tasted good
If I remember
I tried to spit you out
But it was too late
What we had together died
The minute I suffocated you

Restricted you
Smothered you
I don't think chewing on you helped either
So now you're gone
And all I have left
Is a bitter taste in my mouth
Next time I'm looking alone and vulnerable
I'll keep my mouth shut!

He looks a little puzzled but seems glad that I am excited (not embittered). William takes me down to his room to watch *Mike Hammer* on his poxy little portable television. What are we doing down here when all the gang is in the bar and I've just had a poem published, if you don't mind.

William wants to cry on my shoulder again but I am in no mood to mope. I rifle through his bookshelf and set about reading his vast collection of Dick Francis crime novels set in the horse-racing world. From the first page I am hooked.

On a visit to the bar for lemonade, I meet Jack's new girlfriend.

I am surprised, to say the least.

I thought Jack was not the type to commit. He was only too keen to impress upon me how important it was to keep things casual and yet now he appears to be quite open to the idea of settling down.

He says she is his girlfriend, he's quite proud to call her that.

I imagine she must be quite a looker. Jack is thoroughly gorgeous and he has beautiful women throwing themselves at him on a regular basis. I ought to know. I was one of them (maybe not beautiful, but definitely throwing myself at him). So you can imagine the shock and horror when I finally clap eyes upon her.

Her name is Delilah and she's disgusting. She's filthy, drug-addled, and clearly bordering on the insane. I can't understand why Jack would choose a scrag like Delilah.

I watch her rummage around an ashtray until she finds a good-sized cigarette butt, relights it and smokes it. Could there be anything more disgusting?

'So tell me, Delilah,' I drawl, elongating the name until it practically snaps back like loose elastic, 'what's your real name?'

'It's Delilah,' she says, looking me straight in the eye.

'As in Samson and…?'

'And what?'

'Delilah. Samson and Delilah.'

She looks at me like I am speaking another language. Perhaps I am.

'I'm with Jack,' she says.

'Yes, I know. I was referring to the famous Delilah.'

'Didn't know there was one. Thought I was the one and only.'

I'm not sure if she's referring to her name or her status as girlfriend to Jack. I suspect she's the one and only of that, too.'

'I'm Teddy,' I say.

'Hmm,' she squints at me sideways. 'William calls you Teddy-Bear, doesn't he?'

I sigh. 'He does.'

'Are you with him?' she asks.

'Not right at this moment. He's in his room. I've just popped up here to get a drink.'

'Yes, but when you're with him in his room are you *with* him in his room?'

'No. I'm not his girlfriend, if that's what you're asking. I'm his girlfriend's best friend.'

'And where is his girlfriend?'

'She's in America with *his* best friend.'

'Seriously?'

'Apparently so.'

'So what does that make you, piggy in the middle?'

Wait a minute. Is this disgusting sow calling *me* a pig?

'A free spirit,' I declare. I mean to say free agent but Delilah has me rattled.

She looks dubiously at my brown cardigan and say, 'You don't say.'

I suppose I could go into a whole big explanation of my messy love affairs but Delilah clearly doesn't give a stuff so I let the matter drop and simply say, 'I'm not with anybody.' And technically that's true.

'Just as long as you're not planning on trying anything with Jack,' she says.

'No fear of that,' I tell her.

Should I mention our history together? What exactly would I say, though? I'm not sure what Jack and I were to each other, or even what we are now, for that matter. Besides, I'm not the type to kiss and tell.

And so I grab my drink, tuck Dick (Francis) under my arm, and head back to William's room. As I pass by Delilah, I see her rummage for another butt in the ashtray before finally coming up trumps.

'Must be my lucky day,' she says.

TWENTY-SIX

Rumours are beginning to whirl about William and me. To be expected, I suppose. We are extremely chummy and we spend an awful lot of time holed up in his little cubby downstairs but, like I said, we are more like brother and sister. I like feeling safe around him. No constant badgering after my body, no leaning in, no leaning out. It's all completely above board.

But William is beginning to moan that he needs a girlfriend, now that Sunny is well and truly out of the picture. We have no news and, whilst that is no surprise to me, William has taken it badly and has now decided to move on.

I suggest he waits five days for my bossy friend Helene to arrive, in the hope that he won't turn to me in desperation.

During our correspondence, Dan has noted once or twice that I mention William an awful lot. Of course the reason for that is he's the only male I can mention, since the others all involve sex in one form or another but Dan is not to know that.

I also decide a little flirting with other men in the bar might make my position clear. I am a free agent. I can do what I like. Come and get me boys.

The trouble is I don't really want any of the boys to come and get me. I would rather be left alone, thank you very much. So, in a bid to find a happy medium, I make an effort with my attire (pinching a lovely lilac jumper from the pile of clothing Sunny has left in my flat). I do the eye thing and the lip thing and even brush my hair and then find myself a safe spot at the bar beside Eve's man.

You remember Lester, the beefcake from the building site who gets his hair tipped at a salon.

He's getting drunk at the bar with a friend and the friend is showing quite a bit of interest in me so I am forced to give Lester quite a bit of my attention in an attempt to keep his friend's interest at arms-length.

I am waiting for Lucille and Mick. There's a farewell party at Jack and Sean's flat for Shelley. She's returning to South Africa.

Bebe is spending the weekend in Oxford with Joseph, and William is on duty this evening so I wait for Lucille and Mick to arrive.

They were supposed to be here at eight p.m. but they are late. And I am getting a little bit tipsy waiting...

I am rapidly losing interest in Shelley's party when finally Mick arrives, but without Lucille. They are fighting. He starts getting friendly with two women in the bar who seem quite taken with him (well, he is gorgeous, don't forget) and then Lucille turns up, chucks a wobbly and jumps into a cab to go nightclubbing.

By now it's about two in the morning (yes, that's how long I've been waiting... drinking cocktails in the bar... with Lester...) so Mick and I head off to the party in Cleveland Square.

Sean is totally ignoring me and I am fed up trying to work out where I stand with him so I find my thoughts turning back to Lester in the bar. We were having such a good time, laughing and drinking and mildly flirting but with the certainty that nothing more would come of it. He belongs to Eve and, therefore, I am safe.

There is, however, nothing safe about the place I am in now. And not just because the last time I attended a party here, I ended up in the bathroom with Jack. Sean knocked on the door, looking for a smoke, and Jack opened the door, putting me in a very compromising position. Well, I was in the compromising position before he opened the door but his total disregard for my dignity made me feel quite ill. Why do I let men put me into these positions?

When Delilah, the scrag, starts treating me like her new best friend, I can take it no more. I can't get out of there fast enough and at four-thirty a.m. I return to The Eagle and, before I know it, Lester is walking me home.

I will admit there is a small voice at the very back of my brain trying to warn me that I am about to go down a very treacherous path but I reason that Lester is 'safe'. He has been in a de-facto relationship with Eve for many, many years. Surely he is happy with her and has no plans to stray?

And besides, I have never in my life stolen a boyfriend before. Apart from the unlikelihood of plain and boring me being able to do such a thing, it goes entirely against the grain. I am the owner of six brown cardigans, for goodness sake. Have you ever heard of someone with six brown cardigans doing such a thing? Of course not.

And, let's face it, I'm not Sunny. Men don't see me as a desirable alternative to their girlfriend and women don't ever see me as competition. You can take my word on that.

Actually, now that I think about it, Sunny has never really been the 'other woman' because as soon as she sets her sights on a man, he instantly leaves his girlfriend. Of course, it's usually all in vain. Sunny never sticks around for long.

Besides, I am a feminist. Women are my sisters. Solidarity, and all that stuff.

And yet, there's a tiny thrill tickling my belly. I am being naughty. I am being wicked. I am doing what everyone else around here does, thinking only of myself and caring not a jot if I hurt someone else's feelings. Somewhere inside of me I think I am just massively relieved that it's finally not me that's getting hurt anymore.

So I take Lester back to my flat. He gives me a story about losing his key and not wishing to wake Eve and I fall for it hook, line and sinker.

Joan is spending the night away so the living/bedroom is empty. I offer Lester my bed. He takes it. In all innocence, I put on my nightie and retire to Bebe's bed in the other room, so as to give the man his privacy. But he follows me.

'I thought we could share a bed,' he says.

'But that's ridiculous. There are three beds in this flat. Why would we squeeze into one?'

'Because I want to squeeze you, that's why.'

Oh.

For a large, bulky man he moves surprisingly fast. He's at my side, sliding my slip of a nightie off and kissing me in the nape of the neck before I've had a chance to even catch my breath. My head is a little fuzzy from all those cocktails.

My thoughts tumble through my head like this: Sean is treating me like dirt again, Jack took my dignity over the bathtub, Delilah is now my new best friend, Mick is toying with Lucille's heart, William wants a new girlfriend because my friendship is not enough, Sunny is off in America and all I have left is a lilac sweater, Bebe is miles away with a man who kills monkeys, and I am alone in this flat. I am alone in London. I am alone.

Lester is being very nice to me, so attentive and gentle and his arms are so muscular and firm that I feel quite safe and protected when he takes me in his strong embrace, and those kisses are so warm and soft and... oh!

At seven o'clock a knock at the door rouses me from my bed. I put on my nightie and answer it. It is Eve. She is looking for her man. I have a tiny little heart attack and then invite her in. In a way, I'm quite relieved she's here. I don't think I really want him, to be honest.

I act like nothing is wrong and offer her a calming cup of tea. I babble along in a friendly, relaxed way saying something like, 'We knew you'd figure it out. It was so nice of him, such a gentleman, to walk me home so late at night. I get so worried. And then he realised he'd forgotten his key and he didn't want to wake you. And I was so relieved because I hate to be alone in the flat. I get so worried. He said you'd figure it out and wouldn't fret. It's wonderful you found the place. I've been meaning to invite you around for ages. He's sleeping in Bebe's bed. Perhaps we shouldn't wake him. No? You'd rather go on in? Well, of course, you know best…'

I'm not sure she's buying it but I can see that she really wants to. She wants to believe that the man she loves is not breaking her heart.

It's not until they leave that I realise my nightie is inside out.

TWENTY-SEVEN

I have a nice, peaceful breakfast, which is more than I deserve, and at nine o'clock Lester returns to fill me in on the details.

After the party, Mick returned to The Eagle to spend more time with those two women in the bar. Lucille turned up and proceeded to wreck the bar – throwing furniture and smashing glasses. Boy, has that girl got spunk.

William called downstairs to Eve's room to get Lester (because he's big and burly) to come upstairs and help stop the fracas. Eve shot upstairs, demanding to know where her man was, and Alan, the little weasel, sitting at the front desk with a perfect view of the comings and goings of all involved, tells them he was last seen walking me home. All Eve knows is that I live somewhere in Gloucester Terrace so she proceeds to knock on every basement door in my very long street until she finds me. That's determination.

Now Lester wants to start a secret affair. I don't think I'm wildly attracted to him. He doesn't seem my type. He's a beefy, tattooed Birmingham lad with not an artistic bone in his body. But he seems quite keen on me and after Sean's hot and cold behaviour, I quite like being wanted, plain and simple. I think Teddy would quite enjoy snogging in dark corners and meeting for clandestine drinks in out-of-the-way places.

This is what happens when you let your standards slide. It's a slippery slope into murky waters and you end up sloshing around in the mud with the rest of the muck.

I have become a mistress and every fibre of my being is outraged. But Teddy is elated. Finally, she is crowing, finally we fit in.

I don't wish to alarm you, but I think Teddy is starting to take over my life.

Naturally I write a poem revelling in every sordid detail.

My love for you is dangerous
Seduction in deceit
Your fire keeps my body warm
Regardless of the 'heat'
Your crystal eyes and subtle strength
Send shivers down my spine

Each night I dream of your yielding arms
Always encircling mine.
But my love for you is dangerous
You are not mine to hold
Though my body aches with burning desire
My sheets are always cold
When I'm in your arms, embracing your warmth
All the dangers I dismiss
Through the fear of detection or rejection and pain
I risk all for the touch of your kiss.

Before I have time to properly consider my (rather reckless) behaviour, Helene flies into London. Four months ago I would have said that Helene and I had much in common. Her birthday is the day after mine, we met in secretarial school, we both come from nice, stable families, and I can guarantee there will be a brown cardigan or two packed neatly in her case.

But now, well, much has changed, as I'm sure you would agree. I turn up at Heathrow Airport dressed in blue – blue jeans, blue cardie and electric blue wool coat. Helene, dressed in a chunky knit sweater and sensible walking shoes, looks unimpressed.

'Have you gained weight?' are the first words she says to me.

I take her to Wimpy's for dinner. It's the British version of McDonalds, although they have that, too. In fact, Helene thinks the amount of fast food restaurants within a mile from home can be measured around my girth.

It takes me a moment to realise what she's doing. She is judging me. It's been a while since anyone has done that to me. That's what makes London so liberating and fun. I've been free to do what I like, free of judgement or expectation. No guilt. No regrets. No excuses. No explanation. No worries.

But now Helene has arrived and her fierce judgement of all that I do is devastating and debilitating.

I want to run screaming from my beloved Wimpy's. I want to tell Helene she can take her crummy attitude and never darken my door again. I want to protect my precious self-esteem and kick this nasty bitch to the curb. But I do none of that. Instead, I take her to The Eagle and introduce her to my new friends. It does not escape her attention that most of them are men. She thinks William is nice but there are no sparks flying between them.

I am sure my friends have recognised the evil that has attached itself to me, ready to suck the happiness out of my very soul but in keeping with their non-judgmental ways, they say nothing and bravely welcome her into the fold.

Knowing how difficult it was for me to make friends in this town, I am expecting Helene to be eternally grateful for the relatively easy transition but no, the ungrateful cow is having none of it.

I take some time off work to show Helene the sights but I don't think she likes what she sees. She keeps complaining about the grime and the crowds and says it's much too cold. I have Options Magazine calling but I have to turn them down (I know, I know, all those gorgeous male models!) so Helene's constant whinging is beginning to annoy me.

As a birthday gift, I present her with some very expensive, opulently jewel-encrusted lizard-shaped earrings from Liberty Department Store. I wept as the shop assistant lovingly wrapped them in tissue paper.

We missed each other's twenty-first celebrations but only by about two weeks, and I was certain the exchanging of gifts would occur once we were re-united. This is our twenty-firsts, don't forget – a milestone event.

Helene, however, has brought me nothing. She says her presence here in London is presents enough. I weep again at the thought of those Liberty earrings but this time for an entirely different reason.

I decide we need some space so I sneak off to the movies to see *Ruthless People* with Lucille and then I hang out at The Eagle with Jack, William, Mick, Sean and Lester until two a.m.

Helene is not impressed.

I've got tickets for Helene and me to go to The Furys Concert with Joan. Things have been tense all round so I'm hoping this will improve everybody's mood.

When Joan moved into the flat, she was aware that it was only for a short time. She knew she'd have to leave when Helene arrived. But when the time came, she didn't want to go. She tried to get Bebe to override our agreement, which, besides being an underhanded, devious thing to do, was rather baffling when you consider how much she disliked me.

I want her to see that for me it isn't personal and that I'm willing to be friends despite all of her animosity although, now that I think about it, why am I bothering to be nice to someone who's been nothing but horrid to me?

I guess that's what happens when you try not to judge others.

I bought these tickets for Helene in a desperate bid to show her a good time. I know an Irish folk band isn't really our cup of tea (another strike against Joan, I'm afraid) but I'm open to all new experiences in London and I was hoping Helene would be, too. But no such luck.

As I sit wedged between these two hard-faced harpies, it begins to dawn on me that Teddy could be the best thing that ever happened to me. Because Teddy is not the type to sit back and take all this crap. Teddy is gonna go out and find herself some fun.

It's December and winter has come a-calling. I take Helene for a walk through Hyde Park to Buckingham Palace and she seems much happier with the one-on-

one time that I'm devoting to her. Still no news from Sunny. Bebe is spending every weekend in Oxford. Rose, the barmaid, is backpacking through India. Shelley has returned to Kenya. And Mick has gone home to Tweed Heads so Lucille and I have more time for fun. This, however, is not going down so well with Helene.

I think she's a little miffed that I've made so many friends in her absence so she decides to latch on to one particular person and give me the freeze. The first time she meets Lucille I'm not around so she thinks we haven't met. Consequently, that's the girl she chooses to replace me. She's rather furious when she discovers that Lucille and I are tight. We even celebrated our birthdays together, something Helene had wanted to do with me. As I said, Helene's birthday is the day after mine (and Lucille's is two days prior) so we really should all get along famously but Helene is quite possessive and does not like to share.

But if she's jealous of my female friends, that's nothing compared to how she feels about the men.

Perhaps that's why she insists we spend an entire day shopping and then the evening out with the girls. Bebe has only a few more weeks left of her assignment and then she's moving to Oxford. Joan has free tickets to The London Symphony Orchestra and against my better judgement I agree to go. I figure at least Bebe will be fun (and we have so little time left together) but she turns out to be the most trouble of all. She has a dreadful asthma attack and we have to take her to the hospital in Paddington. They want to keep her overnight but she refuses to stay so I spend a sleepless night listening to her breathe.

I don't know, men seem a lot less hassle than this.

A postcard arrives from America and Helene gnashes her teeth in envy. You know, I think she liked it better when I was brown and invisible. When we met at the secretarial college in Melbourne, we discovered we both travelled in from Pixy Point and decided to do the commute together – an hour's train journey each way. I don't really recall us talking much and, now that I think about it, I did manage to get through *The Lord of the Rings* trilogy during that time, but Helene still thinks she knows me better than anyone else. The fact that Sunny and I have been friends since we were ten is neither here nor there as far as Helene is concerned. Anyone can see, she will reason, that Sunny and I have nothing in common. She must have thought that I'd been kidnapped and taken to London against my will. Perhaps she even thought she was coming over here to save me. Perhaps she still thinks that. Or perhaps she just didn't like the idea of me having so much fun without her. Now that I think about it, she did make the decision to join me shortly after Sunny left. So a postcard addressed to Teddy and Bebe must really stick in her craw.

'Why does everyone call you Teddy all the time?' she seethes.

'I like it.' (Go figure!)

'Well I don't and I'm not going to call you that. It's undignified. Your name is Theodora and that's how I shall address you.'

'Fine but if you do then no one will know who you're talking about.'

Even Sunny has accepted my new nickname without a moment's hesitation. Perhaps she knew it would set me free.

Dear Teddy and Bebe (Sunny's postcard begins),

I'll give you a quick run-down of our amazing journey. We drove from New York down the coast to Miami and The Keys. We then drove another car through the southern states including Texas, Las Vegas, and the Grand Canyon and up to San Francisco where we dropped the car off. We then hitched down to Los Angeles and San Diego. We have met some great people. Americans are very hospitable and they love an accent. We are now taking another car up to Wisconsin and will stop at Denver and the Rocky Mountains. Will spend my 21st in New York but our money is running out so we will be in England for Xmas probably.

All my love, Sunny xxoo

P.S. Also went to Disneyland.

She's alive! You know, I had my doubts there for a while but (blast!) she won't be coming home anytime soon so I am stuck with stick-in-the-mud-Helene. And I have a cold. Too much stress, perhaps? Helene blames my late nights and partying. I blame Helene. I wrap myself up in my chunky chocolate brown cardigan, the one that pills a lot but is nice and cosy and warm on account of all that chunkiness, and get stuck into my reading. Everyone at The Eagle has been swapping books, which is why I've got Bob Woodward's *Wired: The Short Life and Fast Times of John Belushi* and the boys are reading Alice Walker's *The Color Purple* and *The Women's Room* by Marilyn French. And everybody is devouring Dick (Francis).

I join a new secretarial agency called The Grosvenor Bureau that specialises in media assignments. My first job is at Readers Digest. Helene doesn't have the skills to join an agency like mine and she's not keen on the fast-paced world of temping so she finds a rather boring job in a boring office working for very boring people. It reminds me of Mr Nichols' accountancy firm back home. I expect they wear a lot of brown. Helene can't do shorthand and her typing speed is only 30 words per minute (whereas I type 100 wpm) so I suppose it's to be expected that I get the better jobs. Oh, and I make an excellent cup of tea.

I think it irks Helene that she can find no fault in my professional life. Luckily, though, I am giving her plenty of ammunition in my private life. She has just found out about my secret affair with Lester and, frankly, she is appalled.

'It's what everyone does in London' just doesn't cut it with Helene.

I'm not sure if it's the tattoos, the muscles, the working-class background or the de-facto status that is upsetting her the most, or if it's the fact that I am doing something indiscreet and undesirable.

'And obscenely indecent,' adds Helene.

I must admit, she is taking all the fun out of the affair.

In an attempt to appease Helene (something Teddy would never do but, I fear, is entirely necessary if I am to survive the next few weeks), I agree to take her to a party that does not include any of the men from The Royal Eagle. My lovely, sane, disciplined (and only slightly rebellious) ex-flatmate Liz may have left the country but I am still in touch with a friend of hers and she's having a party in Notting Hill full of ordinary, respectable, educated and well-behaved people. I put on a cream blouse and beige slacks and lower my expectations.

As you can imagine, the party is a bore but then I hear it… the most delicious Liverpool accent. It's the Beatles – Paul, John, George and Ringo – all rolled into one. His name is John, naturally, and I am in love with that accent. Turns out he is in love with mine.

'What accent?'

'Aren't you Australian?'

'Oh. That.'

We are soon deep in conversation and I discover he plays the saxophone, just like Sean, but this is the only thing that they have in common. John is ordinary, respectable, educated, well-behaved... and rather scrumptious, if I do say so myself. Now, you would think that Helene would be thrilled to her frilly knickers that I have found a decent chap to occupy my attention, but you would be wrong. Don't forget she's a jealous, rather vindictive, bossy little sort. I don't think she likes to see me happy. I think it actually pains her greatly. That would explain the frown and the constant attempts she makes all throughout the night to make me look shabby in front of John. But it doesn't work.

I invite him back to the flat and we kiss in the kitchen until four a.m. But that's as far as it goes. No sex, no broken teapot, no tortured poetry, just a nice, simple, romantic snog. And then John leaves and I put myself to bed (alone) with my skin tingling and my heart pounding and my head swimming and my toes tickling and a great big grin on my face.

Is that the gnashing of teeth I can hear from Helene's side of the room?

TWENTY-EIGHT

John returns in the morning at a more respectable hour… and so does Lester! I leave them both in the sitting room and rush into the kitchen, ostensibly to make tea but really to have a breakdown. I am frantic and beg Helene to help me but she refuses, muttering something about it being my bed and lying in it.

Who can think of sleep at a time like this?

Luckily, my cool head prevails and disaster is averted. In the end, I calmly entertain my two gentlemen callers and John is none the wiser. Lester, however, has sussed it out and doesn't stick around for long.

Later, I go down to The Eagle for dinner and have the inevitable confrontation with Lester in the bar. I can tell you, it's very difficult breaking up in public with someone with whom you have been conducting a secret liaison. Finally we sneak out to the fire-escape stairwell and end our messy affair in a frenzied whisper-fest.

I am on cloud nine. John seems positively perfect but not all my friends agree. A group of us go to the cinema in Piccadilly Circus to see *Crocodile Dundee* and William leans over in the dark and says, 'John's not right for you, Teddy-Bear. There's something 'off' about him. Don't you think?'

I don't know what he's talking about. I can only assume that they think John is somehow too tame for daring Teddy. I guess I am enjoying my new lifestyle and all the excitement and fun that goes along with it (suck eggs, Helene) but surely a nice, respectable chap is more in keeping with my true nature. Or could it be that William sees something in him that I haven't spotted yet. Let's face it, I'm lousy at picking winners.

Then again, maybe William's jealous.

Helene is showing quite a bit of interest in Dave, who is still staying at The Eagle, waiting for the completion of his home renovation. I wonder if it will ever be finished. Dave has money and manners and is a lot more mature than us (in both age and behaviour) so I'm not surprised that the sensible Helene is drawn to him. I try to bring the two of them together but Helene is appalled by my crass behaviour.

It seems that Teddy has learnt some very bad habits during her time in London.

'The gentleman always makes the first move,' admonishes Helene.

Is she kidding?

After the movie the others jump on a double-decker and head home but John and I elect to walk. It takes us over an hour. It must be love. On the way, John reveals that his last relationship was six months ago. He then asks me when my last relationship ended.

'Er, on Sunday.'

'Sunday just gone? You mean two days ago?'

'Yes.'

'But I met you on Saturday.'

'That's why I broke up with him on Sunday.'

John is tickled pink.

But enough about men. Sunny is back! We all go to Pizzaland to welcome her home but the others see me paying for John's lunch and they are not impressed. He's finally confessed to me that he's out of work and rapidly running out of money (hence the long walk home last night). He says he will have to leave his flat and go back home to Liverpool but I want him to stay in London and find another job (he's a hotel clerk) so I invite him to sleep on my sofa until he gets back on his feet. This, of course, does not go down well with everyone else, especially Helene (because our beds are in the same room as the sofa), and Sunny (because she was counting on sleeping on that sofa). Of course

I am always going to put Sunny above any man so I assure her she can have the sofa and in a stroke of genius I declare that John can bunk with me.

'I'm not having the two of you bumping and grinding right in front of me,' chokes Helene.

'Who says we're going to bump and grind? We've only just met.'

When John is (hopefully) out of earshot, Helene says 'He can't be trusted. He's just lost his job. He has no money. I'm worried he's just staying the night so that he can rob us.'

'Why? Have you got the Crown Jewels stuffed under your mattress or something?'

'He could be a rapist. Or even a homicidal maniac.'

'Sounds like most of the guys we meet,' I joke.

Personally, I think she's overreacting. We go to a boring, straight-laced party and I meet a regular guy and suddenly he's Jack the Ripper. I really can't see the danger of him sleeping in a flat with the four of us (me, Helene, Sunny and Bebe). If anything, I'd say he had more to worry about than us.

And with that marvellous bit of logic, everyone is happy. Actually, no one is happy except me but what do I care?

'We need a rule for this sort of thing,' Helene says firmly. (Helene loves her rules.) 'No men allowed overnight. It's not appropriate, considering our beds are a mere few feet apart.'

Not appropriate... with this lot? Oh the tales I could tell. They would make Helene's toes curl. But I must admit she does have a point. It is a rule already enforced by Mrs Quist and one that I, in the beginning, was totally in agreement with. I don't, however, expect any funny business to go on between us. I consider it as just helping out a friend, like what I do for Sunny. The sofa is always available for her when she is between ventures so why can't I do the same for John? Are they forgetting that he is a gentleman?

I'll even wear my flannel pyjamas, guaranteed to act like a bucket of cold water to even the most ardent flame.

I survive the night without being raped or robbed or murdered and in the morning we all squish into the kitchen, making tea and toast and talking about broken teapots. Sunny notices it's broken, you see. Helene thought it had always been like that but Sunny says, 'Not always.' So, of course, I have to explain.

'Sean broke it.' I try to sound nonchalant.

'No, he didn't,' says Helene. 'You've only just met him and this pot's been broken ever since I've been here.'

I am sure Helene thinks my life did not begin until she came here.

'I said *Sean*, not *John*. Perhaps you have a build-up of wax in your ears.'

'Perhaps if you didn't talk with a mouth full of toast,' Helene gripes. 'So how did *Sean* break the pot?'

'He sat on it, I think.'

Any further speculation is thankfully avoided as John squeezes himself into the kitchen. He looks so deliciously dishevelled first thing in the morning. I try not to sulk because I realise this will probably be the only morning I see him like this. He scans the Classifieds for a job and Sunny says she needs one too and it occurs to me I probably need to find work as well so I jump on the phone and call the Agency and tee up a job for tomorrow working at a cable television company that from the sound of it basically involves watching MTV all day. Honestly, I don't know why they make it so hard for themselves. Get an agency, people; they do all the work for you.

Cable TV is brand new in the U.K. (we don't even have it in Australia yet) but thanks to Dire Straits and their *Money for Nothing* music clip, we all know what MTV is and I suspect my assignment will probably entail doing nothing, just sitting at a desk, answering the phone and, really, who's going to be calling a cable company? Like I said, it's brand new. It's bad enough you have to pay for a television licence in the U.K., who on earth would want to pay extra for a bit of rock and roll?

John works in hospitality and although he would prefer to work in a nice, posh hotel, he realises it's easier to get work in a pub so he decides to pound the pavement because beggars can't be choosers, he says. Sunny thinks working in a pub sounds like fun. Is she insane? John says she can do the rounds with him if she likes. Is he insane? Who do you think the publican is going to choose – a pasty-white Brit (hey, I finally got myself one) with extensive hospitality experience or a drop dead gorgeous Aussie who's never worked in a pub before? Well of course they're going to choose Sunny.

By the end of the day, Sunny has a job as a barmaid in a busy pub in Covent Garden and John has to go back to Liverpool. Are you really that surprised?

John seems pretty down, but who can blame him? He's sleeping on a friend's floor tonight. He says my place is too crowded. I feel terrible. I'm sure he overheard Helene's nasty comments but I've got a lot of catching up to do with Sunny, so we make plans for the following night and he slumps off down the road.

I put on the kettle and settle down for a tour through America.

'So we arrived at JFK airport in New York,' begins Sunny, 'and it was so cold. Smoke poured out of the grates in the streets and they cooked nuts on the side of the road, just like in the movies. We had to organise a car straight away because we couldn't afford to stay in New York so we agreed to drive a car for an elderly couple down to Florida whilst they flew. We picked up the car and drove to The Keys and slept in a carpark. Elliott had a brand new sleeping bag so he was nice and toasty. I, on the other hand, did not. I thought I was going to die from the cold. It was minus ten degrees, Teddy, and I was sleeping in a car! After a few nights of me complaining bitterly, Elliott bought me a new sleeping bag. We spent a lot of time driving and Elliott started smoking in the car and making this irritating lip-smacking sound every time he drew back. SMACK! I was so agitated I could hardly speak. So there we were – driving in silence across America.'

I go into the kitchen to make the tea. I'm a little disappointed that this story isn't as much fun as I thought it would be. What about the sights? Did she even look out the window during their long drive to The Keys?

'We drove to the Grand Canyon…'

Great, I think, a lovely story about magnificent vistas and awe-inspiring canyons. Maybe they pitched a tent in the ravine (like the Brady Bunch did) and met a genuine American Indian? Perhaps she has some turquoise beads as a souvenir and every time she wears them she can reminisce with fondness back to a pink sunset and blue rocks stacked like pancakes. Maybe she even bounced down the treacherous path on a donkey, like Alice the housekeeper did. Maybe she took a piece of rock with bird poop from an

American eagle on it. Maybe it's just me who does things like that.

'It's impressive, I'll give you that,' says Sunny. 'A man nearly fell down into the crevice and his wife called out to him to throw her the car keys. We decided to go down into the Canyon and took off merrily at ten a.m. We passed lots of people with backpacks coming back and started to wonder whether we hadn't been a little hasty. After a couple of hours we made it to the bottom but that's probably because we ran some of the way. It was downhill, don't forget. At four o'clock we decided to head back up before it got dark. It was so cold that some giant ice-sheets broke off from the rocks and crashed to the ground. Then it got dark and we couldn't see the edge of the tiny track. And donkey poo made it slippery. And we were exhausted. We had no torch, no food, no drink, and no (insert swear word) idea! At two a.m. we arrived at the gate, literally at death's door. I will never forget the ecstatic relief I felt when I saw that gate. Over the next few days we could barely move our fingers and having shared such a harrowing experience brought us closer together. But soon we were fighting again.'

I go back to the kitchen to search for some chocolate biscuits. I feel the story warrants it.

'Oh, we saw Texas and Las Vegas before we did The Grand Canyon then it was up to San Francisco, hitch-hiking down to Los Angeles, and into San

Diego. A really nice American couple let us crash on their living room floor and even let me make a phone call home to my family. Then it was Wisconsin, Denver and the Rocky Mountains. And finally New York.'

Ah, I think, this ought to be good. Everybody loves New York. They even have bumper stickers attesting to the fact. I wonder if Sunny got me an 'I ♥ New York' sticker.*

'So I said to Elliott, "C'mon, let's go and see the Statue of Liberty," but he said, "No, I've already seen it. You go". But I didn't want to go alone – my sleeping bag cover had busted open and I looked like a bag lady carrying it around. So we ended up shouting at each other from either side of the street. He must have felt bad because he bought me a little statue. I never saw the real thing.'

Egads! What an awful story. I can't help thinking that Sunny and Elliott do not make ideal travelling companions. There doesn't seem to be any tenderness between these two so I can only surmise that they won't be travelling together again but then you never know with Sunny. It's not the journey for her, it's the destination.

---

* In case you're wondering, I got nothing.

And speaking of destinations… Sunny is off to spend some 'quality time' with William. He is over the moon but I am worried his fragile heart won't be able to take another break from Sunny. I go out for drinks with Bebe and the Kiwis from Flat 2. One of their mothers has had a heart attack so the girls have to return to New Zealand. Bebe is also leaving London in two days' time and I will probably never see her again so it's an emotional evening all round.

At midnight I clomp down to William's room to collect Sunny. She doesn't want to spend the night in his room as she thinks it would send him the wrong message but she is still fond of him and doesn't want to close the door on any future opportunities. So I have given them their space but now it's time to let me in.

My bond with both of them is far stronger than their bond to each other. Plus I'm tired. And emotional. I'm upset at losing John, and Bebe. And I know I'll lose Sunny again, too, so I stand at the closed door and knock.

'Come on Sunny. It's time to go home.' (She doesn't have a key and I've got work in the morning so I don't want her waking me at some ungodly hour to let her in.)

'Go away,' says Sunny. (Seriously, that's what she says to me.) 'Leave us alone. Why do you always have to come between us?'

I am stunned. And outraged.

Surely I deserve to be treated better than this. Far from coming between them, I suspect I have been the glue that keeps these two together.

'How dare you,' I holler from the other side of the door. 'How dare you both treat me like this! I have treated the both of you better than you've treated each other and I deserve to have friends who appreciate me, not ones who slam doors in my face and tell me to go away. You want me gone? That's fine with me! I intend to spend tomorrow night with my lovely new boyfriend and the two of you can have all the time in the world together. At least until Sunny pisses off again. And as for sleeping on my sofa, Sunny, you can forget it. I wouldn't have you in my home if you paid me for the pleasure, which of course we both know you never will. So budge up William, it looks like you've got yourself a freeloader, and I hope the two of you never darken my door again!'

It would seem the Teddy-Bear has turned into a grizzly bear.

I stomp up the stairs and all the way home, find Bebe's bowler hat and stomp on it again. What am I going to do when Bebe (and her bowler hat) is gone?

TWENTY-NINE

A tad overboard, I'll grant you, but it's the new me. Teddy keeps rearing her ill-tempered head the minute anyone tramples all over me and I must admit I rather like it. It's virtually impossible to be bland and insignificant when you're making a stand and causing a scene and Teddy seems rather fond of grand statements. Truth be told, I think she does it rather well and it's not like the things she says are completely foreign to me. They're still my thoughts, only now they're rather vocal. I think Teddy has given me the courage to finally speak my mind.

When Sunny comes knocking at my door, I refuse to let her in. So Bebe does. But I refuse to let her sleep in my room. So Bebe lets her sleep on the floor in her room. I lock myself in the bathroom and refuse to come out. Unfortunately, when making a stand, it is sometimes difficult for other people to see the point you're trying to make when all you do is stamp your foot and pout. Sunny is beginning to look like the poor victim and, worse, she's beginning to think like it.

It is John's last night in London and I want to spend it with him but I'm fretting too much about Sunny. It doesn't feel right to be fighting with my best friend, especially when she's about to turn twenty-one (at the stroke of midnight, no less) so at eleven-thirty p.m. I turn up at The Eagle, clomp downstairs to William's room and, once again, bang on the bedroom door.

'Go away,' says Sunny, again.

'No. Let me in. We need to sort this out.'

Reluctantly she opens the door and reluctantly she forgives me. And I'm guessing that reluctantly she lets me buy her a drink at the stroke of midnight. I'm not at all sure what she's supposed to be forgiving me for but I think it's got something to do with me shouting at her. Apparently I had no right to feel hurt and betrayed. I had no right to think that I was being treated unfairly. I get no apology from her or William and once she's had her drink they both disappear back into his room.

I walk home alone and in the morning I say a teary farewell to Bebe (and her wonderful bowler hat).

'Does this look bent out of shape to you?' she says.

And I honestly answer, 'Yes.' Because that is exactly how I feel.

She's off to Oxford and won't ever be returning to London. We've been sharing this flat for six months and I am going to miss her. I get the impression, though, that she is happy to be moving on. London is a little too racy for her blood these days.

Speaking of racy, I race over to John's friend's flat to say another teary farewell. John is returning to Liverpool. It's all rather taxing, I must say. Although our little romance didn't have much of a chance, I give our farewell kiss my all. I then go to Portobello Road market with Helene to buy Sunny a birthday gift (I thought she'd still be in New York so hadn't bought anything yet) and to stock up on party decorations. I've decided to throw her a little bash in the bar. It can be hard to get the gang motivated so I figure if I hold it in the bar then my job is halfway done.

I decorate the bar and put candles on the cake and then we wait. And wait. And wait. Sunny is still downstairs with William but I figure she has to come out eventually and in the meantime we'll just have the party without her. Things have been a little awkward with Lester since we ended our sordid secret affair but he says there's no reason why we can't be friends so I let him buy me a drink... or two. Helene is playing coy with Dave and I have learnt my lesson so leave them both to it. Dave gallantly buys her a drink and

Jack nudges me and says, 'We all know what it means when a bloke buys a girl a drink.'

What? What does it mean? Lester's been buying me drinks all evening. What does it mean?

Eventually, William and Sunny walk into the bar and we quickly gather ourselves and shout, 'Surprise!'

'Thanks,' says Sunny, giving a wan smile.

Then arm in arm with William, she walks out the door. Apparently he's taking her out to dinner in a nice restaurant, to celebrate her twenty-first. Are you kidding me? What is that meant to be, if not a slap in the face to me?

I sit in the bar and sulk a little. Helene's attention is focused on Dave. I want to go home. I don't have the heart to sit in a room full of people all having a good time but I am much too tipsy to risk walking through the mews alone so I accept Lester's offer to see me safely home. Oh, give me a break. What else can I do?

Can't you see that I'm all confused? I don't know which way to turn. I've lost everyone that mattered to me – John and Bebe and William and Sunny. Even Helene has turned her back on me. They are all doing what is best for them but what is best for me? At this point, Lester is the only one who's being nice to me. He tells me I look very sexy in my brown cardigan and no one has ever said I look sexy in brown before. Those are very intoxicating words for someone who's a little intoxicated. Lester says he misses me. He says I make his heart flip and his mind race and my poetry leaves him weak at the knees. I suggest he might have a fever but he takes me into his ridiculously muscled arms and squeezes me tight and tells me that he cannot live without me and NOBODY has ever told me that before. Not ever.

I dissolve into a puddle on the floor and let Lester have his way with me. It is not a pretty sight.

THIRTY

There is a new man on the scene but this one is safe with a capital S, capital A, capital F and capital E. SAFE. His name is Brian, and he is Lucille's younger sister's boyfriend so he's a year younger than us and so bland as to put my brown cardigans to shame. He even makes Alan at the front desk seem exciting. If you looked up dag or dweeb or dork in the dictionary his bland mug would pop up every time. Please, I am trying to explain here; this boy is an absolute zero.

So Helene decides he can join us for lunch at the pub.

Alarmingly, he seems rather desperate to get himself a girlfriend, which makes him an even bigger zero. Surely he must expect Lucille to tell her little sister if he strays during his visit to London? I get the feeling, though, that this is just about the most exciting thing that's ever happened to him and he's a little reluctant to have it all end. ('Be careful what you wish for,' mutters Teddy under her breath.)

Brian is nothing like the dishevelled losers that Teddy is attracted to so Helene has declared him fit for our company. So there we are, three nice, respectable people (all in brown) sitting quietly in a cosy pub, eating pies with a knife and fork.

Of course, it isn't long before Teddy becomes bored and scuttles back to The Eagle. Imagine my surprise when I am greeted by William as if I'm a long-lost relative. Well, it has been several days since he's acknowledged my existence. Perhaps he thought I really had gone away. Sunny has taken a room at the Nags Head pub in Covent Garden (her new job) so it seems I'm back in favour again. But it feels a little off. You can understand why, can't you?

So I have myself an early Sunday night. I know, it's practically unheard of.

It's almost Christmas and Oxford Street and Regent Street have the most amazing decorations but our flat is still tinsel free. Helene makes me soup and tells me that a quiet night, in careful contemplation, might just do me the world of good. Normally I'm not one to take her advice but she's behaving very much like a nun lately and it's quite soothing, if a little unsettling.

The other day she told me that God moves in mysterious ways.

I don't think I'll ever understand men not if I live to be one hundred and three.

And why, as Helene would so eloquently put it, am I running around like a dog in heat?

Helene has written me a note from work. Does anyone else think that's bizarre? She says she was bored but I'm thinking more like passive-aggressive, but okay, we'll go with bored:

December 23, 1986

Dear Theodora,

Sorry it's been so long since I've written. With one thing and another I just haven't had any time. Weather is terrif and the people I'm working with aren't too bad either. I've just finished writing two letters and three postcards. It's only 11:30. Shame, isn't it? What will I do with my afternoon? I think I'll have to get my skirt dry-cleaned as it is starting to pill. It's not actually 11:30...it's 11:25.

I was wondering if you would like to join me for a drink tonight. A Christmas drink together would be good. Or perhaps we could go down the street and buy some Tia Maria and relax at home in front of the fire. Maybe we should save the Tia Maria for Christmas Day. We could get some Coke instead. It's cheaper.

Simon and I are both sitting here with nothing to do. If he doesn't stop asking me the time I will crush, kill, destroy him. Sorry to waffle on like this but there's nothing else to do. My writing is an absolute disgrace. You don't have to agree with me. Oh, for God's sake don't go on about it. Well, if you're going to be like that then I'm going to sign off.

– Hel.

What the hell is that all about?

To tell you the truth, Helene is driving me a little nuts. She's like one of those stalkers that jump out of a cupboard when you think you're alone. She is questioning everything I do and everywhere I go. And she hates absolutely everything. I mean, is that even normal?

Thank God I don't work in the same office as her or else I'd throw myself out the window. Every morning, Lucille, Helene and I catch the tube together to work, which has a nice symmetry to it, considering Helene and I forged our friendship on the train ride into Melbourne, but all the same I am thankful that I'm the first to alight. Lucille tells me, in quiet confidence, that Helene won't even allow her to read the billboards inside the train.

I hate to say this but I'm beginning to regret kicking Joan out of the flat in favour of Helene.

Helene finally cracks and throws tinsel all about the room.

I receive a ton of Christmas cards from friends and family back home, not to mention all my new friends and family over here and I must admit I sort of flaunt them in front of Helene. Her paltry little pile on the corner of the mantelpiece is all the evidence I need that she is a pain in the neck and I'm not the only one of that opinion.

I watch her read all my cards with a permanent scowl on her face. So many names that mean nothing to her. I think she's beginning to realise that I had a life before she got here. Helene has a habit of hoarding her friends, keeping them away from others, but surely she can't alienate me from everybody? If I know Helene, she's going to give it a darn good try.

She finds a card from Liz. It says:

Dear Teddy-Bear and Bebe, and anyone else who's there (especially Mrs Q and her yappy, chocolate-thieving companion),

Have a Merry Christmas and an extremely drunken, obscene, rude, hilarious, naughty, cheeky, shameless and therefore enjoyable New Year. I know you tarts will live up to your reputation and my expectation of you as members of the New London Massage Parlour and I hope that you have informed Mrs Q that she is to be the new Madam.

Teddy, you quiet little early-sleeper; I wish to know whether you have had your literary works printed as yet. Bebe, I wish to know whether you're still going to Africa, my friend has written and said you haven't gone yet. And I also wish you to know that I miss being in London and learning to be a tart from you girls. Just drop me a line when you have time and none of your slack-bag excuses. That's final!

Oh, and Teddy, I hope you had a wonderful 21ˢᵗ Birthday.

Helene eyes the card suspiciously.

'What does she mean about Massage Parlour and Madam and tarts?'

'Oh that's just a bit of nonsense. She and Bebe got terribly drunk one night and when I came home I found a silly note on the door. They'd decided to turn the flat into a massage parlour. Pretty pointless anyway, one was tucked up sweetly in bed and the other was weeping on the loo.'

'Hmm.'

I can read a thousand disapprovals vibrating through that one sound.

Sometimes it is best not to speak of my life in London preceding Helene. She doesn't exactly appreciate it.

Come to think of it, I have changed rather a lot since I stepped off the plane in Heathrow with my six brown cardigans and Heathcliff heaving in my underwear. It must be disconcerting for Helene, she likes my brown cardigans, and clearly she does not like Teddy.

Teddy is loud and dresses inappropriately. She stays out until four in the morning and has secret affairs with practically-married men. She invites men to share her bed and shouts at her friends when they upset her. Teddy stands out like a sore thumb. Helene is discreet and lady-like and always in control and Teddy refuses to be tamed. Okay, so Teddy is my rebellion. My chance to kick up my heels and try new experiences, to have a little fun, to be a little wild, to test the boundaries of who I am and who I want to be. But, how much of Teddy is really me?

And when do I stop being Teddy?

THIRTY-ONE

We are down one flatmate at the moment since Bebe moved on to Oxford. Mrs Quist shall find us a new one, tout de suite, and I realise this will be my sixth flatmate.

But it's Christmas Eve so I have more important matters to attend to, like a party. First I have dinner at The Eagle then I call the family back home because even though it's still Christmas Eve over here, it's Christmas Day in Australia. Then Lucille and I hightail it over to a party a few blocks away. Along the way, Lucille finds a shopping trolley by the side of the road and decides to make a grand entrance, wedged inside it.

'Always best to arrive at a party in style,' she says.

Sean is at the party but I've had enough of his on again/off again nonsense so when he decides to get it on with me, Lucille steps in between us and says, 'Get lost, loser. She doesn't want *you* anymore, she wants *me*.'

I do?

Lucille then goes into surprisingly graphic detail about our planned evening culminating in me dressed up like a Geisha girl in Hyde Park and her taking piccies of it. She must be drunk. I mean, seriously, could you even make that stuff up sober?

Unfortunately all this talk of Geishas and Polaroid pictures is getting Sean excited and, before you know it, he's suggesting a threesome. On Christmas Eve! Does that man have no respect for the baby Jesus?

Later that night (or early morning, I suppose) when the party is well and truly over and we're all tucked up in bed, Sean comes a-knocking (which thrills Helene no end). 'Fancy a nice cup of tea?' he says, eyeing the broken teapot. I slam the door in his face. What did I ever see in that guy?

In the morning, Helene informs me that we have a new flatmate.

'Don't I get a say in the matter?'

'Not when you go out boozing all night.'

'You say that like it's a bad thing.'

Helene is trying to cook a turkey in our tiny little roasting oven but the oven has died (the turkey's not doing so well either). She races up to Mrs Quist's flat and Mrs Quist races down with another portable roasting oven. She must have a cupboard full of them, just waiting for such an emergency.

The two of them flick switches and move around the ovens and poke the turkey and tut-tut-tut under their breath as I gingerly make the tea.

'Is our new flatmate nice?' I ask.

'Yes dear,' says Mrs Quist.

'Is she Australian?'

'Yes dear.'

I'm surprised there are any of us left in Australia. We seem to all be squeezed into London. 'What's her name?'

'Zara.'

'That's an unusual name. Is it her real name?'

You can understand why I would question it.

'I don't know, dear. Why don't you ask her this evening.'

'She's moving in tonight, on Christmas Day? Isn't that sacrilegious, or something?'

'I don't think so, dear. Enjoy your turkey.'

I'm a little peeved that I have not been included in this arrangement but Helene says I have no one else to blame but myself. In the spirit of Christmas, I decide not to deck her. We move the table into the living room and open out the extension leaves and Helene does a lovely job of setting it, so all is forgiven. Brian and Sunny are joining us for lunch. I don't think they've actually met yet. Sunny is coming all the way from Covent Garden by cab, as there is a transport strike.

All my other friends have made plans elsewhere and at this point I'm regretting that I didn't take up Aunt Flavia's offer to spend Christmas in Crowborough. Teddy had a hankering for a large gathering of boisterous odd-bods but this little foursome is positively snoozeville. Hence, it's no surprise that I fall asleep right after lunch. Helene does, too. Then again, it could have something to do with the bottle of Tia Maria we polish off. Sunny and Brian are left alone to make their own entertainment. What will they do?

Fall in love, that's what.

Brian, you may remember, has been trying to hook up with anyone who will have him but until now no one's been interested, probably because he's dweeby and desperate. Sunny is now living far away in Covent Garden, so far away that even William has lost interest in her. He never was the type to work hard for anything. But Sunny likes men with a little hunger in their eyes, and what do you know, there's Brian – so keen he's about to bust out of his brogues. I get the feeling, too, that she's losing interest in the Nag's Head. It's a lot of stale cigarettes and sticky booze and not quite as glamorous as expected. She's only seen one theatre star, John Hurt, and I think she's seen the resident ghost more often than that so I guess she's feeling a little lost and lonely. Still, is this any reason to go and fall in love with Brian?

Brian, for God's sake!

I'm not sure I'll ever get over the shock.

Later that night, Helene and I welcome Zara into the flat. She is dressed all in black with her long, black hair piled haphazardly on her head. She looks like the lead singer of The Cure. A little scary, but I like her. Helene is behaving as if Zara is her own private discovery, like a toy she got for Christmas that she doesn't want to share. She found her and she, alone, agreed to have her move in and so she is trying her very best to keep the two of us apart. She has told Zara that I am difficult to live with. Nice.

I get a telephone call from Dan and Helene explains to Zara that he is my boyfriend in Australia. I then get another telephone call, this time from John and Helene explains that he is my boyfriend in Liverpool. Shortly after that, Lester calls in for a quick visit and Helene explains that he is my boyfriend in London. After that, William calls me up on the telephone and I glare at Helene. 'Now you can't say that he's my boyfriend.'

'I don't know what he is,' retorts Helene and I slink off, defeated, to Lucille's.

I decide to forsake all men on New Year's Eve and welcome the New Year with Sunny. It seems fitting, somehow. Since beginning this adventure, we have both spiralled out in different directions and I quite like the idea of starting 1987 together. Last week Brian invited me out for a special dinner on New Year's Eve. 'Just the two of us, Teddy,' he said. I imagine he said the exact same thing to Helene. Naturally, we both turned him down flat. But Sunny, ah Sunny, she does it to me again. She goes out to dinner with Brian and I descend into a funk.

It takes all of Lester's coaxing to get me out but finally I schlep on down to The Eagle and join the gang in celebrating a brand new year. Lucille, whom I am to understand is working as barmaid on this night of nights, is dancing on the table and even Helene is cracking a smile so all in all it's a good start to 1987.

But then I find myself at the end of the bar with Dave. Helene is still waiting for the gentleman to make his move and for whatever reason Dave has not made it so I guess Helene's nerves are a little raw. Perhaps that explains her hostile reaction to me sitting so close to him at the bar. I shiver a little and Dave gallantly drapes his sheepskin coat around my shoulders. He says something funny. I laugh. That head-flung-back-mouth-wide-open type of laugh that people do late at night when sitting in a bar, knocking back the alcohol. At no time did I transfer any liquid into his mouth and at no time did I find myself even the tiniest bit attracted to him so I can categorically state that I was not flirting with him. But I'm afraid Helene has taken note of every little nuance – every twitch, every blink, every sigh and every smile – and has rapidly come to the conclusion that I have just had sex with Dave, right there on the counter, right under her nose. How else can you explain her violent reaction, her death stare, her hard pinch, her hissing in my ear and that thunderous look on her face.

'Back off,' I growl. But she doesn't. She squeezes my arm and yanks so hard that I fall off my barstool. 'What do you think you're doing,' she spits in my face.

'What do I think I'm doing?' I splutter, as Dave helps me to my feet and rescues his lovely coat from the sticky floor. 'What do you think you're doing?'

Does it need to be said that I am so very tired of everyone treating me like this? I take a look at Helene, standing there with hands on hips, mouth tightly pursed and pure venom radiating from her eyes and from somewhere deep inside I feel Teddy stirring within my bones. She is saying, 'They drag us out of our flat and force us out of our funk for this?' and I feel a steel rod shoot through my spine. It lifts my chin up, straightens my back, squares my shoulders, pushes out my chest and brings a fire to my eyes.

In a voice that freezes the booze in the glass I say, 'Dave is my *friend*. We have talked late into the night many times and we have shared many stories. I have written him a poem about the housekeepers disturbing his slumber. We have exchanged birthday cards and Christmas cards and we have watched episodes of

Return to Eden, right on that couch over there (that alone makes us bosom buddies). I am now sitting at the bar with him because – let me make this perfectly clear – WE ARE FRIENDS. I don't know why you think you have a prior claim on him, or what you think is going on, but last time I checked you had no say in what he does or what I do and if the two of us decide to share a drink and a laugh together, you, my dear, have no say in the matter whatsoever. So you can stop grabbing my arm and pushing me around and giving me daggers and spitting in my face. You can stop trying to make me do what you want and you can stop interfering in my life because right here and right now I am letting you know that I have had enough. Either you back off, sister, or I am going to give you a whole heap of grief. You got that? Well? Have you?'

Helene narrows her eyes at me. 'You are such a bitch when you're drunk,' she hisses.

'At least *I* wait til I've had a drink.'

Lucille falls off the table and all eyes slide away from me and over to her. She lies on her back like an upended turtle and laughs so hard she pees.

'Welcome to 1987,' I sigh.

THIRTY-TWO

My head is not in a good place at the moment, judging by my bleak poetry.

Quietly I let myself in
You could have heard the drop of a pin
Turning, I bolted the door
And moved silently across the tile floor
Standing, surveying my gloom
Moonlight splashing the room
Sleeping, his face dark and dull
Swiftly the crack of a skull
Never had time for a shout
Quietly I let myself out

Too busy guzzling
Into my neck nuzzling
Took the bottle, opened the cap

Did you think I fell into your lap?
Drinking your fill, your lips you moisten
But you didn't read the label. It said I was poison

She likes to stab and shoot you down
When you smile, she likes to frown
She's poison and she cuts your throat
In your sea of troubles she sinks your boat
Although you find her such a thrill
Beware, the lady likes to kill

Such a large appetite
Do you really eat so much?
Judging by your bulge
I'd say it's all in your crotch

And judging by the hostilities coming my way courtesy of Eve, I am guessing my secret affair with Lester is perhaps becoming not so secret any more. Unsurprisingly, his frequent disappearances are beginning to register with her.

One night she accidentally-on-purpose nudges my elbow and spills my drink. Another night she talks loudly about the ugliness of brown. I tell my chocolate cardie not to take offence but you know how sensitive chunky cardies can get.

And let's not forget the awkward conversation where Eve brags about the sexy red underwear Lester's given her for Christmas. She looks at me smugly as if to say, 'I've won. He wants me more.' But I know that's not true.

How many times has he whispered in my ear, 'I want you more than anything else in this world'? Teddy lifts her head up and gives me an enquiring look as if to say, 'Shall we?' but I push her back down into the deep shadows of my twisted psyche and tell her not to be so cruel. Eve is clinging desperately to her rat boyfriend and even I don't have the heart to stick the knife in.

'I got my boyfriend some Union Jack boxers from Harrods,' I tell her. 'I wanted to send home something that was British.'

'You have a boyfriend?' She is suddenly very, very interested.

'Yes. He's waiting for me back home.' I take out the photo that I carry in my wallet and show it to her. A gorgeous six-foot blonde – bronzed and hunky and insanely attractive – smiles broadly back.

'Oh my God,' she says.

'He's very athletic,' I explain (as if it weren't achingly obvious). 'He surfs in summer and skis in winter and he's got a terrific sense of humour. (Teddy lifts her head again as if to say, 'And that's not sticking the knife in?') Most of the time he's all I ever think about.'

'I can see why,' she sighs.

And then she smiles. And I know why. She is thinking that any girl who has a gorgeous guy like that would not waste her time on a bloke like hers and I have to say she has a very good point.

What the hell am I doing with Lester?

'So how was dinner?' I ask Sunny.

'Okay, except Brian told me I wear too much make-up and he'd booked a room at some crappy hotel.'

'What? He took you to a hotel room on your first date?'

I've got to say I am shocked. I didn't think old Dweeby was the type. He seems so square and, oh, what's the word? … SAFE! What the hell happened?

Sunny shrugs. (Talk about noncommittal.)

'Did you sleep with him? What does William think about this?'

'It's no big deal. He's going back to Australia tomorrow. It was just a bit of fun.'

But Sunny is wrong. It is not just a bit of fun for Brian. He's probably thinking the same thing everyone else on this planet is thinking. How does a skinny, ugly runt like him wind up with a drop-dead stunner like her?

I spend the day at Thames TV, typing up copy for the News Department. Every time a news anchor grabs his papers or glances down at them, I get a tiny thrill knowing that I typed that stuff up. I could care less what the news is actually about, just as long as there are no errors in my copy. I'm actually the first one to hear the news, too. When a reporter on the scene calls up from a phone box to file his story, I am the one that takes it all down, word for word.

I've gotta say, I love my new Agency, The Grosvenor Bureau. All of these media assignments are pretty cool and every Friday night all the temps drop into the office in Grosvenor Square to share a glass of bubbly after work and let the Manager know how things are going. It's a much smaller agency than Kelly Girl but the assignments are just as good, if not better.

So, this being a Friday, I call in for champers and a chat and then head off to The Eagle where I am not surprised in the least to find Brian sitting in the bar.

'Haven't you missed your flight?'

'I decided to stay.'

'Of course you did.' I look across at Sunny sitting shell-shocked by his side and wonder how she's going to get out of this. William is unravelling at the seams. I am dragged down into his dungeon so he can wail and whine about Sunny and I guess there is a part of me that's rather pleased that I am back in favour and the two of them are no longer slamming doors in my face, but overall I'm kinda over the whole damn thing.

'I envy you, Teddy-Bear,' he sniffles.

'Why?'

'You never seem to get bogged down by love.'

Ah, but looks can be deceiving, can't they? The thing about me is that I don't tell guys how I really feel. I just write bad, angst-ridden poetry. The truth is, I was deeply hurt by Jack, torn in two by Sean, devastated by Max, heartbroken by John, sick to my stomach by Lester, betrayed to the core by William, and full of longing for Dan.

All in all, I would have to say my love life is like a car wreck – lots of carnage and twisted metal and me whimpering, 'What the hell just happened?'

And Helene would be the cop yelling that it's entirely my fault.

Have I mentioned how tired I am? I flop onto William's bed and go in search of Dick (Francis, that is) but I've read all of the books in William's bookshelf and there's nothing worth watching on the telly. To make matters worse, William won't stop moaning about Sunny's so-called betrayal.

Sitting in that windowless, airless, basement room with a man who has held onto the fantasy of a girlfriend for far too long, I realise I am beginning to miss the simplicity and boredom of my six brown cardigans.

'I can't believe she'd sleep with Brian,' he says

'I guess people do strange things when they're out of their comfort zone,' I reply, 'and have sex with the most unlikely person in the room.'

To be fair, I'm mostly thinking of Lester when I say this but William is not to know that and so, unfortunately, he gets the wrong end of the stick.

'You know, you're right Teddy-Bear,' he says and proceeds to rip our clothes off.

My first thought is that William is having a stroke or has lost his mind. My second thought is that he might be trying to make Sunny jealous in a bid to win her back. My third thought is that he must be bored, and perhaps a little horny. My fourth thought is, 'Oh my God, not another one!' and my fifth thought is, 'What a shame there is no window or I could have thrown myself out of it and be done with all of this.'

I am very, very tired (and a little tipsy from that glass of champers at the Agency) but I still manage to shout out, if rather feebly, 'Stop, William. I don't want to have sex with you.'

'Why not?'

I don't want to hurt his feelings...

'I already have a boyfriend.' The words are out of my mouth before I can stop them.

'You mean back in Australia?'

'No, I mean here.'

'You mean that guy from Liverpool? He's not even around anymore.'

'No, I have a boyfriend still here.'

'What, here in London or here in this hotel?'

'Both.'

'Do you mean Jack? I thought that was all over now that he's with Delilah. Or do you mean Sean?'

'No.'

'You can't mean Max. He hasn't been around here for ages.'

'Can you please stop giving me a rundown of all my disastrous hook-ups? You're beginning to depress me.'

'Who is it, Teddy-Bear? Not Alan?'

'Are you trying to make me vomit on your bed?'

'Then who?'

'I'd rather not say. You'll just get mad.'

'I'll get mad if you don't tell me. I thought we were best buds. Don't we share everything?' (He's got a nerve, hasn't he?) Is it Dave? Is that why he's still around?'

This is getting ridiculous. William is not going to give up and I am getting tired of the third degree. I am secretly pleased, however, that he hasn't worked out who it is. But this is where I make a huge mistake (actually I make two). I decide to put him out of his misery.

'It's Lester.'

Now, it might have escaped your attention (it certainly escaped mine) that William has been working at The Royal Eagle Hotel for many, many years. And so has Eve. They are – as William points out to me in no uncertain terms – friends. Not hanging-out-in-the-bar friends, but I-got-your-back friends. And William is absolutely furious that Lester is cheating on her. And he can hardly believe that I am involved in the whole sordid mess.

'I thought you were better than this,' he says.

Must be the brown cardigans. They give off a certain proper impression.

'I would give anything not to be involved with him but he's like that *Return to Eden* miniseries. He's so addictive, that I can't stop.'

'Well, I'm going to put a stop to it right now,' says William, heading for the door.

'No!' I fling myself on top of him and push him to the bed. 'No, no, no, no, no!'

All I am thinking is that he must not leave this room. If he goes upstairs and confronts Lester it will all be out in the open and everyone will know what an awful person I am. And I will never again have words like, 'I want you more than anything else in this world' whispered lovingly in my ear.

Then again, I could be wrong.

William grabs me in a tight embrace and begins to ardently kiss my neck. And he whispers in my ear... 'I want you more than anything else in this world.'

Oh crap!

THIRTY-THREE

So here comes mistake number two. I sleep with William. And it is awful. Not least because right in the middle of it I get the worst leg cramp I have ever experienced in the whole of my rotten life. We are talking pain so bad that I beg William to cut my leg off.

I push him away and scream in agony and seriously want to curl up and die (but none of that has anything to do with the leg cramp). I am mortified.

'This is going to ruin everything,' I groan.

'No it won't.'

You have never seen two people back-peddle so fast. We could have won the Tour de France.

William walks me home and promises me – absolutely, positively promises me – that nothing will change between us and I desperately want to believe him because I value his friendship more than anything else. I want to believe that I'm not just a drinks-in-the-bar buddy. We are like brother and sister (except for the sleeping together bit) and I desperately want to believe that we can get past this awful, dreadful mistake.

But I am wrong.

Our friendship is ruined.

It has begun to snow and the temperature plummets to minus ten degrees. I put on thick woollen tights, trousers and socks, a skivvy, a sweater a cardigan, my winter coat, hat, gloves and scarf and run into Mrs Quist on the landing who tells me to rug up so I return to the flat and add several more layers before waddling out to Wimpy's for brunch with Sunny, and the whole sordid mess is revealed. I can't quite believe it but the instant William returned to The Eagle he blabbed to Alan (who sees all at the front desk) and the blabbermouth with no life of his own then told everyone else. And they say women can't keep secrets.

William has seemingly painted me as a wanton harlot, seducing poor Lester whilst laughing in poor Eve's face, and I'm not sure but I think he's made out that I seduced him, too. Good Lord!

To make matters worse, Sunny is now upset with me for sleeping with her ex. I would have thought that was the only thing out of all this business that made sense. William and I have been very close friends for six months, we do everything together and we make a good match, so it should have been the most natural thing in the world for us to become a couple but I have to admit it felt so very, very wrong the instant we did it. I guess he's just not Teddy's type and I realised a long time ago that she's the part of me that chooses who we sleep with. And as for Sunny getting her nose all bent out of shape, are you kidding me? I point out to her, as gently as I can, that she only actually dated the man for a few weeks before flitting off THREE TIMES with his BEST FRIEND. And now she's hooked up with (I can barely keep my burger down) Brian, right under William's nose.

'Don't pretend we both don't know what comes next.'

'I don't know what you mean.'

'Yes you do. Brian's just gotten a job at The Eagle and it comes with a shoebox that he has optimistically squeezed a bed into. You're not happy working at The Nag's Head, you want to come back to Paddington but you don't want to work. I can see the wheels churning in your brain, Sunny. I predict it goes something like this – you hide in Brian's room and he gives you anything you want because he's just so blown away by the fact that you're willing to sleep with him.'

'People in glass houses,' sniffs Sunny.

'We are never to speak of this unfortunate incident ever again,' I stress.

I am too ashamed to show my face at The Eagle and I feel utterly betrayed by William so I adopt a 'screw you' attitude and give the hotel a wide berth. This is not the only drama I have to deal with. I've gone and done a rather foolish thing. No, not that thing, I'm talking about another foolish thing.

I have told Dan not to wait for me. Well, I had so many men circling me (like flies to a rubbish dump) that I thought it was a little greedy of me to keep Dan on the backburner. Now, of course, it has all blown up in my face and what I really need is a few reassuring words from Dan to make me feel wanted again. You know the ones – I love you – I miss you – I want you to come home – but I have told him not to wait and he has responded with:

So you don't want me to wait for you. It took some getting used to. It's hard to take Europe means more to you than I do. Maybe there's someone special to you over there. Probably William. I don't know, you seem to write about him all the time. I don't think I mean too much to you (correct me if I'm wrong). I don't know why I felt so strongly about you but you're so far away, I couldn't show you how I felt. I really miss you heaps. I think I might even LO... No, I can't say it but it might explain how I feel about you. I just hope that when you do decide to come back we can be friends and I hope you still keep writing to me. I know you've got your own life to live and it's hard to take that I'm not part of it but I tried to tell you just how much I care about you and now there's nothing left inside of me. I just wish you would come back. I guess I'm not that important to you.

Keep in touch, love Dan.

I cry myself to sleep but tears on my pillow won't wash away this mess. In the morning I write another letter back to Dan instructing him to ignore my last letter because I was a silly fool to think I could ever let him go. I tell him that if I could I would pack the whole of London in my suitcase (along with my six brown cardigans) and rush back to Bitterly Bay just so I could see him again.

Wait, dear Dan, please wait, I beg. *I think I LO you, too.*

Pathetic. I am pathetic.

But I am on an emotional roller coaster and at this point I'm just glad I haven't puked in my hair. I feel a little annoyed that everyone has painted a scarlet letter on my chest when clearly my behaviour is not that different to theirs. Don't they remember Sunny running off to the south of France with Elliott, or Bebe spending the night with Mick? And what about the way Jack and Sean treated me? And let's not forget, I'm not actually the one who is cheating on Eve. That would be Lester but no one is giving him a hard time about it (not even Eve).

Helene is of the very firm opinion that The Eagle is bad for me – a den of iniquity, she says – so she thoroughly approves of my abstinence. We decide to take up ice-skating.

Queens Ice Skating Club is about a fifteen-minute walk towards Bayswater (in the opposite direction of The Eagle). We take out memberships.

Zara is working behind the refreshment counter at The London Palladium Theatre and gets us free tickets to a performance of *La Cage Aux Follies*.

Zara has a habit of breaking glassware in the flat so we've taken to stopping by at the pub after our weekly food shop so that she can pinch the glasses.

There's also been a fair amount of traffic in our flat.

Lucille's hot water goes on the blink so she comes to our flat for a bath. But we don't have hot water either, so we boil the kettle and heat pots of water on the stove and run to and fro filling up her bath.

Sunny and Brian visit quite often in order to escape their tiny shoebox room and the Manager roaming the corridors (don't forget Sunny is not supposed to be living there).

One week they join us ice-skating.

Another week Jack and Sean join us.

Alan goes to the movies with Helene.

Lester moves a television from Lucille's flat to mine. Even Eve pays us a visit, although I think that's to make sure her boyfriend moves the television as intended.

Our affair, however, continues unabated.

I feel crummy about the whole thing but somehow I can't seem to get rid of him.

THIRTY-FOUR

It's Lester's birthday. I write him a poem:

It's not until you cut the cake
That you realise your age
As you blow out all the candles
You think it's just a stage
But the frustration of those wasted years
Soon will turn to rage
And by the time you see your fate
You're trapped behind the cage
Your life reveals an open book
And as you turn the page
It's not until you cut the cake
That you realise your age

Clearly I am trying to get rid of him but he doesn't take the bait. I tell him I don't want to be a mistress anymore but he misunderstands and turns up on my doorstep one night positively elated. He has left the bitch (his words, not mine).

I am appalled but he insists we go out to a fancy restaurant to celebrate. I want to set the record straight at once but Teddy is hissing in my ear that finally we get the fancy restaurant. 'Put on some lippy and shut the hell up,' she says. So I put on some lipstick and I shut the hell up.

Lester says he has taken a room at The Eagle but I don't believe him. If he had really broken up with Eve she would never have let him stay at the hotel. Perhaps they had a fight and he agreed to sleep in another room until they both cooled down and now his plan is to spend the night with me. I tell him to stop wasting my time. I tell him I don't want a boyfriend. If I did then clearly I would not have chosen someone who already has a girlfriend. I just wanted a chance to do something so out of character that when I'm ninety-four, drooling into my withered lap, I can say that once I did something truly shocking. And even though the nurse will simply scrape the porridge off my chin and say, 'You're losing your marbles, dear. Anyone with six brown cardigans would never do such a thing', the point is I will know (and hopefully I will remember). One day I will stare out the window of the old folks' home and remember that a practically-married man with muscles thicker than my thighs once whispered in my ear that he wanted me, more than anything else in this world. Actually, thanks to William, I'll probably also remember with unmitigated horror that he, too, whispered those words in my ear. I imagine when I'm ninety-four that I probably won't be able to hear a whisper.

Anyway, Lester returns to Eve and I continue to stay away from The Eagle but, like I said, it appears The Eagle cannot stay away from me. Or at least those who frequent the place can't. Everyone, except for William, finds their way to 133 Gloucester Terrace until the night when it all comes to a head.

It begins at four-thirty p.m. when Lucille pops in to tell us there will be drinks at The Mitre pub for Reebok (who's heading back to Australia next week). Reebok got her nickname (courtesy of Bebe, of course) when she returned from a trip to America with a pair of outrageously expensive runners. Apparently they are all the rage over there.

At six-thirty p.m. Helene answers a knock at the door. She calls out that some ugly, hairy guy is accosting her at the front door and I race through the kitchen, heart thumping and hopes rising.

Could this be Max, ready to forgive me at last?

But my hopes are dashed. It's only Joseph, Bebe's boyfriend, down from Oxford for the day. Apparently he's a little insulted by being described as ugly and hairy so doesn't stick around for long. After he's left,

I tell Helene about the experiments he does on monkeys and how he considers it humane to shoot them in the head and she says she's glad she called him ugly and hairy, and regrets she didn't throw in short and fat and smelly.

But then she admits that she actually thought Joseph was my latest suitor and I realise that Teddy's reputation is not one that I am entirely comfortable with. Which brings us back to that old chestnut – what the hell am I doing with Lester? And when he calls at the flat an hour later, I say as much to him. 'What the hell are we doing?' I wail. He can give no answer and so I tell him that it's over.

Naturally this leaves me a little flat. Helene and I head off to The Mitre but I'm not in the mood to kick up my heels. I'm in for a shock, though, for sitting with the group is William and I haven't quite worked out what I would do if I were to meet him outside of The Eagle. To tell you the truth, it very rarely happens. William just expects everyone to come to him but I think our estrangement has shown us both that life does not revolve around The Royal Eagle Hotel, as previously thought.

Perhaps it worried William that, like the Pied Piper of Hamelin, I was leading the others away and whether he was forced to follow or to intervene before things got out of hand, it seems that he has decided to forgive me. I am more than happy to put the whole mess behind us and so graciously accept his forgiveness (!).

At midnight I find myself back at Wimpy's with Sunny (like you do).

'What happened to everyone?' I sigh, digging into my burger and fries. 'They used to be so interesting and cosmopolitan.'

'That's just your opinion,' mumbles Sunny through a mouthful of meat.

'Where are all the fabulous people?' I moan.

'Eating burgers at Wimpy's,' grins Sunny.

And who can argue with that.

By the time I get back to the flat, Helene is there with a new guy called Jimmy. He's Scottish, very tall and skinny and a little manic. Helene seems quite taken with him. He's got an Aussie friend with him who's very dishy (of course). Apparently she met them at The Mitre pub and invited them back to the flat. I am astonished. How is this not just like Sunny and me bringing Douglas and Kev back? What is it with The Mitre pub?

You remember how Doug stole Sunny's money and tried to flush the coins down the loo?

At least this time, Helene won't get robbed. For starters, there are too many people coming in and out of the flat. And secondly, Helene hides her money under the mattress. She never was the trusting type.

I don't have a chance to chat, though, which is probably a good thing. I need a dishy Aussie bloke like I need a hole in the head. My head, however, is filled with other things. Lester is back and he has that determined glint in his eye.

We kiss and make up. I know, I know, I am so pathetic.

THIRTY-FIVE

A few days later, my total repulsion of the whole male species drives me to break up with Lester yet again only this time I think it will stick. I mean, now I am well and truly turned off by men and I have Helene's new man, Jimmy, to thank for that. I absolutely, one hundred percent cannot stand him.

He actually physically causes me pain whenever he enters a room. My eyelashes hurt. And my teeth. And my toenails. Even the very tips of my hair scream out in agony whenever he is near. He is just so completely and utterly horrid. What the hell is Helene doing with him? I wonder if this is punishment for me subjecting her to Lester for so long?

Jimmy, however, is on another level all his own. He struts, he boasts, he preens, he blags, he leers, he jokes, he talks about himself non-stop and he thinks he's God's gift to women (so obviously he's clinically insane). He is so full of himself that everything he says and everything he does grates on me to the point of madness but Helene is crazy about him so I do my very best to be nice to him.

I would rather have my fingernails pulled out one by one.

Zara has also fallen in love, with an Irishman named John. She has a separate bedroom to ours so is exempt from Helene's rule. You must remember the rule?

- NO MEN ALLOWED OVERNIGHT -

Instigated the night my Liverpudlian came to stay. Odd, though, how Helene also seems to be exempt from this rule. Jimmy spends the night in our room. Our beds are practically side-by-side so I am forced to listen to Jimmy and Helene having sex.

Luckily it doesn't take long.

It seems that Helene and I have done a complete role reversal. All I want to do now is hibernate in my flat and become addicted to EastEnders on the telly. I start to believe that maybe I have tamed the beast within, the one named Teddy, when I receive a letter from Dan and Teddy goes into overdrive. It starts off nice and simple, he talks about the weather (forty degrees Celsius), water-skiing at the lake, how much he misses me and wishes I were coming home and then he adds an *oh by the way* at the end of his letter and talks about a girl named Tiffany who appears to be rather interested in him and, not to worry, he'll try ignoring her and hope she goes away...

I feel the fire burning in my belly, racing through my veins and exploding in my head. And Teddy says, 'I am going to kill that bitch! If she lays one hand on Dan, I will tear her fingernails out one by one and stick them in her eyeballs. I will rip her lips off and shove them down her throat, then kick her in the teeth and make a necklace out of them. Seriously, she'd better keep her hands off my man!'

Using remarkable restraint, I carefully fold the letter and place it in the pocket of my embroidered beige cardigan. I smooth down my hair, pick at an imaginary thread from my brown knit skirt, and then slowly walk into the kitchen to make a cup of tea.

I have a lot to think about and this is no time for Teddy to overreact.

Where has this part of me (that I now call Teddy) been hiding for so long? Why did she never show her face in Bitterly Bay? Why is she now calling all the shots? Is it a good thing that I have found my voice and now refuse to be bullied or is Teddy going too far with all this carrying on?

And what about this business with the men? I could have sworn that Teddy was all for casual sex and bad poetry and not letting the heart get hurt but could it be that she, too, has serious feelings for Dan? Has she found that hidden spot in my heart where I stashed Dan for safekeeping?

Has she had enough of all these games? Because, to tell you the truth, I think I have.

I decide a girls' night out with Lucille and Zara will keep me safe from men but it all goes horribly wrong when we meet some sleazy guys in Notting Hill and Lucille tells them we're lesbians.

It starts at the Mitre pub (which, in hindsight, is probably not the best way to start things) so by the time we reach the Notting Hill pub, I am three sheets to the wind (drowning my sorrows, you could say). A couple of sleazy guys at the bar won't leave us alone so Lucille comes out with her shocking news.

'Get lost, creeps, we're lesos.'

Now you may remember she tried this tack with Sean on Christmas Eve and it got him all in a lather so, I don't know, maybe she's trying to have a little fun but either way it rapidly gets out of control. The men refuse to leave us alone and we find ourselves having to pretend all night. Nothing too salacious, you understand, just stroking hair and nuzzling necks and the conversation goes a little like this…

'Ooh, I love my lesbian girlfriend.'

'Yeah, my lesbian girlfriend is hot.'

'She's so sexy.'

'Yeah, she really turns me on.'

'Yeah.'

'Ooh yeah.'

Then Zara runs into an old friend, Terrence, and we go upstairs with him to a private club but the sleazy guys aren't about to let us get away so they follow. They try to break into the club and a huge fight breaks out. I cower under a table, the police turn up and Terrence's face is badly cut. We scarper back to Lancaster Gate where, incredibly, the thugs are standing right outside The Mitre Pub. We'd have to walk right past them to get home. Zara and Terrence calmly cross the road and keep walking but Lucille and I are too freaked out to move. It's all right for them, the boys hardly got a look at them, but we're forced to make a detour and hide in The Eagle for a couple of hours. We finally set out for home at around two a.m. but somehow end up at Jack and Sean's place.

And incredibly we are still playing our lesbian charade, which completely puzzles the boys and who can blame them? They both know from first-hand experience that this simply isn't true. It is a bit odd that we keep telling everyone we're lesbians. I think Lucille just likes shocking people and don't forget I'm horribly drunk and by this stage too busy vomiting to make any sense of it.

By the time I stagger home, the sun is coming up and Helene is standing in the kitchen, making coffee, giving me that judgemental stare of hers.

'Bebe went home yesterday,' she says.

'What? Back to Australia?'

'Yes, that's what I said.'

'But she didn't even say goodbye to me, not a word. I had no idea she was going.'

'She asked me not to tell you.' Helene looks like the cat that ate the canary. Naturally she would have kept this secret from me.

'But why?'

'Perhaps you didn't know her as well as you thought you did,' says Helene, smugly. 'I guess she just wanted to see her *friends* before she left.'

I am stunned. When did Helene become her friend? And when did I stop?

I lie down on the bed and the room starts spinning as I try to absorb all this. Dan is seeing another girl back home, Lucille and I are lesbians, and Bebe has gone home without saying goodbye. What is going on with the world?

I feel really sad that Bebe left things this way. And why have Lucille and I become lesbians? That's just stupid.

As I lay my head wearily upon my pillow, something crinkles in my ear. I lift the pillow and find a letter hidden underneath it. It's from Bebe. It says:

Dear Teddy, my plan is to wait until you leave the flat and let Helene think I've come to see her. Whilst she's making a pot of tea, I shall feign a trip to the loo and hide this letter under your pillow so if that's where you've found it then my plan will have worked. The trouble is, you see, that I'm hopeless at goodbyes. Especially when there's every chance we'll never meet again.

It is my sincere wish for you that you have friends most special surround you, friends who love you and are willing to stand by you... no matter what. And, my dearest, that this will be a truly wonderful year for you, filled with so much happiness and laughter and travelling and sightseeing. Go for it, Teddy – show us all what you are really made of.

And who knows, maybe we'll meet again on the other side.

My love and wishes always, God bless, B.B.

Bebe was a true friend and Sunny and I were so lucky that she moved into 133 Gloucester Terrace. She helped me find my voice (thanks to that ridiculous nickname) and I will never forget her. It hurts when people move on but it's the nature of the beast.

We are all here for such a short time and that is especially true for the people in London. We are travellers, adventurers, explorers. We came to London to experience all the best that life can give but none of us, myself included, expected to live here forever. We have homes and families and friends (and boyfriends?) to return to. And it is only right that Bebe is returning to hers.

Even Lucille is leaving, in one week's time, so once again we go down to The Mitre and I try to drown my sorrows. Once again, I vomit my guts up and Helene takes me aside and says, 'What's up?'

Where do I begin?

I must confess I've hardly eaten a thing all week. It's a combination of feeling fat (from too many Wimpy burgers), losing my closest friends, sick with worry that back home Dan will succumb to Tiffany's charms, being followed home from work every day by Lester begging me to take him back, and, finally, having Helene bossing me about morning, noon and night. She spent the first month here telling me how awful my friends were, the second month trying to steal them away from me and now that she has driven every man from my hearth, she turns around and practically shoves her man down my throat. Is it any wonder I can't keep my food down?

I take a day off work to recuperate then head down to Wimpy's for a midnight feast. My eating habits are back to normal, if you can call them that!

THIRTY-SIX

It is Valentine's Day. I get a wake-up call at eight-thirty a.m. from Australia, a wake-up in more ways than one. It is Dan, and I am over the moon.

'Oh Dan,' I gush, 'I think of you every moment of the day and I would die, absolutely die, if I never heard from you again.'

'Now that's what I wanted to hear,' he says, sounding absolutely delighted.

He has sent me a beautiful Valentine card, pink with two red love hearts and inside he has written, *You mean more to me than anything. Don't ever forget me, love Dan.*

My heart is filled with happiness again.

I just want to be loved without the pain and it seems the only way I can do that is to keep the object of my affection at arm's length. It seems like a fair solution to me.

Helene, Lucille and I go to Le Beat Route nightclub in Soho. Once again there is a thumping disco beat blaring in one ear and Lucille rabbiting away in the other and I still adore her. And my heart is lighter than air because Dan loves me.

Jimmy and his Aussie mate have been calling in almost every night so just for something different we decide to hang out at Lucille's place. It will probably be our last time. She lives about ten doors down but her place is a dump. Actually, everyone lives in a dump. I think it's a traveller's rule. Our place is a palace in comparison but we try to keep it as messy as possible in keeping with the traveller's code of conduct.

Jimmy is stoned. He has a laughing fit over nothing and then writes me a poem. It is awful. It begins, *Hi there brain, are you awake, sitting in the court of veins*, and goes downhill from there. I must be giving him even filthier looks than usual because he writes, *who picks whose fun? Who has the right to decree?*

I tell you what, Jimmy, if it were up to me, you, my creepy friend, would be history.

The next night we go to Moriaty's pub for another goodbye drink for Lucille. If she doesn't get on a plane soon, I could end up an alcoholic!

'I'm going to miss you, Luce,' I blubber. 'I've never had so much fun in all my life.'

'Don't worry,' she says, 'you and I are going to be friends for the rest of our lives.'

And beyond, I hope.

It is now the middle of February and Aunt Flavia in Crowborough has extended an invitation for me to stay with them over the Easter break.

Helene and I have booked a tour through Europe that begins on Easter Monday so we will have to terminate our lease and this seems an ideal arrangement.

We're on a 10-week package tour for 18-35 year olds with a company called Autotours. It costs $2,500 and takes us to France, Spain, Italy, Venice, Yugoslavia, Bulgaria, Turkey, Greece, a yacht in the Greek Islands, Austria, Hungary, Germany, Liechtenstein, Switzerland, Amsterdam and finally Belgium. We leave April 20 and return June 25.

Aunt Flavia also informs me that I have a second cousin dying to meet me and I realise I have many relatives in England that I intended to visit but am now rapidly running out of time. It makes me appreciate that one day it will be me going home.

But in the morning it is Lucille. She flies back to Perth and forfeits her life as a traveller, duly passing on her backpack and sleeping bag to me for my European trip. I feel as though a little piece of Lucille is still with me, especially since she has left a large stain on the sleeping bag (actually it wasn't her stain but one she inherited from the last owner).

And the following day there is another reminder of her. A friend of hers, named Suzy, needs a place to crash for a couple of hours. She has travelled from South Africa for an abortion and needs to rest after the procedure. I have to go to work but Helene stays home to look after her and then kindly lends out her winter coat as it is freezing outside. Suzy promises to return it but, guess what? She doesn't.

I know it was only a cheap coat, bought at the market (everyone wears them – tweedy, old, smelly, second-hand men's coats that I wouldn't be seen dead in) but I am still astounded that after all the kindness afforded her, Suzy could not somehow return that coat.

I get another letter from Dan and, once again, Teddy goes into a tailspin. It appears that Tiffany keeps inviting herself along to Dan's activities, the latest one being a houseboat at Pixy Point with a group of friends, who all appear to be encouraging the relationship.

'Dan is going out with a lampshade.' At least that's what I tell Zara.

'A what?'

'Well, maybe not a lampshade but her name's Tiffany, like the lampshade. It's a stupid name.'

'And Teddy-Bear isn't?'

'That's not my real name. It's just a silly nickname I got saddled with over here.'

'Well, there's nothing you can do about that,' she reasons, and I'm not sure if she's talking about the nickname or the fact that another girl is sniffing around my beloved.

'You don't know what it's like,' I moan. 'Leaving the man you love behind.'

'Yes I do,' says Zara. 'I have a boyfriend back home, too. Matter of fact, he's coming over here in about six months' time.'

'What about Irish John?'

Irish John has been sleeping over nearly every night. He's not devastatingly handsome, not unless you like pale men with pointy features and black, greasy hair that droops over his eyes but Zara is no oil painting, either, unless you go for scary Robert Smith types (he's the lead singer of The Cure).

'I have no idea what I'm going to do,' says Zara.

Cripes, and I thought I had problems!

I go to the movies with Sunny to see *Ferris Bueller's Day Off*, and tell her that I am falling in love with

Dan. She tells me that I am most definitely not. I am in love with the idea of being in love.

Sunny hates messy love affairs. She would never have done the ridiculous juggling act that I was trying to pull off with my Liverpudlian and Lester (and William, for that matter). I like that she's so pragmatic about love. Do you think this means she won't ever get her heart broken?

I am bored to the back teeth with my latest work assignment, which has been dragging on for far too long. It's a furniture design company called Vitra.

I keep asking my boss at The Grosvenor Bureau Temp Agency what furniture has to do with media but she says they are creative types and very good clients and she keeps talking me into staying longer.

On the way to work one morning I get lost in a blizzard and wonder if this is just a metaphor for my life right now. I bump into an American soldier, standing sentinel, and think *good grief, I've walked all the way to America* before realising I'm at the American Consulate.

I contemplate jumping ship. I've spied an ad in the paper for a video magazine company. I call them up and arrange an interview and take a day off work and make my way to their dingy little office. They offer me the job but I decide against it. It's a long way from home and a permanent position, which clearly isn't feasible for me, and besides, it's really just a lackey job that they've tried to dress up as Assistant to the Manager. And it's nowhere near as well paid as temping.

So I return to Vitra. On the plus side, one of their chair designers is really cute and he frequently walks me to the Tube station after work. I convince myself that he's far too attractive and clearly out of my league and I'm going to Europe soon so I can't even think about men.

Or so Helene keeps instructing me. Every time I even glance at a guy she says, 'Don't even think about it'. So I guess I won't.

I bump into Sean at the Laundromat and we go to the pub for a pint and a chat. He seems very concerned about me. He thinks Helene has too tight a grip on me.

Maybe all this misery isn't just about men. I do hate the way Helene stops me from associating with certain people, one of them being Sean. Even if she's right and he's not the greatest person to be with I do still enjoy his company. He's interesting because he's so odd and so unlike me.

Sean says they miss me. I only ever see him and Jack when I'm at The Eagle and that's not very often these days. He invites me over to his place and we start planning my escape.

Well, something has to give. I am so very, very bored.

I sneak off and spend my evening with Sean, Jack and Delilah.

Sean is still playing his on again/off again games but I just can't be bothered to respond anymore.

Jack is still giving me that seductive smile of his and undressing me with his eyes.

Delilah is still rummaging around for cigarette butts in dirty ashtrays.

But none of it really matters.

I find myself sitting on the loo, staring at the cat poo and not giving a damn about any of it. I just stare into the middle distance and wonder when my pretend life will be over and I can return to my normal life again.

Although it's not much different to hanging out with Helene, Jimmy and his Aussie mate, I must admit I do feel considerably happier away from Helene.

But it's more than that. Down at the Eagle, William notices that I don't write poems anymore. I just sit on the sofa and stare blankly at the big screen. He thinks it is writer's block. He says I am losing my sparkle. He says winter in London turns everything and everybody grey.

And that's when it hits me. I am no longer brown. I am a melancholic, moody grey.

And from somewhere deep inside of me I can feel Teddy doing that silent scream made famous by the Norwegian expressionist painter Edvard Munch.

I look down at my grey knit jumper and my grey knit pants and decide that tomorrow I shall wear my mustard polo shirt. I think it's time for a little sunshine, don't you?

By the way, something has to be done about Helene and Jimmy. They keep having sex in the bed right next to mine and it is creeping me out. I ask them to stop but they just tell me they'll be quiet. Believe me, that is just as creepy.

It all comes to a head one night when Helene is in the bathroom. I am in bed and Jimmy is sitting on Helene's bed, spouting his usual bullshit.

You know, he is convinced that he's God's gift to women and doesn't stop bragging about it so a little idea pops into my head and I begin to flirt.

Don't panic, there is method to my madness.

Now I'm not saying that I'm an expert at seduction but it is surprisingly easy to seduce a man who is convinced that all women are destined to fall hopelessly in love with him. He expects it. And I am sure he has been watching me from the corner of his eye, waiting for a sign.

The other day when I wore my mustard polo shirt underneath my grey jumper Jimmy pounced on it. Not literally, but figuratively. When I walked into the room, he said 'Teddy, what is that racy bit of mustard I see poking out of your cleavage?' which is ridiculous since only the collar of my mustard shirt was showing and that was up around my neck and nowhere near my cleavage. For that matter, I don't even have a cleavage.

All the same, my mustard polo caused quite a stir with Jimmy.

'You are a dark horse, aren't you?' he grins. Well, it's more of a leer and I try to imitate it whilst Helene is occupied in the bathroom. I am sitting in my bed and Jimmy is sitting on Helene's. So I do the leer and I pat the bed and I say in a breathless, seductive drawl, 'Come here.'

He comes.

THIRTY-SEVEN

Before long Jimmy is lying on top of me, trying to kiss me. Did I say before long? More like within seconds! I immediately call out to Helene who catches her weasel of a boyfriend trying to extricate himself from my bed. He pleads innocence, claiming I have seduced him. I point out to Helene that even if that were true, he still chose to climb into my bed, which makes him a low-life scumbag willing to cheat on her.

Naturally she takes his side. You understand why I did it, don't you? Desperate times call for desperate measures. When I think of that bony creep pressing down on me... well, it doesn't bear thinking about. It just doesn't. I don't care if Helene thinks I'm a rat, the end result is worth it. She bustles him out of the flat and tells him that future assignations between the two of them will be done at his flat. I never have to see Jimmy again.

I don't think I can even begin to explain to you how utterly awful he is. He's so cocky and sure of himself, constantly bragging and exaggerating, and he's so skinny and weaselly that just looking at him offends all my senses, even the dull ones. He is always the loudest person in the room and goes on and on about the dullest things and acts like he's just invented the wheel. Once he talked for over an hour about cheese and not even the good stuff. And don't get me started on those crappy poems he writes.

He is a pasty-white Brit who huddles in darkened corners talking existential angst and I absolutely loathe him.

Now you may be thinking this is just jealousy on my part because Helene has a boyfriend and I don't, but honestly, I've had my fill of men. Quite frankly, I'm glad to be free of them. And I don't begrudge Helene her chance at romance. In fact I'm relieved she isn't focusing every second on me. I quite like the breathing space, honest I do. I just don't like it when they both breathe quite so heavily right next to my ear.

And while we're at it, I hate chairs, too.

I am still working at Vitra, the furniture design company, so I guess it's to be expected. There's an interesting guy here, though, who works in the back office with me, some sort of designer. He's Scottish and he's hilarious but in an entirely accidental way. He reminds me of Frank Spencer in *Some Mothers Do 'Ave 'Em*.

He is trying to buy a house in London so that his family can join him but he keeps getting gazumped. I'd never heard of such a thing before. It sounds utterly despicable. In Australia, if you buy a house, put down a deposit and sign a contract then no one can take that house from under you. But here in England, if someone approaches the vendor with a better offer, they just give you your money back and take theirs and then the house belongs to them. Outrageous. How on earth can this be legal? And how can these people sleep at night?

Stewart, the Frank Spencer clone, had only a few days until settlement with the last house he'd found. His wife had packed up their old house and the kids were taken out of school and then someone else came along and gazumped him and his family was left homeless.

I think they're staying with her parents, which must be very distressing.

Poor Stewart looks like he's about to have a heart attack but he talks in such a thick Scottish accent that, even when he's distressed, he sounds comical. I find the whole thing deeply disturbing and insanely funny, like black humour, I suppose.

It's about the only fascinating thing going on in my life so sometimes I do find myself skipping into the office, hoping he's there with more news on the house front. I think he really appreciates my interest in his troubles. I keep telling him, he's better off back in Scotland. London ain't all it's cracked up to be. He says I'm just a restless traveller and blames it on my youth and the fact that I'm an Aussie. He thinks Australians are a little irresponsible. We don't seem to take anything seriously.

I know many would take this as an insult but I am delighted. No one has ever called me irresponsible before. In fact, I'm always accused of being too uptight and taking everything far too seriously. I suppose I have Teddy to thank for this incredible transformation (and perhaps my mustard polo shirt as well).

If you had told me a year ago that one day I would be irresponsible, I would have been horrified. It was very important to me that I behave in a mature and sober fashion. If there's one thing I've learnt from Charles Dickens, besides his love of ludicrous names, it's that life is hard. We must put our heads down, work diligently and be as kind to others as we can.

My aim in life was to keep a low profile (hence the six brown cardigans), and not make any waves, but sitting on a boat in still, calm waters can be a bit of a bore at times. Teddy has shown me how exciting and invigorating rough seas can be. All that lurching about with sea spray in the face can cause a little seasickness at times but most of the time it's just rollicking good fun.

So whose shoes would you rather be in? The sober, hardworking Stewart who keeps getting gazumped in life, or Teddy who likes drinking cocktails and staying out late and gets the occasional sea spray (and vomit) in her eyes but who is categorically, undeniably having the time of her life?

But, and I cannot stress this enough, I still hate chairs.

Dan is getting worried. I have told him all about Helene's crummy boyfriend and he finds it hard to believe I haven't got one, too. He says he's not the jealous type but will get the next plane out and punch his head in. He is afraid I will fall in love and never return. I do the only thing I can do to reassure him that my feelings for him are just as strong as his feelings for me... I write a poem.

> You said I walked out of your life, find me
> You said I'd forget your name, remind me
> They say that love is blind, blind me
> Don't you know that I want you, to find me

A long-distance romance is sheer torture. But then I suppose that's half the fun of them. Before I have time to luxuriously wallow in misery, my Liverpudlian, John, is back.

He is living miles away, working in a large hotel, and hasn't enough time between shifts to travel very far, so I agree to visit him. I see Sunny before I leave and tell her how excited I am but all that changes when I see him again. He is not the same. He looks like a slob and has barely enough energy to stay awake during my visit. He sleeps on a dirty mattress on the floor with cigarette butts squashed into the filthy carpet. I had dreams of him serenading me with his sax but that is no longer possible. He hocked it to get a mate out of jail. It doesn't matter anyway. There is no chemistry between us anymore. By three o'clock I am back with Sunny, wondering what happened. Maybe if Helene hadn't come up with that stupid rule…

– NO MEN ALLOWED OVERNIGHT –

…and he'd been able to stay with me for a few days, John might have gotten back on his feet and stayed in London and that connection we had at the very beginning wouldn't have been severed.

It's just so maddening that the NO MEN rule only applies to me. Especially since I know I would never have sex with anyone else in the room. I never did it to any of my other flatmates and I would never do it to Helene. Some things are private. Helene still doesn't know what happened to that teapot. How I wish she were that considerate.

By the way, she and Jimmy are lousy in bed. He moves up and down like a bored robot and she lies there rigid as a log. Ooh, wasn't that bitchy (but true!).

THIRTY-EIGHT

I swear off men (what is this, my sixth time already?) and make hasty plans to visit all my relatives before Easter. I am still working at Vitra so I only have the weekends free. First stop is Winchmore Hill, an outer suburb of London, to meet my father's cousin and a bunch of third cousins. I live near Paddington Station, which connects to a host of above and underground lines so it's just a hop, skip and a jump away. Actually, I have to get on the Bakerloo Line towards Elephant and Castle and switch at Oxford Circus onto the Victoria Line towards Walthamstow Central then get off at Finsbury Park and catch an above ground train to Winchmore Hill but it only takes about forty-five minutes so once you know exactly where you're supposed to be, it's no big deal. I am a whiz at catching the tube. I carry my London A-Z with me at all times because as a temp I never know where my next assignment will be.

I have a lovely relaxing time and enjoy being amongst normal people living normal lives, none of whom find it necessary to interrogate my every move (yes, I'm talking to you, Helene).

I'd forgotten what being normal was like. Here in London amongst my cosmopolitan friends it's considered dull and boring and creatively stifling to be normal. Everyone goes out of their way to be different. I very much doubt I would have even made friends had Teddy not stepped in. And now that I've opened up my mind, it's sometimes a little frustrating to have to put the brakes on for a bit and wait for the next move.

A cough caught in my throat
A heel caught in the grate
This temporary imprisonment
Just hates to wait
The window in my bedroom
Always sheds new light
Just waiting for the darkness
Is like welcoming the night
A cough caught in my throat
Makes my breathing ill at ease
But if I swallow
Will the cough become disease?

There is a restlessness stirring in Teddy's bones and she keeps prodding me in the ribs, urging me to wake up and get moving. 'Steady on, Teddy,' I murmur. 'Not long now.' I busy myself with the relatives and keep reminding myself that at the end of these visits Europe is waiting.

I spend another weekend at Winchmore Hill and the next weekend I'm at Chelmsford, Essex to visit more of Dad's cousins and second cousins. I take the Central Line all the way. It's a one-hour journey but the view is nice. My twenty-year old second cousin takes me to a nightclub. Luckily Teddy insisted I pack my tight black dress with the zip to the chin. We get home at five-thirty a.m. 'That's more like it,' says Teddy. The next day I dress in brown and join my twenty-two year old second cousin for lunch at a quiet country pub. It can't all be about Teddy, you know.

On April 10 I finish up at Vitra. Freedom at last. I am done with the place. Stewart is still being gazumped at houses, the boss is still screaming for coffee and that gorgeous guy who walked me to the station nearly every evening never once asked me out on a date so I am glad to be out of there. I pack up the flat, pack for my trip and run around London getting visas organised, which is easier than it sounds. For the French visa, Helene and I have to queue up at the French Embassy at six a.m. It's a good thing we get there so early (a recommendation from friends) as the queue eventually stretches for several blocks and halfway to Paris. When the doors open, I am the first person to get my passport stamped. After that we walk past all the people moaning in the queue and go to McDonalds for breakfast.

I spend my last free weekend in Birmingham with Uncle Bill and Aunt Ida. What a lovely way to bow out of my London life.

Dan writes that he is still waiting for me (eighty-six days, seven hours, twenty-three minutes and fifteen seconds to go, he says) but in the meantime he is taking scuba lessons, windsurfing, and jet skiing up at Point Danger. Weather in Melbourne is between twenty-six and thirty-one degrees Celsius every day.

In London we have reached nine degrees, in case you're interested.

Helene is pretty annoyed that I'm still communicating with Dan. She says my attachment to him is pathetic and shows a lack of moral fibre.

'You know, you're not fooling anyone with this lovesick act. You don't care about him one iota,' she scowls.

I tell her to mind her own business even though I know that she won't. Everything I do is her business now. She says she's protecting her financial interests, making sure I don't back out of our trip. It seems to really bother her lately, this trip. She keeps calling it a waste of money and says the thought of spending ten weeks on a bus with me is depressing her.

Depressing her? How does she think I feel?

'Maybe you should go on this trip with Dan instead of me,' she says.

'Oh lighten up, Helene,' I sigh. 'Don't you know that modern girls just want to have a bit of fun?'

Helene gives me a stare that could freeze molten lava and says, 'That's what I'm afraid of.'

I am afraid that Helene is going to take all the fun out of this trip. She gives me an Easter card that says:

Smile. We're going to have fun on our hols.

I don't know why but it has a rather ominous feel to it. And why is our holiday a plural? Are we having more than one?

I stand on the footpath outside 133 Gloucester Terrace and stare down at my old basement flat. Today I say goodbye to it and I have to admit it does break my heart a little. Sunny stands beside me. She says the occasion deserves a moment's pause. We cast our minds back to that sunny day almost a year ago when I looked at the red geraniums in the bay windowsill and said, 'I'm home.' I truly felt it. I give a little emotional gulp and wrench my eyes away.

'It's okay,' says Sunny, linking her arm in mine and gently leading me away. 'Look.' She points down to my feet. 'You're wearing your sensible walking shoes. Everything is going to work out just fine.'

Helene and I spend the Easter weekend in Crowborough with Aunt Flavia and Uncle Reg then make our way back to Paddington on Easter Sunday for our final night at The Royal Eagle Hotel. It feels different this time, like it is no longer a part of me. I have one final drink at the bar and say goodbye to Sunny. She says when I return I can sleep on her sofa. I secretly wonder if she'll even have a sofa.

William has moved to a bigger room. He is no longer in the basement but actually has a view of the sky. I guess he's (literally) moving up in the world. Perhaps he caught the travelling bug and felt the need to widen his horizons, too. We sleep on his floor, ready to meet the tour bus at six a.m. in the morning at the pick-up point on the corner.

Amazingly, for so early in the morning, we have a farewell committee to see us off. Sunny and Brian, and Alan (who sees all on the front desk) stand on the top step of our beloved Eagle Hotel, ready to wave us off in style as Helene and I trudge through the empty lobby at five-thirty a.m., heaving our backpacks and sleeping bags over our shoulders.

Suddenly Helene stops. 'I'm not coming.'

'Is this a joke?'

'No. I've been planning it for some time. I don't think we'd survive the trip together. You're not the same person you were back home.'

'And you've decided to tell me this now? Right when we're supposed to leave?'

'Someone else is taking my place.'

'What? Who?'

Are you ready for this? Helene turns around and a figure steps out from behind one of the columns with backpack in hand. I can feel the blood draining from my face. My knees turn to jelly. I open my mouth but no words come out.

I cannot believe that he is standing here, right in front of me – those clear blue eyes, that sun-kissed blonde hair, tanned face and broad shoulders...

I think I faint.

THIRTY-NINE

When I open my eyes, I am in Dan's arms and he is hugging me so tight that I can barely breathe. He's laughing and kissing me and breathing into my ear, 'It's you. It's you. I can't believe it's you!'

'How did you get here?' I squeak.

'Helene rang me. She suggested I take her spot on the trip. We decided to surprise you.'

'Surprise,' smirks Helene.

'My plane got in last night,' grins Dan. 'I wanted to see you right away but Helene said it would be a better surprise if we waited until now.'

Helene very wisely walks away at this point and is halfway to the lift when she turns back and says, 'Have a great time. I'll leave a number at Reception where you can get in touch with me. Call me when you get back. Bye.'

'We'd better get going,' says Dan. 'We don't want to miss the bus.'

'Enjoy your trip,' chirps Sunny, a little nervously, waving from the top step. Dan waves back enthusiastically and pulls me around the corner. My last glimpse of The Royal Eagle Hotel and Sunny is but a blur.

There are only fifteen of us on the tour bus, which is great, plenty of room to spread out, but Dan's having none of it. He insists we sit side by side. I'm still trying to absorb all that has happened. I suppose I am thrilled to see him again. I have been missing him dreadfully. It's just that there's a part of me that suspects I've just been missing the thought of him rather than the actual person. And, to be honest, Teddy was hoping for a little holiday romance with some fascinating men-folk, perhaps a smooth Frenchman or sultry Spaniard or even a lusty Italian.

As the coach threads its way through the London streets towards the white cliffs of Dover, Dan kisses me, over and over, but I never once kiss him back. I want to but I'm like a zombie, frozen in shock. He laughs at me. I expect he thinks I will snap out of it and fling myself joyously into his arms. But I don't feel it coming upon me at all.

There are only five men on the tour bus and Dan is by far the best looking so a lot of the other girls are already eyeing him off. I can feel Teddy getting all green-eyed and possessive again. Oh sure, no one else can have him but does that mean she still wants him?

'Are you disappointed I came?'

'I can't quite believe you're here.' I pinch him on the arm.

He laughs and puts his hand on my thigh like he's about to pinch it, but then he slowly caresses it and a look of desire ripples across his face. I feel a pull in my loins but I know that's just Teddy looking for a little fun. It still doesn't mean she wants him.

'Tell me the truth,' he says, 'are you glad I'm here?'

His face is inches from my own and I know what he wants. But is it what I want?

'Yes,' I whisper and I give him a tender kiss on his soft, willing lips. I can almost feel his heart melting at my touch.

My heart does nothing, nothing at all.

Sarah-Jane is our enthusiastic tour guide, also known as a courier. She introduces us to Trev, our driver and in no time at all we arrive at Dover and catch the ferry to Calais in France. We spend our first night in Paris and I learn my two favourite words in French – vin rouge (red wine). I'm going to need a lot of the stuff. Dan and I are sharing a tent.

We zip our sleeping bags together but no matter how physically close we get, I know that the emotional distance is still like a chasm between us.

All the same, when he removes his clothes, tipsy or not, I can still appreciate his incredible physique. His broad chest is so smooth and rock hard and his soft hands are so gentle on my skin that I must confess I feel a ripple of desire shoot through my body when he touches me.

'This is it,' whispers Teddy in my ear, 'the moment we've been waiting for.' I can feel her as she grips the back of Dan's hair and pulls him to her. Her fingertips gently explore every dimple, every bulging muscle, every dip and curve and fold.

Dan groans in ecstasy and I feel enormous relief that Teddy has taken the time over the past nine months to diligently practise the art of lovemaking. Were it not for her, I would be a useless log (like Helene) lying rigid on my back and waiting for the man to do all the work.

Teddy has not spent all that time with cads and womanisers for nothing. And now that she is finally with a man worthy of her affection, she is not going to waste a single minute, or a single piece of flesh for that matter.

I feel a shift take place from deep within, as if a final barrier is breaking free and a feeling of contentment washes over me.

'Oh Theodora,' moans Dan.

'Call me Teddy,' I coo.

FORTY

I feel different, bolder, more worldly, and not just because I'm standing at the top of the Eiffel Tower, staring down at all the ants scurrying about below. I feel like I'm fully awake. Dan wants to hold my hand and pull me away from the dangerous edge (metaphorically speaking) but I'm having none of it.

I missed you Dan, truly I did, but I want to see the world and I can't have you holding me back.

At the Galeries Lafayett, a beautiful department store in the 9th arrondissement with magnificent Art Nouveau staircases and a glass and steel dome ten storeys high, I purchase a pair of shiny, black, quilted ballet flats and stuff my sensible walking shoes into the bottom of my backpack.

I send a postcard to Sunny:

Bonjour!

Paris est fantastique! I've seen the Eiffel Tower, the Mona Lisa portrait at The Louvre, The Latin Quarter, The Notre Dame Cathedral, the Sacre Couer flea markets, Place de la Concorde, Opera National de Paris, Moulin Rouge cabaret theatre and the Arc de Triumph. We drank café noir at sidewalk cafés and had a glass or two of vin rouge. The French are tres chic and I'm having an absolute ball. Weather is nice and warm. Eating lots of paté, fromage and frenchsticks. C'est formidable!

Love and kisses, Teddy xxx

PS. Make sure you give Helene hell for what she did to me.

PPS. Dan says hi.

We spend a day at the Palace of Versailles, where Marie Antoinette ate cake (hopefully not in the Hall of Mirrors where every bite would have been amplified over a hundred times) and then tour the exquisitely landscaped gardens. We spend a night in Cognac visiting the Hennessey Cellars then drive through the lavender French countryside into duty-free Andorra. By the time we reach Spain, the cracks are beginning to show, and I'm not just talking about the crumbling buildings. Try as I might, I just can't seem to get enthused about Dan sharing this trip with me.

And then there's Jenny.

Jenny is on the tour with Randy but they are not a couple. He's her brother's best mate, or something like that, and it's not exactly clear why they're on this trip together but she's got that sweet little innocent act down pat and I can see that Dan, for one, is falling for it.

In Barcelona we attend a bullfight and Jenny starts to lay it on pretty thick.

'Oh, no, I can't bear to see a bull in pain. I don't think I can do this,' she whimpers, clinging to the nearest manly arm she can find... Dan's, of course.

'Don't worry, Jenny,' he soothes. 'I'll look after you.'

And does he what. They sit tightly together on the concrete slab and she hides her head in his protective chest eleven times, at least.

'You know, Jenny,' I say at last, 'I'm sure Randy would be happy to hold your hand if you're that affected by it all.'

'No thanks,' grimaces Randy.

It's quite possible I could have clawed my boyfriend back from Jenny's sweaty clutches were it not for that useless matador.

At that very moment he turns his tight buttocks towards the bull and does a tiny half-bow to the audience, which naturally results in the bull charging full pelt and almost piercing his opulently beaded, tight satin pants (embroidered in gold) with one very long and very pointy horn.

All hell breaks loose. The matador trips on his dress cape of satin and silk, Jenny shrieks, everybody else yells 'Ole!' and I leap to my feet and join in with the Mexican wave. By the time I look around both Jenny and Dan have disappeared. I have just enough time to catch them heading for the exit, her tear-stained face looking up appealingly into his kind, concerned eyes.

Crap!

Actually, I decide this is for the best. It will give me a chance to meet my fellow travellers (Hail, fellow travellers!) and, after all, I will be free of Dan for a while. Isn't that what I've wanted from the start?

I discover Sangria, a red wine and fruit drink, and things go rapidly downhill from there. I get just the teensiest bit drunk and stumble upon my perfect drinking pals – Marie, a tiny round New Zealander with a huge zest for life, and Randy, no longer encumbered with Jenny.

We pass out in someone's tent (I think it might be mine) and I wake up with a bunch of love-bites all over my neck. How did that happen? Needless to say, Dan is not impressed.

'You can talk,' I shout. 'You went off with Jenny way before I did anything.'

'I didn't go off with Jenny. I was just looking after her.'

'Well, perhaps you should have been looking after me.'

'How was I to know you were going to get plastered and end up with hickeys all over your neck?'

'I just wish you hadn't sprung all this on me,' I moan.

'That's it, isn't it? You don't want me here with you.'

And before I even have a chance to decide if that's true or not, Dan moves his sleeping bag out of my tent and Randy moves in. Not by choice, you understand. Jenny kicks him out of her tent in order to make room for Dan.

How's that for a kick in the teeth!

FORTY-ONE

I have fallen in love… with a building. It is La Sagrada Familia, a Gothic church designed by Antoni Gaudi and still unfinished. It is magnificent. I could have stood on the pavement and stared at it all day. Sarah-Jane says Gaudi was doing just that when he was killed in 1926. He was crossing the road, staring up at his magnificent creation, when a tram hit him. I don't blame him for being unable to tear his gaze away. I am in love with this building. It has a nativity façade that looks like melted wax with spiky, encrusted spires and inside there are columns that mirror trees and branches, and stained glass windows in the shape of flowers designed to create the same mottled effect as that of sunlight pouring through branches in a thick forest. There are gaps in the floor of the apse, providing a view down to the crypt below and the rosette windows take my breath away. When the church is finished it will have eighteen towers – eighteen!

Actually, it surprises me that I can love something so loud and ostentatious. I couldn't be further from a Gaudi creation if I tried. I am the epitome of dull and plain and near invisible but don't forget Teddy is a part of me now and she has awakened within me a lust for vitality. I consider this to be a good thing.

Jenny wears white cotton blouses and denim jeans with the crease ironed into the leg. In her handbag she carries tissues, lipstick and breath-mints. She must come from Queensland because she has a delicious golden tan. I've been living in London for nine months so I'm as pale as a ghost. When Dan wants to tease me he calls me Casper.

Just be yourself, I whisper under my breath. That's all you can do.

But I'm not that girl from Bitterly Bay anymore, am I? I'm Teddy from London and now I have a little French chic in me and a bit of Spanish vitality as well. I guess what I'm trying to say is that Dan and I need to find ourselves as a couple again because it's not going to be the same as it was in Bitterly Bay. I think we both need a little breathing space. Don't forget, I've only had a few days to get used to the idea that it is not Helene sharing this trip with me. And only now does it dawn on me that I am finally free of Helene.

I have a huge grin on my face as we travel on to the French Riviera. On our way to Cannes we stop off at a traditional parfumerie factory where we learn that most scents are a mixture of flower essences, such as jasmine, rose, lavender, orange flower and tuberose, and civet (extract of cat genitals), ambergris (intestinal goo from whales), bits of beaver, and musk from Tibetan goats.

A little off-putting, I'll give you that, but I dab a little behind the ears and Dan instantly burrows his nose into my neck.

We spend a few hours on the beach in Cannes (where even the filthy rich apparently can't afford a full bikini) and by nightfall we are in Monte Carlo and getting dressed up for a night at the Casino. Before leaving London, Helene had decided that my tight black dress with the zip to the chin was not quite appropriate for Europe so I had returned to Selfridges and purchased an electric-blue, ankle-length, jersey-knit, long-sleeved dress. Apparently electric-blue is the colour of the season (hence my winter coat). The jersey material is perfect for travelling. I simply roll it up and stuff it in the bottom of my backpack and when I'm ready to wear it, I shake it out and put it on. There is not a wrinkle on it. Whilst the other girls queue for the one iron in the campsite and jostle one another as they attempt to apply their make-up in front of the tiny mirror in the toilet block, I pop on my blue dress and shiny, black, quilted ballet flats and join the boys at the bus.

Dan is impressed.

I expect the moment won't last, however, once Jenny (primped and preened and lathered in pink frosted lippy) makes her appearance but I am in for a pleasant surprise. It seems you must be over twenty-one to enter the Casino. Randy and Jenny are only twenty but boys can easily pass for older so Randy has no trouble at all getting in. To help matters along, I slip my arm into his to show the bouncer that he is old enough to be with a sophisticated woman of the world. Perhaps it is my French footwear or the subtle scent of extract of cat genitals but we quickly gain entry without a wrinkle (much like my blue jersey dress).

Jenny, however, is stopped at the door and firmly turned away. It would seem that sweet baby face doesn't work in Monte Carlo. Dan comes across all gallant and chivalrous (damn his sense of decency) and insists we stay outside, too, but I make it very clear that I have no obligation to Jenny and quickly hurry inside. To be honest, I have no desire to see Dan choose her over me although I know, without a shadow of a doubt, that he will.

I don't gamble (too smart, I guess) so someone else gives me some money to play the pokies. I pull the handle and it flashes WIN but no money pops out. I think I must be mistaken so I walk away. After we leave the casino, Marie explains the rules to me. When it says WIN, you have to press either Play Again or Collect Money to get your prize. I wonder how much money I won? (And lost!)

In Monaco we follow the winding roads made famous by Grace Kelly and Cary Grant in *To Catch A Thief* and stop at the spot where Grace Kelly died. There's a brass monument in her memory embedded in the rock. I stand on the narrow shoulder, staring out at the sheer, terrifying drop, and shed a tear for the sheer perfection of Grace Kelly.

Next stop Italy, beginning with the Statue of David in Florence, the Plaza del Signora, Duomo Cathedral, leatherworks, markets and beach (phew!). At The Leaning Tower of Pisa, I take the obligatory tourist snap where it appears that I am holding up the tower and in Rome I send a postcard to Sunny:

Ciao!

Sunday was Spain – Barcelona bullfights, Picasso, Miró, Gaudi, La Rambla Boulevard, and way too much Sangria. Tuesday was Cannes and the French Riviera then Monaco and a Monte Carlo casino. Wednesday was Florence and a peek at the Statue of David, and then the Leaning Tower of Pisa and now Thursday is Rome – the Trevi Fountain, The Coliseum, St Mark's Cathedral, the Catacombs, Michelangelo's Sistine Chapel and The Vatican.

Next on the agenda is a cruise around the Greek Islands. To tell you the truth, I could use the rest.

Love and kisses to all, Teddy xx.

P.S. Streets are so crowded that I'm not at all sure where Dan is but someone far off in the distance is waving frantically so I'm guessing Dan says hi.

Vatican City is recognised as a separate country but it only consists of a church and plaza about the size of a postage stamp. Speaking of which, The Vatican has its own Post Office. I buy some stamps but I can't find the Pope anywhere. Now where is he hiding?

We're meant to rendezvous at a certain spot at a certain time in order to jump on our bus before the traffic police move it along but at the appointed time and place, I am the only one there.

Sarah-Jane has a mini stroke and makes Trev drive around the block, which is an enormous square full of about a thousand cars all trying to turn left. At least we're in the perfect place to have her prayers quickly answered and so it is that the others are waiting at the pick-up point upon our return. From my vantage point in the bus, I can see down on everyone and can't help but notice that Dan and Jenny are holding hands.

I feel a twist in my belly, I'm not going to deny it. It's like someone thrusting a knife in there.

But there's no time to dwell, not whilst Pompeii awaits. What a fascinating place, chock full of phallic symbols. I don't know why, but I keep thinking about Dan as I walk around the ruins. And I notice that he and Jenny are still holding hands, only now she seems to be dragging him along.

As we drive into Naples, Dan rejoins me at the back of the tour bus (where all the fun happens). There's lots of laughter and singing (and even dancing in the aisle) and Randy is teaching me card tricks.

Jenny, the wet blanket, sits straight-backed at the front of the bus, staring quietly out the window.

A year ago that would have been me. In my brown cardigan and sensible walking shoes. That was the girl that Dan fell in love with back in Bitterly Bay. Perhaps that's his type. Perhaps Jenny is better suited to him and if I have any chance of keeping him then I'll have to rein in my Teddy tendencies.

The trouble is, I love the person that I've become. She's fun. And I shouldn't have to change who I am for anyone. And besides, Dan is down the back of the bus having fun with Teddy so there must be some part of her that he likes. At least I hope there is.

Then again, I'm not even sure I want to be tethered to his side.

The weather is perfect as we tour Naples and Sorrento and take a ferry to the Isle of Capri for a spot of sunbathing. I buy a pair of pale blue terry cotton shorts to give my pasty legs every chance to tan. But it is on the night ferry from Brindisi to Corfu where we hit a snag. For starters, there are way too many people squeezed into my cabin. And secondly, someone has produced a bottle of vodka. Yes, yes, I know, the last time I drank Vodka I puked in my underwear so, yes, I am well aware of the danger but surely the rules don't apply when you're in international waters?

After several vodka shots, Dan and I pass out in a bunk together. When I groggily open my eyes, he whispers 'I love you' in my ear.

What do you think about that?

My response, of course, is to issue forth with the most perfectly elegant belch. Everyone shouts 'Salootay!' and someone pours more vodka into my glass so I don't remember anything after that.

I think, though, that I murmur 'delicious' but, before I can get the glass to my lips, Dan covers my mouth with his. I'm pretty sure that's what happens. Pretty sure.

Anyway, when I wake up in the morning, we are lying in the bunk bed together and my glass is still half full. Or half empty. However you want to view it.

FORTY-TWO

We reach our campsite in Corfu and are forced to undergo a complicated Ouzo drinking test before breakfast. I consider a spot of paragliding but fear my heart (or, more precisely, my head) might not be in it.

I really ought to work out what my feelings are for Dan but I must confess I'm having far too much fun to give it any proper thought.

Had I not spent the past nine months in London getting my heart trampled on, I might have jumped head first into coupledom but I know I'm not the same girl that Dan fell in love with back home and let's just say I'm not prepared to let go of Teddy just yet, if ever. I like the strong, fearless woman I've become and if Dan is attracted to weak, fragile, simpering ninnies like Jenny, then perhaps we're not as compatible as he thinks. If, however, Dan does like the 'cut of my jib' then there's plenty of time on this trip to let our relationship blossom naturally. For now, though, I'm more interested in lying on the beach and working on my tan. I've got a long way to go before I reach 'golden delicious'.

The trouble is, Marie and Randy are not the type to sit still for long and before I know it, Randy and I are burying Marie under an enormous mound of sand. Her head and shoulders and arms are free and she's lying on her stomach so she good-naturedly props herself up on her elbows, chin on her hands, and lets us get on with the job of conquering her. Randy pokes a stick in the top of the mound and I sit astride it as he takes a photo. I wave out to sea and Dan, who is fighting waves the size of mountains, breaks a crest long enough to wave back before swimming off to explore a cave in the bay.

I finally roll off Marie and let Randy get on with the task of freeing her whilst I lie back on the sand and attempt a little nap. Jenny plonks down on the sand beside me, hugging her knees to her chest. 'How serious are you about Dan?' she asks.

'I'm not serious about anything,' I reply, refusing to open my eyes and look at her.

'Well, what's your relationship status?' (No beating around the bush with this girl.)

'He's my boyfriend,' I reply.

'Oh.'

She leaves pretty quickly after that.

'Is he really your boyfriend?' asks Marie. I can understand her confusion. I've been hanging out with her and Randy a lot more than with him.

'How should I know?' I smile. 'I was just messing with her head'.

'Women,' laughs Randy and he begins piling sand on my legs.

In order to keep on schedule we do a night drive into Athens and have just enough time to watch the changing of the guards in Syntagma Square. They have colourful costumes (is that a skirt?) and pom-poms on their shoes that wiggle playfully when they jump from one foot to another. Very cute but not sure it makes them very effective guards. We then board a large yacht, called the Esperos I, for a weeklong cruise around the Greek Islands.

We are all bunking together below deck so there's no confusion over whether Dan will be sharing my tent or Jenny's. I think she gave Dan some bogus excuse about why Randy couldn't share her tent so he felt somewhat compelled to bunk with her. He wasn't pleased that Randy was sharing my tent but what did he expect? Even though I suspect Randy was the one to give me all those hickeys, Dan needn't worry. We're too busy having fun with Marie (we're a team, you see) to muddy the waters with romance. Anyway, the situation is now rendered moot. We are all squished together in the sleeping quarters of the boat.

We spend the day sunbathing on deck then dock at Poros for some serious partying at a bar called The Ship. I get thoroughly 'ship-wrecked' and have difficulty climbing aboard the yacht but Dan to the rescue again. He scoops me up into his arms and effortlessly carries me on board. Then everyone plays a rousing game of Chinese Whispers only I forget why I'm putting my mouth to Dan's ear and end up seductively sliding in my tongue instead. He gives me the queerest look and his hand doesn't leave my thigh for the rest of the night.

Kiwis Honey and Harry, the only married couple, are the first to go to bed. When they disappear below deck, I rather loudly tell everyone about the secret poem I've written for Honey's birthday. I then recite the whole blasted thing so it's possible she hears every word. In which case, I hope she likes it.

I know of a woman, both kind and bold
Though now twenty-six, she doesn't seem old
A nurse by nature, she's caring and bright
But I still love to watch her go dancing at night
Like that fancy dress evening, she really looked
happy
Dancing about done up in a nappy
Her interests are varied, her faults are so few
I really like Honey – well, wouldn't you?

Not my best, I will admit, but I am a little under the influence.

A few of us decide to put our sleeping bags on the top deck of the yacht, under a blanket of stars. The water gently laps the side of the boat as it softly sways to the lull of the waves. A warm, relaxing breeze blows in our faces and our toes hook under the railing to stop us from sliding off the deck and into the ocean. It is heavenly.

Dan puts his sleeping bag next to mine. My stomach churns in anticipation but it could be seasickness, or too much alcohol. We don't seem to stop drinking so it's a little hard to tell. It's Dan's birthday, too, so I know he's expecting considerably more than just a poem from me.

He snuggles in close to me and I surreptitiously kick the sleeping bag next to me.

'Oh,' yawns Marie, 'no funny business you two.' She's supposed to be stopping me from doing something I might regret whilst under the influence but clearly she's not too concerned about this.

I kiss Dan on his sun-kissed shoulders then quickly fall asleep, snoring into his neck. I have a plan. As long as I keep him active (sailing, swimming, snorkelling, and dancing) then he won't have time to analyse our relationship. Disturbingly, though, Jenny, the vulture, is still circling around him, waiting for her moment to strike.

In the morning I send a postcard to Sunny:

Yassoo!

From the minute my feet hit Greek soil I have been drinking Ouzo. The minute I stepped onto the yacht, it was Pimms, naturally. One must always drink Pimms on a yacht. I don't even know what Pimms is but I like it. Most refreshing. Anyway, apart from drinking, I have also been enjoying the beautiful Greek sun. Visited Pompeii, Corfu and Athens and now sailing the Greek Islands.

Poros is very small and full of white buildings. Took just an hour to walk around the entire island.

Hydra is where the rich go to play. More white buildings. We swam ashore from our yacht and lay on the sandy white beach amongst the rich tourists then paddled back to our yacht for afternoon Pimms. What a life, hey?

Dassi has nothing on it at all except, surprisingly, a donkey. Honey and I paddled ashore on her lilo and thank goodness there was no one to watch us struggling out of the water. We upended the lilo, got our clothes (tied up in a plastic bag) all wet and I nearly drowned in twenty centimetres of water.

Spend most of the time snorkelling and sunbathing. My tan is coming along nicely and thanks to an all seafood diet (yuck!), I am eating salad every day and have finally managed to get rid of those last Wimpy burgers off my hips.

Randy (the pest) has just written on my arm so I must leave you now in order to throw him overboard.

My love and kisses to all, Teddy xx.

P.S. Dan says hi.

After a week on the yacht, we return to Athens and visit The Acropolis then split into three groups for the hotel rooms. I'm in a room with Honey and Harry, Randy, and Marie. Somehow Dan is in a room with Jenny. How on earth does this keep happening?

I lean over the balcony and shout down to Dan. 'Are you hooking up with Jenny?'

He looks up from the room below. 'Of course not.'

'Well, it sure looks that way. Why isn't Randy in there with her and you in here with me?'

'Jenny says she feels uncomfortable with Randy.'

'That's bullshit. Randy is amazing fun.'

'What's that supposed to mean?'

'It means he's fun, Dan.'

'Are *you* having fun with him?'

'Don't be a dill. I'm having fun with everyone except, apparently, you!'

I slam the balcony door and lie down in the shaded room. Everyone is dozy. It's hot. I'm wearing the cutest little sundress I bought in Poros along with a pair of beaded sandals. It's not like me to wear frivolous footwear but when in Rome... or in this case, Athens... I really thought I was lightening up on this trip and that Jenny's fascination with Dan wouldn't bother me but now I am beginning to get really pissed off.

Randy lifts his head up from the pillow. 'She's a schemer, you know. By the end of the trip, he'll be going home with her.'

'She's picked the wrong woman to steal from,' I growl.

'I thought you didn't want to be burdened with a boyfriend on this trip?' says Honey.

'No, I didn't want my boyfriend to burden me, there's a difference.'

'Huh!' says Marie, once again saying the most intelligent thing in the room without actually saying anything at all.

Marie, alone, is worth the price of admission.

FORTY-THREE

She's right, though. What game am I playing? Dan doesn't know if he's coming or going. I lead him on. I push him away. I think the hot sun is frying my brain.

We travel to Meteora where ancient monasteries perch high on inaccessible mountaintops. A part of me wants to hide away in one of those monasteries forever but we haven't time for quiet contemplation. We're on another night drive, this time to Camp Kavalla. I like the night drives because it means we don't have to worry about who's sleeping in what tent.

Sometimes, though, when I'm nursing a hangover and lying across both seats, Dan will sit up front with Jenny. Sometimes I'm a little preoccupied with Marie and Honey and Harry and Randy and the fun crowd at the back of the bus and at least with Jenny no one else is vying for her attention. She listens to every word he says and is always praising him and stroking his ego.

As long as that's all she's stroking.

We meet another coach tour at Camp Kavalla, which is nothing new – there are plenty of other tour groups coming in and out of the campsites – but this one is running concurrent to ours and everyone is getting along beautifully so we decide to meet up at the various campsites along the way. The other group is with Top Deck, they drive around Europe in a double-decker bus and even sleep on it, although the sleeping quarters are very cramped and there's absolutely no privacy. We arrange to meet up in Gallipoli (where we plan to have a halfway party to celebrate the halfway mark of our trip) and head off to the Turkish border.

But there is a problem.

One of the girls on our bus, Mia, is South African and therefore not permitted a visa into Turkey. Sarah-Jane and Trev think we should smuggle her across the border and everyone seems to be in agreement but I am terrified. What will happen if we're caught? Sarah-Jane thinks that she and Trev might be arrested and thrown into a Turkish jail but the rest of us should be fine.

'But no one else can drive the bus,' says I, completely missing the point that Sarah-Jane and Trev will be rotting in a Turkish hell for the rest of their lives until their teeth fall out and cockroaches eat them from the inside out.

I am really not good at subterfuge. I can't even cheat at cards. I cannot lie. I cannot deceive. I cannot even pretend. Those eagle-eyed Turkish guards (all carrying rifles) will spot my fear from twenty paces. I am sweating in my armpits just thinking about it.

But a plan is devised, nonetheless. Half of us are to go to the passport office and the other half (including Mia) go to the toilets. Then we swap but Mia stays with the toilet crowd. Then we all climb aboard the bus and wait to be waved across the border. And the plan is working beautifully. We all get our passports stamped (except Mia) and we all take a leak in the loo (and Mia takes two) but once aboard the bus, we strike a problem. One of the guards has boarded our bus and is doing a head count. He's got a clipboard with all our names and passport numbers on it. There are sixteen names (including Sarah-Jane and Trev) on that list but there are seventeen heads on the bus. A few people sitting near Mia hiss at her to duck her head down but she is too terrified to move.

It actually occurs to me that Mia might be thinking that if she ducks her head and is caught then the guard will know that she's the guilty party but if she looks completely innocent, he might drag another poor soul off the bus. I don't like to imply that she is that dumb but I do think she would literally throw someone else under the bus in order to save her own skin.

Mia has beautiful caramel skin and dark curly hair and the biggest, roundest eyes you've ever seen and they are now so big and round that I'm sure the guard can easily see the absolute terror radiating from them. He walks slowly down the aisle and I think only the fact that Mia has been to the toilet twice saves her from peeing her pants. When he talks to her ('passport, please') she bursts into tears and is gently led off the bus.

Sarah-Jane and Trev grab her bags and follow her into the office and we spend a tense twenty minutes waiting for them. I know I ought to be worried for Mia but to tell you the truth, I'm a little cross. If she has put my safety in jeopardy, I am going to kill her.

Finally all three emerge from the building and line up against the wall. For one heart-stopping moment I think a firing squad is going to shoot them but instead they're ushered over to a truck driver who is crossing the border from Turkey into Greece. After a few minutes Mia climbs aboard with her bags and they drive off. Sarah-Jane and Trev return to our bus and explain that all three have been let off with a warning and Mia now has to make her way back to the campsite where one of the organisers will put her on a train to Austria. The plan is that we meet up with her there in two weeks' time.

I imagine it's going to be a terrifying experience for poor Mia but, strangely enough, Dan does not feel compelled to chivalrously offer to accompany her on this sad and lonely journey.

We're all a little shell-shocked when we reach Gallipoli and then, of course, we tour Anzac Cove where our brave Aussie and Kiwi soldiers were massacred, so that doesn't lighten the mood any. As we stand on the clifftop, I stare down at the sheer drop and wonder how on earth anyone could have scaled that, with all their gear strapped on and the Turks firing on them from all angles. A few of the gang climb down and I don't know how but they eventually climb up again. The whole thing makes me sick. After that we walk to the spot where rows and rows and rows and rows and rows and rows of white crosses stand. Rows and rows and rows. A little Turkish boy with a wooden gun shoots at all the crosses.

We then rest back at our campsite and meet a grizzled old Turk who was once an Olympian volleyball player. He cheerfully challenges all the men from Autotours and Top Deck to a game; all of them on one side, just him on the other.

Our boys think it's going to be easy but he thrashes the pants off them. He never even raises a sweat. One by one our boys remove their sweat-soaked tops so in no time at all there is an audience of eager women watching the game.

Dan, of course, easily has the best body and is the best athlete but, unfortunately, this means he's getting an awful lot of female attention, which is pissing me off somewhat.

And then Hopper removes his top and his gleaming muscles momentarily distract me. Real name James Hare, he's called Hopper in reference to his surname and also because he likes to hop from one girl's bed to another, or so the rumour goes.

Hopper is almost as hot as Dan. He's a little shorter, hair a little thinner, but then I doubt there'd be a better specimen than Dan on the whole of the planet. Hopper, though, is garnering almost as much attention and that gives me a thought.

This is how you fight fire – with fire. I can try to outmanoeuvre Jenny all throughout the trip but that's just making me do all the work. I'm way more fun than she is and clearly I've already captured Dan's heart but Jenny is clever. She isn't trying to steal Dan from me, you understand. She wouldn't dream of trying to split us up. Oh, no, no! She merely needs a *friend*, someone to protect her and help her.

She is very cleverly keeping her true motives hidden from everyone, even Dan. If I were to challenge her, I would probably lose because I would look like a bully, picking on a poor innocent waif. She's clever, I'll give her that. But I'm smarter and I fight harder. And I've just come up with a brilliant plan.

Hopper will be my man.

I think it's time Dan got a visit from the green-eyed monster. Make him think about only me for a change and push that pesky princess right out of the picture.

FORTY-FOUR

Me and my stupid plans!

I don't know what it is, but every time another girl looks at Dan I go a little nuts. I think it must be insecurity. I mean, he's just so handsome and wonderful that he could have any girl he wanted. Why on earth would he want plain and boring me? I can't stand to watch the volleyball game anymore (or, more likely, I can't stand to watch the girls drooling over Dan) so I take a shower. I want to feel clean and fresh and be ready for our halfway party. I am still convinced that making Dan jealous by flirting with Hopper is my only recourse. How I'm going to catch Hopper's eye is another thing entirely.

I am in for a shock, though, as I ready myself in the shower block. There's a large floor to ceiling mirror and I haven't seen one of those since we began this trip so it's the first time in a long time that I've taken a good look at myself.

The first thing I notice is that the saltwater has made my hair thick and lustrous and soft. And I'm tanned, too. What I call a golden delicious colour. A honey brown that puts a slight smattering of freckles across your nose. I slip into my tight blue jeans and they fit perfectly. It seems I've slimmed down quite a bit and the jeans are hugging my curves in all the right places. I put on a white top and it makes my tan pop. I add my beaded sandals. I don't want to sound like I'm full of myself but I feel a lot more confident as I make my way to the dining hall. I am beginning to think I might just be able to snag me a Hopper.

The other girls have all made enormous efforts. They have their hair teased out to gravity-defying lengths and they are smothered in make-up and perfume. Most of them are wearing skimpy skirts and revealing tops and the whole thing smacks of desperation. It's not a good look. Why on earth would they think it was? I suppose boys have told them they like short skirts and booby tops and bright red lips but what do boys know? They have immature and underdeveloped minds and most of the time they're not even using their brains.

It would appear that my understated, natural look is making me stand out amongst the overdone baboons. I smile at Hopper and he is at my side in seconds.

Now, this next part of my plan requires some sort of skill in the art of seduction and, as you well know, I have no skills in that area. I decide to get drunk. Things always seem to happen organically when you take rational thought out of the equation. The minute I skull a bottle of red wine I know that I am well and truly committed to my ludicrous plan, whatever may happen. Dan, concerned by my paralytic behaviour, locks me in our cabin. Not a good start, I'll grant you, so...

I vomit. Who didn't see that coming? I'm sharing a cabin with Dan and Randy and Jenny (I figure it's the only way I can keep an eye on her) and I accidentally (on purpose) retch all over Jenny's sleeping bag until Marie unlocks the door and lets me out. I think Jenny hoses down her sleeping bag but I'm in no condition to know for sure. Somehow I manage to host a drunken party in our spewy cabin and somehow Hopper turns up.

'I need to spew, Hopper,' I moan, clearly the sexiest words ever spoken.

'Use my finger,' he laughs.

So I wrap my mouth around his finger and slowly bob my head up and down. He is hooked. Yes, with a guy it's that easy. By the time Dan arrives, Hopper is on my bed, rubbing my chest in a slow, circular motion to help settle my tum.

But Dan doesn't do what I expect him to. He doesn't knock Hopper's block off. He does something most unexpected. He kisses Jenny!

Right, I think, two can play at that game.

And that's when things get totally out of control. Dan invites Jenny into his sleeping bag (because hers is covered in my puke) and I invite Hopper into mine (because I'm a bloody idiot!). Don't forget, I'm practically paralytic and sensible decisions are never made when one is under the influence.

I can feel Hopper's enormous erection rubbing up against my thigh and I hate to be the one to put the brakes on so I'm hoping Dan will crack and put an end to all this nonsense but, once again, I underestimate everything. In hindsight, I think there was already a little passion brewing between those two and I merely put a flame to their smouldering desires. Once in the same sleeping bag, Dan wastes no time exploring Jenny's possibilities.

Oh God, I am so stupid!

In my ridiculously drunken state, I think *stuff him! Who needs him?*

And then I do the absolute worst thing I can do. I begin to moan in ecstasy and Hopper quickly gets me naked. I don't know how that happens. Maybe I pass out for a second. One moment I'm moaning, the next moment I'm naked. And then I turn my head to look at Dan and he's kissing Jenny passionately and also appears to be naked. Crap!

Hopper tries to open my legs but I manage to keep him at bay, still moaning, as I direct his mouth to my left breast, which has the added benefit of getting his boofhead out of my line of sight. I arch my back and release a delighted gasp. *That ought to show 'em*, I think.

Yes, I know, I am an idiot!

Dan is moving, rising up out of the sleeping bag, and I'm sure this is it – he's on his way over to put a stop to it all – but I am wrong. He is merely raising himself up on his arms and straddling Jenny so that he can penetrate her in one smooth, powerful movement.

With a vigorous thrust, he enters Jenny and my heart breaks into a million pieces.

Hopper easily breaks down my own defences and enters me with the same powerful force, the two men grunting and groaning almost in unison.

I just lie there, feeling my mind leave my body, listening to Jenny's tiny excited squeaks as the man I love reaches his thunderous climax on the other side of the room.

What am I to do?

FORTY-FIVE

Honey thinks I'm an idiot but I'm blaming the grog. It seems there's no going back now. Jenny and Dan are now semi-officially an item and she is permanently glued to his hip. Nothing can save me from despair.

Hopper is keen to hook up with me again but luckily he's not on our coach so I don't have to see him all the time. It's bad enough I have to look at Dan every day. We haven't spoken a word to one another. What is there left to say? We have passed the point of no return. There is no longer any trust or loyalty left between us. I have never felt so wretched. I am hoping he falls overboard on the ferry trip from Gallipoli to Troy, but no such luck.

I know it's my fault, too, but what on earth was he thinking? I suppose I have to face the fact that he'd rather be with Jenny than with me. I've been giving him the cold shoulder throughout this trip so can I really blame him?

As Romeo once said, tempt not a desperate man.

We visit the City of Troy with the obligatory wooden Trojan horse and then move on to Pamukkale, which has natural pools of hot water springs believed to contain certain healing properties. Unfortunately they cannot heal a broken heart.

You know, I've never been entirely sure that I loved Dan. After all, we'd only known each other such a short time before I went to London. It's hard to have a long-distance romance but sometimes it's even harder when you reunite. You sort of get into the habit of being apart. Being together takes a lot more work.

I try not to think about him the whole time we're in Gorome, which is harder than it sounds. Have you seen their complex caves and tunnels where whole villages lived underground? They have these fairy mound chimney type things poking out of the ground that look exactly like penises. They are everywhere. Every time I turn around it feels like a penis is poking me in the eye.

After visiting The House of the Virgin Mary on Mount Koressos, an onyx factory, a pottery shop, lots of rugs and a Turkish bath, we do a night drive into Istanbul. I enjoy hanging out with Honey and Harry and Marie and Randy and I imagine this is how it would have been if Helene had come on this trip with me instead of Dan. No doubt, she would have left me for Jenny, too, but it surely wouldn't hurt so much.

In Istanbul we meet up with the Top Deck gang for breakfast at The Pudding Shop, made famous from the movie *Midnight Express*.

I'm hoping that Hopper has moved on to another girl but no such luck. He seems to only have eyes for me. How can this be happening?

We tour the Blue Mosque, another impressive building with good use of mosaic tiles, more windows, more nave vaulting. I hate to say it, but you do get a little jaded seeing one magnificent edifice after another. We have abbreviated them to P.F.A.s – pretty (insert swear word here) awesome (or 'awful' if you're sick of the sight of them).

Hopper appears to be one of those men who feel the need to be the life and soul of the party at all times. Personally, I don't think a hallowed National treasure is quite the place for feeble jokes and forced jolliness. It occurs to me, though, that he might be trying to buoy my flagging spirits, which, whilst admirable, is still a tad annoying.

I manage to ditch him in the Grand Covered Bazaar. With sixty-five streets and over three thousand shops, it isn't hard to do. Whilst he haggles over the price of a fake Lacoste polo shirt, I go in search of Turkish Delight.

We then do a short ferry cruise across the Golden Horn in the Bosphorus Strait, which forms part of the boundary between Europe and Asia. Then it's back to the campsite for a rousing game of Sexual Trivial Pursuit. Honey, being a nurse, is winning. Hopper has bought a leather jacket and 'worry beads', which Turkish men constantly twirl around their fingers. It's supposed to be relaxing but it drives us all crazy.

Randy, my tent-mate, has found himself a lovely young thing (from another tour group) to hook up with, which means tonight I have our tent all to myself. Unfortunately, Hopper thinks this is divine providence. I don't want the others thinking I'm just using him to get Dan jealous, which is the truth, of course, but I certainly don't want Dan finding that out so I'm afraid I'm stuck with Hopper.

In a way I'm glad of the company. Now all I have to do is convince Hopper that our newfound friendship is purely platonic. It's a bit like trying to close the gate after the horse has bolted.

I decide to play it safe and offer to swap sleeping arrangements with a couple on board Top Deck. They jump at the chance for a bit of privacy. It also means I don't have to worry about Hopper and as an added bonus I get to see what it's like to sleep on a double-decker bus. I just need to remember to get on the right bus in the morning.

In the television room at the campsite, they're watching *Mad Max* in German with Turkish subtitles, which is as entertaining as it sounds, but I sneak off to the Top Deck bus for a bit of quiet time and write postcards to friends and family back home. I get to chatting with a few of the girls and a far different picture of Hopper is emerging. He likes women, that's true, but not in a conquest, wham-bam-thank-you-Ma'am way. He genuinely likes them. He enjoys being in their company. Now not only do I have to think about how to extricate myself from him but, more importantly, do I want to?

And let's not forget Dan. Where do things stand with him?

We leave Istanbul and travel back through Greece towards Yugoslavia and celebrate with another party – a 'shit-face' party, which involves lots of alcohol (what a surprise) and wrapping the bus in toilet paper. Dan, who can party with the best of them, is once again sitting with us at the back of the bus. Jenny remains at the front, sitting ramrod straight and never cracking a smile.

It seems whenever I drink I let all my inhibitions go including my distance with Dan. Let's face it, I really enjoy his company, that's why we hooked up in the first place. Now we have become 'best buds' of a sort. I am delighted to discover that this annoys Jenny just as much as our former relationship did.

We arrive in Dubrovnik at one a.m. Everyone is shattered but I'm used to much later nights than this back in London so it doesn't bother me all that much. I have a nice juicy steak for 'dinner' and watch Dan pitch Jenny's tent. I guess he belongs to her now. The Top Deck gang are already at the campsite and it doesn't take long for Hopper to stroll over. I feel obligated to hang out with him. We've got the whole day tomorrow to explore Dubrovnik, which is apparently a very lovely terracotta town, and walk along a wall, which sounds easy enough but it was built in the fourteenth and fifteenth centuries, encapsulates most of the city and runs uninterrupted for over six thousand feet so I think it's gonna take a while. Luckily I still have my sensible walking shoes. Hopper seems keen to join us, so that's that then. I wouldn't say we're an item but we've definitely become friends.

I'm back to sharing a tent with Randy so I'm safe for another night, particularly since I bought a pair of silk pyjamas at the Bazaar in Istanbul that are so voluminous that not only can no one else fit in my sleeping bag but it would take a month of Sundays to wade through all that fabric to find flesh.

FORTY-SIX

W e travel through Zadar (of which I remember nothing thanks to a little too much alcohol) and on to Venice, where I am totally captivated. It has such a romantic, old-world vibe. If you were to look at it logically, you'd probably just see all that mould and it does smell a bit and all that slapping water is a little disconcerting, but the old buildings are covered in a beautiful worn patina, the Venetian glass is rich and opulent, the lace is delicate and intricate and the masks are fantastical and magical and here I am on a dreamy, romantic gondola ride under soft moonlight with... Hopper.

This is not right and I have to do something about it. Hopper and I take a moonlit stroll across the bridges and I decide to clear the air.

'Hopper, I've been thinking about us.'

'Me, too. You know, you're not like any other girl I've ever met. It's easy to talk to you. And you're interesting and fun. I think we're going to be mates forever.'

'Mates?' I let a little bit of relief creep through.

'Sure. You okay with that?'

'Absolutely.' (Phew!)

'It's been fun, Teddy, but even I can see that it's Dan you love. I don't know why the idiot can't see that.'

'I blame that bitch, Jenny.'

'Oh, I dunno, he wouldn't have given her a second glance if you'd let him know how you really feel,' says the incredibly perceptive Hopper.

'Yeah, well, I can't even admit that to myself.'

And I can't, can I? And I think that's because I can't get past the feeling that Dan could do so much better than me. 'Why would he want me anyway,' I sigh.

'You're kidding, right? Why wouldn't he want you?'

'I'm plain and boring and dull as dishwater.'

'Says who?'

'Says me.'

'Well, you're wrong. There's nothing dishwatery about you.'

Have I been wrong all this time about who I really am or has Teddy taken over completely and now I am a different girl?

We enter Vienna in a thunderstorm, which is a little unnerving, and stop at the campsite to make sure Mia has made it safely to camp. She has. She's been hanging out with the camp cook and says it was very lonely taking the train to Vienna. She's glad to be reunited with us but it doesn't last long. We take a river cruise on the Danube, listen to music by Johann Strauss, have a little dinner and a waltz, and admire the girls in their dirndl dresses (full gathered skirts with lots of white cotton petticoats underneath). Then it's off to a funfair where Marie flashes her own knickers to everyone on one of the rides. In the morning we head to Hungary, another communist country that Mia's not allowed to enter. So it's 'Hi Mia, bye Mia' and on to Budapest.

In Hungary everything is 'most wonderful' or 'most impressive' and always 'most important'. We kick our 'most annoying' Hungarian tour guide off the 'most fed-up' bus and head to camp.

There is the most puzzling of buildings at this camp. The women's shower block has no door, just an enormous entrance. It gives a very clear view of the shower stalls within which also, puzzlingly, have no doors on them. So anyone walking past the shower block can get a perfect view of naked women showering. I have no doubt this would explain the popularity of this campsite and the reason why an inordinate number of men find themselves treading the well-worn path outside the women's showers.

Everyone's looking to blow off a little steam so when I steadfastly refuse to take a shower in the women's block, they throw me into the men's, which, funnily enough, has a massive door that the others barricade from the outside. There are three men showering and one by one they turn around to face me.

'Hi there. Nice to meet you. Nice weather we're having. Lovely buttocks, by the way.'

In the morning we make our way back to Austria, picking up Mia along the way, and then do a very serious tour of the Materhausen Concentration Camp.

'You are here,' says the tour guide, 'so that you may never forget what happened and maybe then your generation will not let it happen again.'

We see images that will stay with me for life and I have a better understanding now of how massive the devastation was and mindful of how easily it could all happen again.

I stand in the gas chamber, where the victims were told to strip naked before 'showering'. Filthy, starved, and humiliated, they were herded in like cattle and must have thought that for one brief moment the Nazis were going to show some compassion. The first lot went willingly into the chamber, staring gratefully up at the jets.

I stare into the ovens with unmitigated horror. Human beings, mere skeletons by now, were slid into burning furnaces. Were they still alive? Did they scream or were they unable to summon any sound at all?

And I see horrific photographs. One is of a man with his torso removed. His chest has been reattached to his hips. Can you even imagine such brutality and all in the name of science? Those surgeons must have thought it was brilliant being able to experiment on live humans but, oh boy, the look in his eyes. So haunting. He is staring straight at me, letting me know that this is pure evil at work.

Suddenly an image of Joseph's monkeys in the science lab flashes into my mind.

That's the only way we truly learn, isn't it? By relating things to our own experiences. Making it personal. Sometimes I wonder if Bebe made up most of the things she told me. Did she have a married lover waiting for her back home or could she anticipate that my morals would slip dangerously low in London and was she trying to warn me? I once asked her what she did back home and she told me she helped people die. I (half) jokingly accused her of being a mass murderer but she said they were already dead. She just helped them understand that.

I pictured her in a hospital at a terminal patient's deathbed with the patient asking, 'When can I go home?' and Theodora saying, 'Won't be long now.'

Were there people like Bebe during the war that helped all those poor, innocent people pass over? There must have been an awful lot of them.

I wonder, too, if Joseph really killed monkeys or if he just said that to get me thinking. Bebe always seemed to be a step or two ahead of the rest of us. Had she anticipated this far ahead?

All I know is that I leave the Concentration Camp a lot wiser than when I entered.

We head to our campsite in Salzburg where the drink of the day is Schnapps and, naturally, a drinking contest is soon underway. Each of the little shot glasses has a number underneath. All participants skull their drink and then we look underneath and the person with the highest number pays for the round. I have budgeted for one round so I'm in until my number comes up… but it never does. I never get the highest number. And so I go on drinking Schnapps until I'm called away for bus cleaning duty.

With Dan.

'Guess you'll miss Hopper when we get to Tyrol,' he says. (Autotours and Top Deck will be parting company. We're going to a private chalet in the Austrian countryside for a few days of R&R.)

'Sure. I'll miss all the Top Deck gang. They're lots of fun.'

'But you'll miss Hopper more?'

'No.'

'Why not?'

'Why would I?'

'Because you're in love with him.'

'Don't be daft.'

Dan stops sweeping. 'Are you telling me you're not in love with Hopper?'

'Of course not. We're not even sleeping together.'

'But you're sharing a caravan.'

'No we're not. I'm sharing a caravan with Honey and Harry. Hopper only asked if he could share my bed because it's so big and offers more privacy than his bus. But we're in our own sleeping bags, Dan. Nothing is going on. And certainly not with Honey and Harry in the van.' (I don't think I'll ever get those images of Helene and Jimmy out of my head!)

'But you did it that night…you know…when I was there…with Jenny…'

Dan looks out of the window and blushes. I guess he's as mortified by that night in Gallipoli as I am.

'That was a mistake, Dan. I was trying to make you jealous.'

'I was plenty jealous.'

'Yeah, but I didn't mean to drive you into Jenny's arms like that.'

'I stuffed up. I realise that now.'

'It's my fault, Dan. I've been such a bitch to you on this trip.'

'No, I shouldn't have sprung it on you at the last second like I did.'

'It's not entirely your fault. You had Helene whispering in your ear and she had an ulterior motive.'

'She did?'

'Yes. She wanted out of this trip and you were the solution. Not to mention she knew it would piss me off. Helene likes causing trouble, you know. To be perfectly honest, I am glad you're here on this trip instead of her.'

Dan perches on the arm of one of the bus seats and his voice goes all hoarse and soft. 'I really missed you. That's why I jumped at the chance to be with you again. It's killing me that you don't want to be with me.'

'But I do, Dan.'

This is the perfect time to proclaim our love for one another and end this silly nonsense but, as always, there is a rotten fly in the ointment. Jenny walks onto the bus and ruins the moment. God that girl has rotten timing.

'Oh Dan, there's a cockroach in my caravan…'

And once again it's Dan to the rescue.

FORTY-SEVEN

We are in Salzburg so we watch the films *The Sound of Music* and *Amadeus* and then spend the morning doing *The Sound of Music* tour and everything Mozart.

At one point, we dance around like lunatics in the glasshouse from *The Sound of Music*, leaping from one bench to another and singing at the top of our lungs, and then I twirl into Dan's arms and give him a lusty kiss. I feel this may be my only chance, so I seize it.

'That's so you don't forget this moment.'

'Don't worry,' he says, 'I'll never forget it.'

And I know for certain that now I have a chance.

After that, it's off to the famous water gardens at Helbrunn Palace. We all get wet but the boys have been playing with water pistols since Italy so we're used to it by now.

By afternoon we are all cultured out. Some of the gang hike to Hohensalzburg Fortress, some head off to McDonalds and the rest of us make our way to the community pool. Need I remind you how great I look in a bathing suit now?

Jenny is doing her poor little simpering act and making a fuss over Dan's impressive dives from the very top diving board but Dan isn't doing it for accolades. He just loves the thrill of it.

I challenge him to a diving competition (on a much lower board, might I add) and I can tell he's more interested in my athletic, competitive spirit than he is in Jenny's weak little machinations.

'Have you ever kissed underwater?' I ask Dan.

'No.'

'Me neither. Let's see what it feels like.'

'Okay…'

We spend the next few days in the Alps, in a three hundred year old chalet on a mountainside in Archenkirch, Tyrol.

Dan goes bike riding and luges down a mountain. Is that the correct verb for hurtling down a massive slide on your backside? It's the same luge as what they use in the Winter Olympics but, this being spring, there's no snow or ice on the slide.

Jenny tries keeping up with Dan but I have no intention of letting him see me all sweaty and terrified so I develop the best relationship with a deckchair that I have ever had in my entire life.

Marie and I spend the entire day sleeping in the sunshine, reading, and eating chocolate. When Jenny returns to the chalet (after trying to keep up with Dan), she is totally shattered and disappears to soak in a tub for a few hours. I have been taking the sun all day and look delightfully bronzed and refreshed. Later that night we trek down to the village pub and I dance the night away with Dan.

We are all sleeping in a massive dormitory, except for Honey and Harry. Being married, they get a room to themselves but they hate it. They want to be with the rest of us.

I am beyond delighted that Jenny cannot drag Dan off to her tent. In fact, we'll be sleeping in one large dormitory at the next few campsites. Chalets are very popular in Germany and Switzerland, too.

The days go by in such a blur that it's not until Switzerland that I stop to draw breath and send a postcard off to Sunny:

Guten Tag to all my lovely Londoners,

After several days relaxing in an Austrian chalet, we roared into Germany and got active at the Olympic Stadium in Munich. Visited a traditional German beer hall where the steins are as big as your head and EVERYONE (even the teetotallers) got plastered. And what's the perfect cure for a hangover? The Glockenspiel at Marienplatz with its forty-three bells and thirty-two life-sized figures rotating through a complicated clock mechanism for fifteen minutes, ending with a very small golden rooster crowing three times!

Then it was on to Liechtenstein, where we trekked through a picturesque village and up a hill to Neuschwansten Palace – the inspiration for Walt Disney's fairytale castle.

Next stop was Luserne (a crying lion statue, a gallery bridge), then Brienz (wood factory) and finally into Lauterbrunnen. Rode a rickety, slow train up the Jungraujoch (pron. Youngfrow) mountain to the 'top of Europe', over three thousand metres above sea level. Saw amazing ice sculptures and had a snow fight in a blizzard.

How's your day going? Why didn't you tell me travelling was this much fun? Missing all the gang, with love, Teddy xxx

PS. This postcard is a mess but it was all right when I sent it.

PPS. That was Randy's idea of a joke, ha, ha!

PPPS. Dan says hi.

I am in chocolate heaven. So many Toblerones, so little time! After looking at Swiss Army knives and cuckoo clocks – and in Bern, bears in a pit – finally we are on our way back to Germany.

Personally I love the crisp, clean air, the towering mountains, the never-ending supply of chocolate and the neutral sleeping quarters but there's only one week left in our trip and I'm running out of time. If I'm to sort out my feelings for Dan, I need a clear head and a little breathing space.

Our plans to travel to Berlin have been scuppered thanks to a visit from the Pope. No tour buses allowed in. Unless we're prepared to enter on foot, carrying our camping gear, cooking utensils, luggage and food supplies, then we're out of luck. We take a vote and it's unanimous – stuff Berlin.

I don't know how a country can expect us to drink their beer by the barrel-load and then expect us to walk anywhere.

We stumble aboard the bus and doze our way onto the autobahn (except for Jenny; she's still sitting ramrod straight at the front of the bus).

Dan sits next to Randy as they devour a copy of *Penthouse* that has somehow found its way aboard the bus.

I'm sitting opposite Dan with a table between us.

'What's so sexy about thrusting your private parts into our faces and letting it all hang out?' I gripe.

'It's like a train crash,' says Dan. 'You can't look away.'

'Well, if you like that sort of thing...'

'I don't like it when it's obvious. I like plain, brown packaging with all the va-voom hidden underneath.'

'Plain brown packaging?'

'The more layers the better.'

'I have six brown cardigans, you know.'

'Yes, I do know that.' Dan grins at me. 'And I like it when there's lots of layers to a person so that you never get bored. I hate being bored.'

'Is that a fact?'

'I like women who aren't afraid to be different from the pack,' says Dan, 'like wearing pearls to a nightclub, that sort of thing. I like women who have strong minds and fearless hearts and have no idea how breathtakingly beautiful they are. I like women who keep me on my toes…'

'Hi, my name's Candy,' says Randy in a high voice, reading from the magazine, 'and I like the colour pink…'

'Brown,' I interject.

'And my ideal man would be big and strong…' says Randy in his high voice.

I stare at Dan and slowly nod along as Randy continues. '…and love to travel and be funny and sweet and hopelessly romantic.'

I keep nodding as Dan and I stare deeply into each other's eyes, neither one of us blinking until Jenny calls out, 'Dan, can you help me up here?'

Without taking his eyes off me, Dan calls back, 'Nope. I'm busy.'

And we keep our eyes locked on each other until the bus rumbles over the cobblestones of Heidelberg.

Marie leans over the seat behind Randy and says, 'I like piña coladas and getting caught in the rain.'

Randy throws the magazine onto an empty seat. 'How can those *Penthouse* pets compete with real women,' he laughs.

FORTY-EIGHT

In Heidelberg there's a huge castle perched on the side of a mountain. How on earth did they build that? The town looks so Gothic and old, like it belongs in a fairytale. And what about all those cobblestones? This country is mad for cobblestones! At the campsite, the Top Deckers are waiting. As I've mentioned before, the boys on our bus have been playing with water pistols since Italy. Well, the Top Deckers have now armed themselves with high-pressure water pistols. We take a break from squirting water at one another to have dinner in a concrete pavilion when the Chinese, who have to be better at everything than everybody else, attack us with a fire hose. So it's wet roast beef and soggy potatoes for dinner tonight. Luckily I'm wearing my all-weather anorak.

The next day we take a relaxing cruise up the Rhine River to St Goar. Another party involving alcohol (this time with a giant glass shaped like a boot) and I don't remember much after that. It's hard to believe I wasn't much of a drinker before I went on this trip. I still can't believe I missed a whole town. To think my only memory of Zadar will be the concrete shower block at the campsite, where I sat under a cold shower for about an hour trying to come out of my coma. I think after this trip I'll probably never touch a drop of alcohol again.

In the morning we leave St Goar and head to the border for Holland. Only five days until our trip ends and every one of us is shattered. Every morning, as the bus set out for a brand new destination, Trev would put Talking Heads on the tape deck and David Byrne would moan to us in that all-is-lost tone that we were on a long road going nowhere. And many is the time one of our bleary-eyed travellers would raise their head (myself included) and say, 'Just where in the hell are we going?' And many is the time Trev would answer, 'Stuffed if I know.'

This invariably would get us into tight corners, sticky situations, hair-raising clifftops and on one memorable occasion in the delightful (yet terrifying) position of having a dozen gorgeous young Italian men jostle the bus through a tightly-packed alleyway in a rather dubious back street in Naples. At least I think it was Naples. It's all a bit of a blur at the moment.

And yet every morning David Byrne would again remind us that a long, long journey with quite possibly no end in sight was all that lay ahead. Now, of course, the end is in sight but we are all too weary to acknowledge it. Most are asleep on the bus, but Honey and I are wide-awake and passing little notes to each other. I, of course, am angsting over Dan and whether I should tell him how I feel.

My argument is that I'm not even sure how I feel about him but Honey thinks that's bullshit. *You are crazy about him and everyone can see it except you,* she writes.

What am I going to do without you? I moan.

We'll just have to make sure that never happens, she writes.

What are you saying? That we'll be friends forever until we die?

Yes, and even longer, she promises.

Friends for life and in death, too, I agree.

We stop at Cologne for lunch so the letters cease but my mind is clear now. I have got to do something about Dan. We trundle into Amsterdam at about three p.m., pitch our tents for the last time, wash the bus, have a quiet dinner and briefly reunite with Top Deck. They're off to a sex show. We're going on a canal cruise.

And, yes, I'm thinking about talking to Dan but don't rush me.

First we have a free day in Amsterdam to fill with the sights and sounds of everything Dutch. A small group go into a coffeeshop to buy hash cookies and space cakes. The rest of us go culture vulturing. I am especially impressed with Anne Frank's attic. By this stage of the trip we have seen so many historically significant sights and impressive cathedrals that we've taken to calling them 'crumblies'. It might seem like we're being disrespectful but I truly think the brain can only take so much wonder and awe before it starts to overload. So when I tell you that Anne Frank's house is a plain building with a row of photographs tacked on a wall, you may think it wouldn't have a hope in hell of impressing such jaded travellers. But it does. It is the significance behind that plain wall of photographs. It is standing in her shoes and imagining her fear and courage and despair.

It is knowing that a plain brown cardigan is never just a plain brown cardigan.

In the afternoon we all meet up again in the main square and help the stoned ones onto a bus that will take them back to the campsite for a long, long nap. Did I mention that Jenny is part of that group?

This leaves Dan and me (finally!) alone…

In a crowded town square…

Surrounded by pigeons.

We talk.

'I love you,' says Dan, right then and there, out in the open.

'Oh Dan, that scares the life out of me.'

'It does?'

'Yes. I have spent the whole time, ever since I first met you, running away from you. I am terrified of falling in love. I will do almost anything to avoid it. It was kinda easy in London because you were so far away. I could tell you how I felt without panicking. But, even then, I still don't think I could admit it to myself.'

'What are you so afraid of?'

'I guess I'm afraid that if I'm with you then I won't be me anymore. You'll expect me to climb up every mountain you see and cross every stream and God knows what else.'

'I don't always have to be climbing,' said Dan. 'Sometimes I like to lie down.'

I smile nervously. 'Please don't break my heart, Dan.'

And Dan says, 'I wouldn't do that to you, even if I could.'

And that's when I know, without a shadow of a doubt, that Dan is the man for me. Because love will soar to the highest mountain, cascade over rolling hills, glide along majestic rivers until it fills your heart with bliss and leaves a tingle in your toes. Love is all about the bliss. And all we can do is grab it with both hands and squeeze everything we can out of it. And it doesn't matter what packaging it comes in, even a plain brown one will do.

And I can fight it no longer.

'Oh, I love you, Dan van Runkle. I really, really do.'

'Does that mean we're zipping our sleeping bags together tonight?' he grins.

'Yes, Dan, we're zipping our bags together.'

And our lips collide in a symphony of song so passionate and pure that all the pigeons in the square take flight in fright.

It gives me a spectacular thrill, too.

FORTY-NINE

Not even a sordid sex show can destroy my bliss. Why are people drawn to such things? It seems so sleazy. I suppose it's out of curiosity but why on earth would you care? It's definitely not my cup of tea.

But Amsterdam is heaving with sex shows so whilst the others pile into a dingy bar to see a stripper slice a banana between her thighs, Dan and I stay on the bus and make out like crazy. When everyone gets back on board, they tell us all the gory details, which I think is just as repulsive as seeing it for yourself but I say nothing. Not even when they tell me that Hopper took a bite out of the banana. Secretly, though, I'm glad I didn't end up with him.

On the way back to camp, we pass through the Red Light District where prostitutes sit in shop windows in their underwear. When they get a customer, they close the curtain.

'See that Teddy?' says Marie. 'Even the pros have the decency to use a curtain.'

Everybody laughs (except Jenny) and we promise not to kiss so much in public. Thank goodness we're back to sleeping in tents.

I send my last postcard to Sunny:

Goedemorgen Sunny, and all my lovely London friends,

Said goodbye to our fellow travellers at Top Deck Tours yesterday so all a little sad. Then we had to get up before the crack of dawn for the Aalsmeer Flower Auction, which began at six-thirty a.m. and was really rather boring. Just a room full of international buyers all bidding for tulips. Then at ten a.m. we toured the Heineken beer factory. Too early to start drinking, even for us. Actually, that's a lie. It seems it's never too early for a drink in Europe. As our tour guide Sarah-Jane says, it's five o'clock somewhere in the world. We had lunch in a little fishing village called Volendam, then toured an Edam cheese and clog factory. Somehow the two go hand in hand in Holland.

We're off to Brussels (where the highlight seems to be a statue of a boy pissing in a fountain), then up to the Belgian port of Zebrugge for a ferry ride back to England. Can you believe my trip of a lifetime is about to end? We're all a little nervous about the ferry because of that awful accident three months ago when some idiot forgot to close the doors and two hundred people drowned but we're looking forward to coming home. We'll be arriving in Paddington around eight a.m. on Sunday. Wonder if you're still at The Eagle, if so I'll see you then. Love to all, Teddy xxx

PS. Dan says hi and see you soon.

And just like that it's over. After ten exhausting, non-stop, incredibly phenomenal weeks we all climb wearily from the bus, the boys unpack our luggage, and we mill about with tears in our eyes, saying our goodbyes. I am devastated to be parting from my new pals, especially Honey and Harry, Randy, and Marie. We have already exchanged addresses with promises to visit. Dan can't wait to go to New Zealand. He's already talking about bungy-jumping and white-water rafting. And I don't know what's come over me, but it actually sounds like fun.

Dan and I grab our backpacks and turn the corner for home – in this case, The Royal Eagle Hotel.

And there is Helene, waiting on the bottom step of the hotel. I have mixed emotions about seeing her, that's for sure. She seems surprised to see Dan and me looking so cosy. I bet that wasn't part of her plan.

'Hello weary travellers, how was the trip?' she says.

'Phenomenal,' says Dan. 'You missed the adventure of a lifetime.'

'I'm not so sure I would have seen it that way. I'm sorry, Theodora, but I just didn't want to be around you anymore. In fact, I would have been happy if I never saw you again. I really didn't like the person you'd become.'

I am more than a little stunned by her honesty. 'So what are you doing here?'

'Oh, I've had plenty of time to think about it. It's this place, London, it changes people and, really, you're probably not that much different from everyone else around here.'

'I am different, Helene. But I like what I've become.'

'I do, too,' Dan chimes in.

Helene looks a little huffy but she keeps her tongue, so clearly she has a hidden agenda. I wait for the axe to fall.

'Are you heading off to your aunt's place now?'

'Not right away. We'll spend the day in London. Why?'

'Um... I'm kind of between places at the moment. Things didn't work out so well with Jimmy. I've been renting a room at The Eagle but I'm running out of money. I thought I might stay with you for a while.'

She's got to be joking. 'Sorry Helene but Dan's staying with me. There isn't room for you.'

'Oh, so you and Dan are still together?'

'Of course.'

'I just thought…'

'Save it Helene.' Can you believe she is still trying to cause trouble for me? Doesn't this girl ever stop?

'What if you two share a bed and I take the other?'

I look at her dumbfounded. It actually takes several seconds for me to speak. 'I don't do that sort of thing, Helene,' I slowly answer.

Can ya believe it?

Suddenly the glass doors open at the top of the steps and William peers out.

'Teddy-Bear? Is that you? What a sight for sore eyes you are.'

'Come on, Dan,' I grin, 'it's time you finally met William Abernethy.'

I leap into William's arms and we hug each other tight, both of us grinning from ear to ear.

'What on earth are you doing up at this time of the morning?'

'A little birdy told me you were coming,' grins William, breaking free to shake Dan's hand.

'You mean Helene?'

'No, no, no, nobody talks to Helene, I mean your postcards to Sunny. We've all been reading them. And this must be the boyfriend from back home. We know all about him, too. You are a dark one, Teddy-Bear. We should have known that's why no one here could steal your heart. Dan, is it? You must be quite an exceptional man to have captured our Teddy. I am thrilled to meet you.'

Dan slaps William heartily on the back, nearly knocking him over, and says, 'Mate, you have no idea how great it is to finally meet you.'

'Time for breakfast, I think,' coughs William. 'Alan will spread the word that you're back and it won't be long before the gang's all together again.'

With Alan spreading the word, we should all be reunited by lunchtime.

'By the way, where's Sunny?' I ask William.

'Oh darling, Sunny is squatting in some hideous council flat in Whitechapel.'

Honestly, you go away for a few months and people fall apart!

By evening we're reunited with clean sheets and a long, hot shower and it feels brilliant to be back in comfortable surroundings. Aunt Flavia is delighted to be rid of the sour-faced Helene and welcomes Dan with open arms. His sunny disposition and eagerness to join in energises the entire household.

The next day we travel back into London (two hours, forty minutes) for a reunion lunch at The Lone Star restaurant with all the gang from Autotours and Top Deck for one final goodbye. It's so strange seeing everyone for the very last time.

I'm wearing my Greek sundress, French flats, and around my wrist are the worry beads I pinched from Hopper in Turkey (it was the only way to make him stop). My hair is still lustrous and soft and my skin is bronzed and glowing. Dan has a proprietary hand around my slim waist and I am not pulling away.

Jenny turns up and tries to give Dan her telephone number. 'Do you want to lose your teeth?' I challenge and she hastily backs away. Later on she whines to Honey that I stole the love of her life and Honey has to explain that we've been working on our relationship for a year and that he is, in fact, the love of my life and I am his. I guess she didn't know that bit.

I feel bad for her until Randy tells me that she has a boyfriend waiting back home. I hug Randy and Marie and promise that I will never get paralytic again, since they won't be around to keep me safe. They both seem very glad to hear that.

After lunch I take Dan over to Jack and Sean's place. Only Sean is home, sitting on a dirty mattress in his tiny box bedroom. I notice one of Emily Oliver's scarves hanging on the doorknob so I guess she's still around. He wants to hear all about our trip but I only give him the highlights. He says he might go to Amsterdam this weekend. I think he probably will.

There's no need for goodbyes just yet as we're all getting together tomorrow night at The Eagle for a final catch-up. I can hardly believe that it's finally me who's going home.

In the meantime, though, Dan and I have some sightseeing to do. It feels strange doing all the touristy bits again but seeing them through different eyes. I also show him places where I've been and worked. It is so unbelievably odd. Am I a local or a tourist?

And, of course, I take Dan to 133 Gloucester Terrace and show him my basement flat. It feels so strange, standing on the pavement, looking down into the window at the bed where I used to sleep. Dan likes the red geraniums in the pots on the windowsill.

I wave to the top floor apartment. 'Goodbye Mrs Quist,' I shout.

Goodbye basement flat.

William has two spare tickets to a Genesis/Paul Young concert at Wembley Stadium. I know Genesis is the big drawcard but I actually have a bit of a crush on Paul Young, wherever his hat may be, so I'm keen to go but I haven't forgotten how unappreciative Helene was when I bought those Fury tickets for her so I check with Dan first.

'Sounds like fun,' he says.

Dan and I sleep on the floor in William's room and the next day we catch the tube to Whitechapel for lunch with Sunny in her council flat squat. It's in a very rundown area and I'm a little concerned for our safety. What on earth is Sunny doing here?

Squatting, it would seem. She's dyed her hair a harsh platinum blonde and is wearing black leggings under an oversized purple shirt. She looks so pale and sickly. She makes us lunch in her squalid kitchen with the peeling yellow wallpaper and a pink tatty scarf draped across the window. She's got a big square piece of wood in the living room propped up on some bricks, covered by a blue and white checked tablecloth. I guess that's a table then. On it is a Walkman, a gigantic box of matches and a dirty ashtray. In the corner there's a pot-plant. I think it's plastic.

Sunny tells us ex-cons broke into the squat and stole all their belongings and I have to stop myself from running out the door. I think Sunny sees all this as some sort of adventure, living on the edge and all that.

We talk about our travels. It seems Sunny has also done a little trekking in Europe (in her typical half-arsed, roundabout way).

Brian didn't want to go anywhere so Sunny went off to France on her own, trying to find work on a yacht. But she ended up back in London with – as she put it – her tail between her legs. It was a bit embarrassing, actually, as they'd all thrown her a going-away party. Finally Brian agreed to travel with her so off she went again. Only he kept wandering off without her. She was accosted in Rome, slept on a mattress in Naples full of dirty needles, and had her bags stolen in Greece. And it was all so tedious, she says, those long train journeys, forever waiting to get somewhere.

Tedious? Europe? I suppose sometimes you have to make your own fun. I tell Sunny about night drives and hoedowns at the back of the bus, drinking games, ouzo for breakfast, Pimms cocktails on a yacht as the sun set over the water and toes hooked under the railing, vodka parties on ferry crossings, running through The Louvre, lying on the floor in the Sistine Chapel looking up at Michelangelo's masterpiece as loud American tourists stomped all over us, dead-ants at The Trevi fountain, yodelling atop the Youngfrow, serenading on a gondola, a t-shirt swapping game through the endless tunnels in Italy, flashing knickers at a funfair, bad-taste parties, epic water pistol battles involving every tour bus in camp, casinos, cathedrals, porn mags, cat genitals, silk pyjamas, worry beads, singing, laughing, hugging, kissing, making friends and falling in love, stonking great hangovers and life-changing experiences... but never, ever, ever a dull moment.

'We're flying home on the sixth of July. Don't forget you've got a return ticket, too,' I remind Sunny.

'I'm thinking of cashing in my ticket and going on safari in Africa.'

'Of course you are, Sunny,' I smile. 'Of course you are.'

Sunny accompanies us back to The Eagle for our final night in London. We stop at Wimpy's for my last

Wimpy meal. Ah Wimpy, I think I shall miss you most of all.

In the bar at The Eagle, William buys us a round (and puts it on his bar tab). Jack strolls in after finishing his dinner shift and informs me that he has married Delilah.

I am gob-smacked. 'Why would you go and do a thing like that?'

He shrugs. 'Why not?'

'But you could have any girl you want.'

'I still can. Marriage doesn't mean monogamy.'

Uh, yes, it does.

Then again, around here of course it doesn't. How silly of me. To be perfectly honest with you, I'm more concerned about his clothing. It seems a lot of dirty, scraggly Delilah has rubbed off on my handsome friend. I just hope he doesn't catch some incurable disease. He's wearing a pair of 'boy toy' leggings, the kind that Madonna wears. Judging by the cigarette holes, I'd say they belong to Delilah. She is definitely not a good influence on him but he seems happy enough.

He leans in close and whispers, 'How about one for the road?'

I knock back my tequila like a seasoned pro and say, 'How about not?'

Lester appears at my side. 'Can I buy you a drink?'

'No thanks,' I reply.

For a moment we hold each other's gaze and a thousand words are spoken in the silence. I will never forget the time when two sensible ships sailing stoically along the straight and narrow, for the briefest moment, sped wildly down the rapids before steering back to safe shore. I will never again become involved with another woman's man but when I'm ninety-four and dribbling soup down my chin, I will remember my wild moment and not regret a minute of it.

Do you think Lester will ever think about me when he's ninety-four with soup dribbling down his chin? I hope so.

Sean is on duty at the front desk so I decide to take him a drink and say my goodbyes. He has written me a poem on the back of an invoice slip. It says:

Teddy ♥
Time is not lost
It's merely waiting, checking the cost
A moment cannot last
In an instant it's past
Memory is the holder of dreams
To attain it, sleep is the means
So, in your slumber, remember our kiss
Then you'll forget not our bliss

It would seem Sean is fond of memories, too, but then he whispers, 'Let's get down and dirty on the linoleum.'

On the linoleum, I kid you not.

I return to the bar and say my final goodbye to Sunny. I'm a little worried about her and Brian returning to their squat in the dark but she seems unperturbed.

'Have a safe trip home,' she says.

'You, too,' I implore.

I do hope that I will see her again.

In the elevator, I tell Dan and William about Sean's proposal. Dan laughs but William says, 'He wanted to have sex in the lobby of The Royal Eagle Hotel?' I can't believe he's so shocked. It doesn't surprise me in the least. You know I think it's the first time William has ever behaved like an Assistant Manager.

Dan wraps his arms around me and holds me tight. I twist around and we kiss. He lifts me up off the ground. I wrap my legs around his hips. We kiss again.

William makes it out of the elevator just in time...

And in the morning Teddy is gone.

FIFTY-ONE

F ast forward back to the present day: I closed Theodora's diary and let the words 'Teddy is gone' die on my lips. Theodora was still sitting in a jail cell, refusing to talk but it didn't matter. Her diary had spoken volumes. I now knew the truth. Theodora could never have killed the man in the shed. He was the love of her life. And his name was Dan van Runkle.

True, the years had taken quite a toll on him. He was no longer blonde and broad-chested, more like pale and skinny and extremely weather-beaten, but then he'd lived a lifetime in Theodora's rather imposing shadow and that would take a toll on many a robust man.

And fancy Theodora thinking she had left all traces of Teddy back in London. Couldn't she see that every bold statement, every fierce determination and fearless venture had Teddy written all over it?

I was as sure as I ever could be that Teddy was sitting in that jail.

I raced down to the courthouse, ready to fling myself upon the mercy of the court.

Yes, I was being overly dramatic, but can you blame me?

This is the greatest love story never told, I thought to myself, and it was up to me to bring about a happy ending. Dan was gone but he was not just going to fade away. He was still a prominent figure in her life. She just needed to be reminded of how much he really meant to her.

I don't think I even wiped the chocolate stains from around my mouth. I was that intent on reaching her in time.

But I needn't have bothered.

Theodora had already been released and was standing with the girls (Sunny, Honey, and Lucille) on the steps outside the police station, breathing freedom into her lungs.

'You're out,' I said breathlessly, holding onto my side where a stitch had formed.

'I am,' said Theodora. 'Lack of evidence. I guess I have you to thank for that.'

Oh, yes, the diary. I had completely forgotten, in my haste, that it was still in my hand. I clutched it protectively to my chest.

'The only diary those silly constables found was Aunt Ursula's weather diary and I bet that made for very dry reading,' said Theodora.

'Perhaps it's just as well they didn't find yours,' I said. 'It's probably a little too racy for their blood.'

'So you read it,' said Theodora, narrowing her eyes at me.

'I may have skimmed a few pages.'

'I suppose now you think you know all of my secrets.'

Theodora scowled at me and I tried my best not to wither under her stare.

'I know how you really feel about Dan,' I said, trying to sound a lot more confident than I felt.

'You don't know anything,' said Theodora, dismissing me with a wave.

At the mention of Dan's name, the others became quite agitated.

'Exnay on the anDay,' said Honey.

'I know what you're saying,' said Theodora. 'You've already explained Pig Latin slang to us.'

'We don't ever talk about D.A.N.' whispered Sunny, spelling out his name.

'I do know how to spell,' said Theodora.

'Well, you said we weren't ever to mention his name so I thought I ought to spell it instead.'

Realising I'd unwittingly stirred up a hornet's nest, I quickly tried to change the subject. Dan, or at least Theodora's feelings about him, would have to wait until a time when she was more inclined to examine them further.

'Look,' I said, 'we don't have time for any of this. You'll be late for your own funeral if we don't get a move on.'

'Oh yes, the service,' said Theodora, pulling us along as she headed for the graveyard. 'They better not have started without me.'

'As if they would ever dare do that,' said Sunny.

The funeral was a small affair and only Aunt Ursula seemed pleased to be there. The plot chosen was in a quiet corner of the Bellwether graveyard. The man in the shed (I couldn't quite bring myself to call him Dan) stood by himself under a tall tree at the very back, looking a little lost without Theodora by his side.

'You will be happy here, I said, 'surrounded by your dearest friends.'

Funerals are eternally fascinating to me. They serve a dual purpose for the one who has died. Firstly, they allow the living to say their final goodbyes. To give 'closure' for the family and to allow them to openly grieve. In Victorian times, a widow could wear mourning black for years (usually made of silk and crepe) to show even complete strangers that she was grieving deeply for a dearly-departed loved one. Queen Victoria, of whom these times refer to, wore black for forty years after her husband died. That's an awfully long time to mourn. Even for a monarch.

As time moved on, the colour of the cloth lightened to grey, then mauve, and finally white. Jewellery was limited to jet – a hard coal-like material sometimes combined with the deceased's woven hair.

That's why witches wear black, because we are always dealing with the dead.

But there was another purpose to funerals that those left behind to grieve had no knowledge of. The dead person (unseen by the living) is reunited with those that have died before them and that can be quite a jolly affair.

It's a strange dichotomy for a hedgewitch to witness. The living, usually looking like death warmed up, all morose and miserable with pale, drawn faces and puffy red eyes, and the dead, looking positively delighted to see their long-lost relatives and friends again. There's a lot of laughing and hugging and celebration. Well, there's no other word for it than party. That's what the dead are all about. Kicking up their heels and having a darn good time.

And there I am in the middle of it. Watching these two opposing sides respond in entirely different ways.

I looked across at the lively mob of dead people and in particular at the trio of ghosts that were recent additions to the afterlife as they mingled amongst the deceased.

But unlike the three ghosts that had visited Ebenezer Scrooge in *A Christmas Carol*, these three ghosts were portents not of doom but of delight.

First, there was Lucille, carrying a cushion in her arms, beautifully embroidered with the words REST IN PEACE. She had fallen asleep in a room with a silent gas leak and never woken again. Apparently the last words to her canary were, 'Do you smell something funny?'

Standing beside her was Honey. She'd taken her husband to the hospital to see about his prostate. She thought he'd died but he hadn't. She had. A sudden heart attack that no one saw coming, least of all the orderly who'd arrived to wheel her husband into surgery. He'd ended up wheeling Honey down to the morgue instead. This was in New Zealand. Technically, her body was buried there but her spirit was here in Bitterly Bay on a long-overdue holiday.

So was Lucille, for that matter. She lived on the other side of the country but she, too, was taking an extended holiday in Bitterly Bay.

And so was Sunny. She still slept on Theodora's sofa between her many travels abroad and interstate (now happily solo) but she lived most of the time along the coast where she was swept out to sea one blustery day whilst standing on a particularly perilous rock. She had seen hundreds of swimmers caught in nasty rips and so when it happened to her she barely panicked. Kept herself nice and calm. That is, until the sharks began circling.

So what, may you ask, brought all three of Theodora's ghostly friends to Bitterly Bay? Why Theodora, of course, or, more precisely, this funeral.

I'm sure the man in the shed would be touched to have them all attend his funeral but, sadly, this is not the case for we are not at the man in the shed's funeral for the simple fact that he is not dead.

Theodora is.

FIFTY-TWO

When I said 'You will be happy here surrounded by your dearest friends,' I was, of course, referring to Theodora (and not the man in the shed). Aside from the crows, I don't think he cared much for company and so the ghost I was talking to was Theodora.

Once again, she was on an adventure into the unknown and, once again, her fearless, fun-loving friends were on this adventure with her.

As I already explained, it is my job as a witch to help the dead come to terms with their new state of being and that is what I have been doing with Theodora. The police, at least the officers who had passed away, had been questioning her in an attempt to jog her memory. They had no idea how she came to be found on the garden path at the rear of the Bellwether house with an enormous pair of gardening shears and what looked like the remains of a corpse half-buried under the blackberry bush.

Was her throat slit?

Was that her blood splattered all over the blackberry bush?

No one knows for certain because it was the man in the shed who found her, or so he claims, and he is not telling anyone anything. Did he kill her? I must admit it's possible.

You remember me telling you at the very beginning that no one would have been surprised to learn that Theodora had murdered the man in the shed? Well, I suppose the same can be said for the man in the shed. Because of Theodora's rather forceful personality (that's a polite way of saying she was a pain in the neck), it's entirely possible that the man in the shed's patience was stretched to breaking point. I doubt it would have taken much for him to snap.

Usually I'm on top of this but I've had a lot on my plate lately what with Honey's heart, Sunny's sharks, and Lucille's leak. I really thought the police would have come up with a lead by now. They're treating her death as suspicious but no one seems in any hurry to investigate it further.

Justifiable homicide seems to top the list.

And I must admit, the man in the shed had a lot on his plate of late, too. He was also dealing with the death of Aunt Ursula. She had left behind her in this world a rather tangled mess. She was a hoarder and the nursing home was only too happy to dump it all in the man in the shed's lap (or, to be more precise, into the Bellwether's already crowded hallway).

Had Theodora marched down that pathway demanding he be rid of that millstone round his neck?

And had the man in the shed taken her literally at her word?

But if I was right and he was her beloved Dan, then he would not have considered Theodora to be the cause of all his troubles. If her diary revealed nothing else, surely it showed us that Dan loved her.

And if he loved her then why on earth would he kill her?

I was standing in the graveyard, still thinking I was the only one who knew just what the man in the shed meant to Theodora (and what she meant to him), when I happened to look down at her freshly-turned grave and I realised with a shock that she had been buried beside her husband... the love of her life...

Daniel van Runkle.

'Oh,' I said. 'He's dead!'

But, as I have said, the man in the shed was not dead. Well, to Theodora and the others he was. When life continues on as it has always done, many times the dead will mistakenly believe that those who are still alive are dead whilst those whom they can see clearly must somehow be as alive as they feel they are. It's confusing, I know, but imagine how confusing it is for me with one foot in one realm and one foot in the other. Is it any wonder I sometimes make mistakes?

Here, however, was clearly the grave of Daniel van Runkle and that must mean he was not the man in the shed.

'He died on our honeymoon,' said Theodora, noticing my shock. 'We were travelling through New Zealand, catching up with Honey and Harry and touring around the islands with Contiki Tours. We'd gone bungy-jumping, white-water rafting and hiking across an ice glacier. If it was risky and exciting, Dan was doing it. He jumped out of a helicopter on skis and went barrelling down a mountain before smashing into a tree. He didn't know what hit him.'

Theodora looked down at the gravestone nestled beside hers. 'I always wanted to be buried next to him,' she said.

I felt a little sorry for the man in the shed. It would have been impossible to follow in those giant footsteps.

'Call it wishful thinking,' said Theodora, perhaps reading my thoughts. 'He was his best mate,' she explained, and I knew she meant the man in the shed. 'We grew closer through our grief and hoped that somehow we could move on with our lives but we never truly got over losing Dan.'

Having (shamelessly) read her diary, I could easily understand this and suddenly I could see their relationship a little clearer. United in their loss, they were just trying to muddle along without him. This strange, twisted friendship they'd formed was not like any other I'd ever seen before but did that make it any less real? She had his back and I have no doubt he had hers and that kind of loyalty does not usually end with a sharp blade between the shoulders.

What if the man in the shed had, indeed, cut his neck shaving and had run out to the path seeking help and what if Theodora had run to his aide, slipped on his blood, and somehow wound up with a pair of gardening shears sticking out of her chest? Was that sort of thing not possible?

Of course, how a rotting, festering corpse ended up underneath the blackberry bush is another matter entirely. Did Theodora have a hand in its demise? As I've said, she's certainly capable of such a diabolical deed and no one would be in the least bit surprised if the decomposing finger of blame were to be pointed in her direction.

But who am I to judge?

You have to admit that for all her bluster and complaining, for all her denials and savage criticisms, Theodora is a truly remarkable friend and ally. I told you at the very beginning that she was slightly outrageous. Too loud, too blunt, too scathing and scornful, yes, she was all of that and more but in spite of that, or more precisely because of that, she was also the best type of friend you could ever wish for.

Just ask the girls. Honey and Lucille have been friends with Theodora for over thirty years and both of them are well acquainted with the Teddy side of her nature; Lucille in London and Honey in Europe.

And don't forget Sunny who's weathered forty-plus years of friendship with Theodora (and Teddy) and any other personality that might be lurking within her.

Or you can even ask me, for that matter.

For such a deeply flawed individual, is it not astonishing how many long-standing, lasting friendships she has managed to sustain?

Give me a friend like Theodora van Runkle any day of the year. Deep loyalty like hers deserves deep loyalty back. And for that reason alone, I am ashamed to have even considered Theodora capable of committing such a terrible thing as murder.

It's just that she's the type of person one should never underestimate. Had she been found guilty of such a crime, I have no doubt we would have all rallied together around her and given her our strongest support.

Even the man in the shed would not have done less. I don't suppose we'll ever learn his actual name but perhaps an introduction could be made, if discreetly enough, without scaring him away.

And so I fell in step beside him as the coffin was slowly lowered into the ground.

'Hello,' I whispered. 'I believe we are neighbours of a sort.'

'Yes,' said the man in the shed. 'I believe we are. I've seen you with your crows. Magnificent creatures.'

'Why, thank you,' I smiled.

'You were a good friend to Theodora, weren't you?'

'Yes,' I said. 'We were very good friends. From the moment we first met, a bond was forged that not even death can sever.'

'She called you B.B., didn't she?'

'Yes, she did. But my name is Birdy Black.'

'And what brought you to Bitterly Bay, Birdy Black?'

'Why, Theodora, of course.'

I always considered myself to be a gypsy, home was wherever I lay my hat, but Theodora developed a rather unhealthy attachment to that hat and somehow her love for Bitterly Bay seeped in and I found myself being drawn to its violent seas and moody skies. Not to mention the inordinate number of dead people roaming about the place.

'I'm glad you're here,' said the man in the shed. 'I'm feeling a bit lost amongst all these mourners.'

'It can be a little overwhelming,' I conceded, 'but never fear, I'm here to help all sorts come to grips with the business of death.'

'Do you think she's with him now?'

I glanced across to the others but they were well out of earshot so I chanced it and said his name aloud. 'You mean Dan?'

'I do.'

Theodora had once confessed to me that she knew the instant she laid eyes on Dan that he was the man for her. A tiny explosion burst in her heart and the blood in her veins, every fibre of her being, tingled and throbbed and fizzed and popped. She never felt so alive. But it frightened her.

So much so that when Sunny suggested they travel to London together, Theodora happily accepted and fled as fast as her frightened feet (in their sensible shoes) could carry her.

'I think she knew,' Theodora had said, referring, of course, to Sunny. 'She always did know me inside and out. She said this trip would be the making of me and she was exactly right.'

Theodora thought she was running away, you see, but Sunny knew that what Theodora needed was time and distance and new experiences, to broaden her horizons, discover who she really was and what she really wanted.

I think Sunny always knew it would lead Theodora back to Dan.

'You know, I miss him every day,' said the man in the shed. 'He was such a great mate and he loved Theodora to death. I guess she and I thought if we stuck together we'd be able to keep his memory alive.'

I nodded sympathetically. I'd heard it all a million times before.

'He's been dead for so long,' said the man in the shed, 'do you think he's forgotten her?'

'Who could ever forget Theodora van Runkle?'

As the shadows hugged the edge of the graves, I watched a ghostly figure draw near to the ghost of Theodora and the years seemed to fall away from her.

'Teddy? Is that you?' said Dan.

And Theodora melted into his arms and whispered, 'Yes!'

They left the graveyard together, not once looking back.

'Come on,' said Sunny, linking arms with Lucille and Honey, 'those two are going to take forever to catch up. Let's grab a cup of tea at Mrs Dimple's teashop.'

'Is it Tuesday?' asked Lucille.

'Every day is Tuesday,' said Honey, 'Haven't you noticed?'

'Good,' said Lucille. 'What book shall we read today?'

'I've just managed to get my hands on a rather juicy memoir…' said Sunny.

When the last of the mourners had left the gravesite, I was left to stand alone beside the man in the shed.

'Come on,' I said, 'it's time to let go of Theodora.'

And the man in the shed did.

THE END

There are some who do not fear death
For they are more afraid of not really living

Ancient Proverb

Kerry Mitchell

www.ingramcontent.com/pod-product-compliance
Lightning Source LLC
Chambersburg PA
CBHW030341120726
47901CB00007B/1871